*P*romises to *K*eep

Pam Giordano

DEDICATION

To my beloved daughter, Kim Mulicka, whose promises
died with her.

In years to come I'll have my house in Carmel
And use my voice and my hands
To please the eyes and the ears of passersby.

Kim

SHAKESPEARE

In this novel, I have extracted quotations from "The Bard," William Shakespeare. Shakespeare was my stimulating teacher on rainy afternoons, my dependable visitor in the midst of a pandemic, and my steadfast companion in the middle of the night. His compelling words reflect life in all its pathos and power; its contempt and confusion; its licentiousness and levity.

CHAPTERS

Part One

1940 to 1957

Merriweather Twins

CHAPTER ONE

*"We came into the world like brother to brother
and now let's go hand in hand not one before
another."*

The ball signaling the beginning of the new decade was slowly
descending in Times Square. 1940 would be a time of new
beginnings for everyone. There was a growing enthusiasm in the
air as the large, boisterous crowd dispersed the excitement. The
country would finally recover from the emotional pain and
deprivation its people felt so acutely over the last several years.
Now, there was a renewed promise of Saturday matinees
complete with chocolate drops, and Christmas might once again
be a time of childhood wonder and excitement.

News of war continued to flash angrily on the horizon, but it
seemed like a long way away tonight. Now, the revelers worked
at putting any thought of war and privation behind them and
gathered to celebrate the here and now.

In the bedroom of a magnificent mansion in Manhattan, the
wealthy and privileged Henry Merriweathers, owners of the
largest and most prestigious bank in the city, were awaiting a
real cause for celebration of their own. Henry's wife, Elise, was
struggling through the last stages of labor with their first child.

Earlier in the day, before the pains began in earnest, Elise passed
the time recalling every moment of the news that would change
their lives forever. She thought about how she and Henry long
ago gave up on the idea of producing a much-wanted child and
heir to the family fortune. They mourned the fact for years.
Eventually, they finally came to understand that it was not to be.

Just as it appeared that the Henry Gerald Merriweather name was
doomed for extinction, a hugely surprising event took place.

Elise, well into her forties now, decided to visit the doctor for what she perceived to be a general malaise. After a thorough examination, the doctor confirmed what he expected.

"It's not uncommon for women to feel exhausted during this time," he said, smiling.

Elise bristled. "You're treating me like an old woman," she bellowed. "I don't remember my mother experiencing this when she was going through her change!"

The doctor stood back, surprised by her response. Then, he gave Elise a quick hug. "My dear, you are not going through menopause. You, dear friend, are pregnant! My best guess is about three months along."

After a few moments of paralyzing shock, Elise flew into the doctor's arms. "Dr. Miles…Robert…please tell me this is not a joke. I wouldn't be able to bear it if…"

Doctor Miles interrupted. "It certainly is no joke, dear. Get used to the idea that there will be a new person in your life. Things will change for you, dramatically. How do you think Henry will feel about this?"

Henry. The thought of her husband escaped her for the moment. Now, she could only imagine his reaction to the news he was praying to hear for so long.

"Henry's waited for years to hear me say the words. We gave up on ever having the

family we once dreamed about. Now…now, my husband will be the happiest man on earth! Thank you, Robert. Thank you, dear Robert!" Elise kissed the doctor over and over, causing him to become a bit red in the face.

"God bless you, my dear," he said. I know how much you and Henry wanted this. But don't thank me. Go home and thank

Henry!" he said, jovially, and ushered the new mother-to-be out of his office.

Elise's car was waiting, but she motioned the driver on and decided to walk. She wanted a few moments of her own – a private time to take in all she'd heard, a cherished time between her and the baby growing inside.

The spring day seemed even more beautiful, and Elise didn't want to miss a thing; the smell of new earth, the happy sounds coming from the playground, the sight of the ice cream shop that offered her favorite treat. She decided to go into the shop and purchase several containers of her favorite.

When she finally arrived home, Elise found Henry in the kitchen pouring a glass of lemonade. He didn't hear her come in and was somewhat startled when he felt an arm go around his shoulder.

"Stop right there," Elise said, taking the glass from him.

"It's only lemonade!" Henry responded, both startled and annoyed at the intrusion.

Elise retrieved a bottle of wine from the cabinet and poured two glasses of their favorite.

"For you," she said, handing him a glassful.

She took a bowl from the cupboard and scooped a large portion of ice cream into it.

"And for me!" she said, shoving a generous spoonful of the rich strawberry sweetness into her mouth. She followed with a large sip of wine.

Henry was stunned by Elise's strange behavior. "Elise! What are you doing? This is not like you. Why all the exuberance? Are you trying to tell me that you've fired the cook? I know you've had a problem with her taking an afternoon drink or two, but she makes a killer Beef Wellington. And our parties! Why, even the Parkers say…"

"This isn't about the cook, Henry, it's about me! Well, really, it's about us! Well…when I think about it, it's about all three of us."

Henry put down the wine he hardly touched. "Will you please tell me what's going on, Elise. I don't understand this uncharacteristic behavior."

"Uncharacteristic, Henry? Is that what you call a woman who is…well, who is in a family way?"

Henry still could not comprehend what he was hearing. "Why are you so vague? Get to the point, Elise. I can't stand this emotional ping-pong."

Elise took Henry's hand and placed it on her stomach. "This is what I mean, Henry. I…we're going to have a baby!"

The room began spinning as Henry tried to absorb what he just heard. All at once, his voice bellowed throughout the halls. "It can't be! It just cannot be! After all these years? This must be a mistake! I mean, there have been times in the past when you thought you might be…I mean, at your age…oh, this is just not coming out right."

Elise took Henry's hand and danced around the room. "No darling, there is no mistake. According to Doctor Miles, our baby will be born sometime around late December."

Henry took Elise in his arms. "When and how did this happen?"

"Henry, dear, I'm not exactly sure when but I do think you know how. Or is there something your father didn't tell you? And why in the world are you crying?"

Henry enveloped his wife, putting her head on his shoulder. "Elise, do you remember our honeymoon, when we stood in the

Vatican Chapel in such a state of rapture it brought tears to our eyes? Today, darling, right this minute, God has blessed us with a moment of even greater proportions. I just can't contain the tears." Henry reclaimed the wine. "To us, darling, and to our child – our son. To Henry Gerald Merriweather IV."

Elise winced. "Perhaps there is another thing your father should have mentioned. There is every possibility it could be a girl. What shall we do then – send her back?"

"We might have to!" He bent over and kissed Elise's stomach. "A girl would be just fine if she's as wonderful as her mother." He stood tall. "But, my dear, it won't be a girl. Merriweather men make Merriweather men. It's tradition. I knew it would happen sooner or later."

Henry's visit to the mansion chapel became a daily occurrence for the remaining months of Elise's confinement and he took great pains to see that all would go well with both mother and child. He convinced Doctor Miles to take up residency in one of the luxurious guest rooms. The servants' quarters housed two nurses. Henry would see that nothing would go wrong. It had been a difficult, tedious time for Elise, who spent the last months within the confines of her bedroom suite. Henry continually referred to the baby as "our boy" causing Elise to feel the enormous pressure of delivering a son. She also understood that delivery at her age could result in complications. She prayed only for a healthy child.

And now, in perfect synchronization with the falling ball, Elise's labor pains worsened. Henry paced and moaned until Doctor Miles ordered him to stop. "For God's sake man, who's having this baby? Elise should be the one moaning! Either behave yourself or leave. This baby is coming any time now."

Henry took to the chair in the corner of the room. Finally, at midnight, Henry Gerald Merriweather IV let out a loud cry and was introduced to the world. There were shouts and cheers in an atmosphere of elated commotion. Henry kept darting between his wife and his son.

"Look at him!" he shouted, proudly. "These are Merriweather hands! And his eyes! He's got his grandfather's eyes!"

Elise just smiled, exhausted from her ordeal. "Why Henry," she teased, weakly. "You'd think I hadn't a thing to do with it!"

Henry finally realized he had been unintentionally shutting out his wife. He sat next to her, stroking and kissing her hand. "Well, I just haven't gotten to the best part yet. Our boy is going to have your wonderful personality – your tenderness, and your unwavering devotion. Together with my head for business, this young man is going to do us proud."

Suddenly, Elise shrieked in pain. "Doctor!" shouted Henry. "Come at once! Something is wrong with Elise!"

Doctor Miles responded immediately, examining his pain-ridden patient. "There's nothing wrong, Henry," he said, calmly, "but I think you'd better prepare yourself. There's another child coming."

Henry felt himself getting dizzy. His legs were giving out from under him and he did everything he could to keep himself from falling over. The anxious voice of Doctor Miles brought him around. "Come on, man, rise to the occasion! We need to concentrate on mother and baby now. Please wait outside. We'll be sure to call you the instant this one comes."

Doctor Miles nodded to the nurse. "Get ready, Noreen, this one is coming fast."

It wasn't long before Doctor Miles announced the birth of the second son. "Elise was a real trooper, Henry," he said. You take good care of this woman. She deserves to be spoiled."

"You can be sure I will, Doctor. Elise means everything to me."

"Look, Henry," Elise said, smiling but in a voice that told of pain and total exhaustion, "This is more than we bargained for. Did you have to pray that hard?"

Henry smiled, broadly. "This will be Gerald. Henry and Gerald Merriweather – my sons."

"Don't you mean our sons, Henry?" Elise said, weakly, then drifted off to sleep.

When all the confusion calmed a bit and everyone had a chance to marvel over the events of the evening, Doctor Miles and the nurses whisked away the babies for cleansing and complete examination.

"Well, my dear, you've done a remarkable job," said Doctor Miles. Women of your age rarely have uncomplicated births, especially with twins. And, they are identical. It won't be long before you'll be able to tell them apart, however. A mother instinctively knows."

Elise just shook her head, but she could hardly see for the tears that were filling her eyes. Henry's eyes were filled, too. He held her hand tight and kissed her over and over. In the communion of that moment they were never more a part of one another.

Henry and Elise remained in the embrace for a long time and, after the twins were cleaned and examined, they were placed on the bed between their parents. "Look, Elise," said a surprised Henry, watching the babies fuss, "they're hungry already. What shall we do?"

Elise laughed. "Why, we shall feed them, of course. I've already asked Dr. Miles to send another nurse. Each of the boys shall have his own, and the nurses will take care of everything – for the moment. But I want it understood that when I am feeling stronger, I shall be as involved as possible with their care. I've waited far too long for this and have no intention of giving it up."

The happy, contented babies continued to thrive. Their father hovered over them, making certain that, even at the tender age of three months, nothing would come in the way of his plans for them. One afternoon, Henry slipped into the nursery as Elise was holding little Henry, singing to him.

"Elise, you are just going to have to stop spoiling that boy," insisted Henry, smiling. He tried to pretend he was joking with her, but Elise knew him well enough to understand that his teasing could be a directive in disguise. She felt a bit offended; it was an insult to her intelligence. She looked down at the child, lovingly.

"So, why shouldn't I spoil Henry a little? Seems as though you have Gerald all the time and you rarely visit Henry's room. It's not fair, dear. You must not show even the slightest bit of favoritism, especially since the boys are twins."

"Nonsense, Elise! They're just babies. As long as they're being held, I'm sure they don't care who's doing it." But Henry understood what his wife was saying. *She's right. I am favoring Gerald. I don't even realize I'm doing it. I must be more mindful of that.*

He looked at Elise, soberly. "I'm sorry, love. You're right of course. I don't do it consciously. Somehow…" Henry did not continue with what he was going to say – that Henry, Jr. must not be aware of any outward sign of affection from his father, even now. He would have to ride his progeny hard if the boy were to be the next head of the family business and steward of the huge fortune that went with the title.

Henry's thoughts ran on through the many tomorrows that, he believed, would seriously affect his son's life. Affection spoils everything. It makes a man weak and vulnerable. He will need to be as strong and dynamic as any proud Merriweather. Henry continued to convince himself what he was doing was the proper thing to ensure success.

Elise interrupted his thoughts. "I know you mean well, Henry, but it won't be long before little Henry will be able to understand that you favor Gerald. Babies are good at that. Quite honestly, I was afraid you'd favor Henry, his being your namesake. Yes, I'm more than a bit surprised by that."

Elise went over to him and kissed him on the cheek. "I know, dear. I can't imagine you'd be deliberate, but we both need to be aware that it is going to be somewhat challenging to raise twins, especially identical boys. There will no doubt be family expectations and other conflicts they will face. But I feel confident that the same God that sent them to us will help us do what is right for both of them, and for each of them.

Elise walked over to the crib, picked up Henry, and placed him in his father's arms. Henry held his son for a few moments, patting him on the back in tandem with the ticking clock – one, two, three, four, five, six. Then, he handed Henry over to his mother and went to get Gerald.

Henry decided to leave the bank early one spring day for a stroll through the park. It was the kind of day that was perfect for taking in all the sights – giggling young lovers holding hands; sunlit daffodils and scarlet tulips; children flying brightly colored kites. Inside a fence, a mare held her head proudly, coaching her new foal.

Henry walked closer, interested in observing how they worked together. The mare seemed to be coaxing and prodding and nudging, her way of establishing discipline. *See,* he thought, *that mare knows what she's doing. She's letting her foal know that there is to be no nonsense, and her foal is responding beautifully.*

Henry continued walking, all the while thinking of his boys, the sweet innocent children who had no understanding of how their father was preparing to set up their lives. Henry walked over to a bench and sat down, allowing his thoughts to race as he formulated a plan.

The boys are three now. It's time Henry begins to toughen up. He's just like his mother, sensitive and undemanding. I love him, of course, but he must learn early on that this is not the stuff Merriweathers are made of.He'll get nowhere at the bank if he remains soft. But he won't remain soft. I'll see to it.

Henry put his head back, taking in the afternoon sun, happy with his plans. Gerald will be mine. He is the son I can enjoy. We'll do all of the things men do together. When it's time, I'll have him work abroad with a few of our foreign clients while Henry will remain in Manhattan and run the entire business. It's a masterful arrangement, and the sooner I begin, the better it will be for everyone.

Henry rose and began walking home with a new resolve. I'll begin today. The boys should spend time apart so they do not influence one another.

He ran up the steps and through the front door, shouting "Elise! Gather the nurses and come to the study at once!"

Elise answered his call immediately, fearing that something dreadful happened. "What is it, Henry? What…"

"It's nothing terrible." Henry took his wife's hand and led her to a chair on the nearby patio. "I have a proposal, dear, and I know that you will be excited about what I have to say. We're going to make some changes in the boys' schedules."

Elise sunk back in the chair. "Oh, for heaven's sake, Henry, the way you're carrying on one would think you'd done something really extraordinary. If it's only a matter of changing their bedtime…"

Henry cut her short. "Well, that's part of it – a very large part, actually. You see, Elise," said Henry, pacing with his hands behind his back, "I've concluded that the boys are missing a sense of individuality. They should not go on seeing themselves as a mirror image of each other. It will not be good for either of them to walk in their brother's shadow. It is vitally important that they are separate and distinct, no more alike than siblings that are not twins. To that end, I think we should rearrange their daily schedule, so they spend less time together and more time alone or with other children."

Henry tried to read the expression on Elise's face, but this time she showed no emotion. He couldn't be certain she was buying what he was offering. He made a clumsy attempt to turn the conversation.

"I just had word that my sister Inez and family are moving here from Boston. What a great opportunity for the boys to know their cousins! There's Edward and little Sally and…"

Elise bristled. "Let's get back to the issue at hand, Henry. What exactly do you plan to do? Why are the nurses here?"

It was clear she was annoyed. How could her husband, the man that always shared everything with her, have the audacity to orchestrate this entire arrangement without even consulting her? She was beginning to see a different side to her husband, a side she very much disliked and wished she did not have to know.

"It's all very simple," Henry answered. "Nurse Anna, Henry ordered, "you will see to it that little Henry is the first to rise. After his morning routine you will work on constructive play, then lunch and an afternoon walk. Dinner for him will be at 5:00 and bedtime will be set at 7:00."

My Lord! Elise was dumbfounded. What is he doing? Where did this come from?

"Nurse Maude," Henry went on. "It will be your responsibility to set Gerald's schedule apart from Henry's. They should be doing different things at different times." Henry looked at each nurse. "Do you understand?"

The nurses looked at Elise quizzically, but she was too shocked to respond immediately. Finally, she found the words to confront her husband.

"Henry! What in the name of all that is good and holy are you suggesting? The boys adore each other, even now! If you keep them apart they will be devastated."

Henry walked over to Elise and gave her a light hug. "I know you must think it a bit strange, dear, but I've been studying the research on identical twins. There's a lot going on in that field lately, and our boys will benefit from the new evidence. It's all about individuality now. Each of our boys will have a chance to grow and thrive in his own skin."

Henry could tell Elise was hurt. He tried to interject something that might mitigate her bad feelings. "You know how much you've always believed that I was favoring Gerald? With the new schedules in place, we'll both have time to spend with each of the boys. And…and, tell you what! Sundays will be for all of us. No nurses, no schedules – just plenty of time to enjoy one another. Alright?" He lifted his wife's chin and kissed her forehead. "Alright?" he repeated, his voice rising.

Elise could tell from her husband's tone she did not have a chance. She could reject the idea totally, but she understood Henry's character and knew it would result in having him brood and become sullen until she finally relented. It would be best for everyone to just give in and save the rest of the drama.

"If you insist, Henry," she said, in a voice that betrayed the hurt she was feeling. But Henry did not recognize the pain. He had gotten his way.

It was not in Elise's character to be devious, and she thought about it often. The boys are mine, too, and it pains me to not have them together. I will do what I need to do.

When Henry was away and occupied with business, Elise would go off on holiday to their home in the country and have the boys' nurses deliver them to her. She knew she was doing the right thing when she watched them together. They loved each other so, but Elise knew it would only be a matter of time before Henry would find out about the arrangement. Soon, they would be describing their country visits to their father. Elise could not risk a confrontation. She was not sure of how Henry would retaliate. Her once loving, attentive partner was now a shadow of the man she had known and loved deeply. His goal now was not in her happiness, but in the assurance of keeping the Merriweather name alive and well. He never once deviated from his ambition.

For the next few years, Henry kept his promise about having the family together on Sundays, but the time they spent seemed forced and stilted. Gerald continued to remain at his father's side. The two would go off to the lake, boating, swimming, and fishing, happy to just be together. Henry was required to remain behind to work on the puzzles his father set up for him.

"By the time we return, Henry, I expect to see twenty new pieces fit into where they belong. And don't be crying to your mother for help!" Henry looked at Elise, shaking his finger. "And don't you be pampering him. He has to learn."

He took Gerald by the hand. "Come with me, son. I've spotted a good catch in the creek, just begging to be caught."

Gerald instinctively acknowledged that his father was hurting Henry. But he was growing older and could already understand how to use his father to full advantage. "Can we go to the ice cream store for a sundae after?" he asked, hugging his father around his waist.

Henry smiled. "Of course, son. How about chocolate ice cream with marshmallow topping and, if we get that big fish, a cherry to celebrate."

Little Henry watched the two go off, fighting back tears and wondering what was wrong with him. He hurried to work at the puzzle. *Maybe, if I'm able to fit in thirty pieces, Father will take me next time.*

The child worked quickly to complete the task, certain that his father would notice, but try as he might, he could not gain his father's adulation. Like the puzzle pieces before him, he would be examined and turned in every direction; then tossed aside until there was a place he might fit.

CHAPTER TWO

*"How sharper than a serpent's tooth to have a
thankless child."*

The plan Henry Merriweather set in place for his twin sons since
their birth, eleven years ago, seemed to be succeeding. Separate
activities, separate camps, different friends, caused them to
spend less and less time together, and to drift farther and farther
apart. Young Henry, isolated and lonely, was beginning to find
comfort in being alone, reading or sketching or studying. He was
becoming dangerously serious and introspective; polite and
mannerly, seldom smiling. His mother was worried. She
recognized this behavior to be out of character for such a young
boy. It was almost as though someone had taken away his
childhood and he had been forced to enter the adult world long
before his time.

Gerald, on the other hand, continued to be a happy, gregarious
child, his father's favorite. He was old enough to understand that
his captivating smile and phony adulation could win the hearts of
the household staff, his schoolmates, and his teachers. He was
adept at manipulating those around him to best serve his selfish
needs.

The stable boy told him how much he loved to smoke, so Gerald
pilfered the chauffer's cigarettes and gave them in trade for a
forbidden ride on one of the most dangerous horses.

Gerald learned to use all his wiles with women early on.
"Bessie," he'd say to the old cook, "is that a new hairdo? You're
going to have to beat the guys away!" His remarks resulted in a
whole bag of Bessie's peanut brittle next day.

Elise was very much aware of what Gerald was doing and
refused to fall prey to his machinations. "Gerald, how much do

you know about me?" she asked, one day after learning that her son paid the stable boy to sweep out the stalls – a job she had given him as punishment for forging her signature on his disgraceful report card.

Gerald hesitated. "What do you mean, Mother? I know you quilt beautifully and you're great at bridge. Let's see…you love good books, and…oh, yes, you're the most beautiful mother of all my friends."

"My, my. You are good. But there's something you don't know about me." Elise moved closer to her son, looked directly into his eyes, and dug a finger into his shoulder.

"I'm smart, son. Very smart. I've been around your father's business acquaintances long enough to have garnered a strong sense of how certain conniving persons use others to their own ends. I regret to think that my own son could be capable of adopting such deceitful behavior."

Elise retrieved the comic book that Gerald was holding and threw it into the trash. "It may work for most people but be careful around your mother who is a good deal wiser. I know exactly what you're doing. You may be clever enough to get around your father and the household staff, but you've met a formidable force in me!"

Gerald reached into the trashcan to retrieve his comic book. "Nice try, Mother, but Father will always take my part so…so, just give up, will you?"

Elise, hurt and frustrated by her son's callous disrespect wanted to slap him. Instead, she took a minute to compose herself, then reached for his hand.

"Gerald, I've tried to raise you boys in the spirit of noblesse oblige. You are very blessed to have been born into the Merriweather fortune. We must all remember that, because we are so fortunate, much is expected of us. Sometimes, when children have too much, they become selfish and insensitive to the feelings of others. I pray this could not be true of my boys."

In response, Gerald shrugged his shoulders and rolled his eyes. It infuriated Elise. "Someday, Gerald, you are going to be stung when you least expect it. Someday, I promise, you will cause pain to someone you may care for deeply, and you will regret it. Please recognize what you are doing and put an end to your egregious behavior!"

Gerald snickered. "Whoa, Mother, you're not talking to Henry now. What was that word again?"

"Egregious! And it's about time you started improving your vocabulary!" Her son's cockiness caused Elise to lose control – the very thing she was fighting against. She locked herself in her bedroom, flinging herself across the bed. Her prayer was more of frustration than supplication. *Please, God! Please help me to understand this child. I'm afraid for him. He doesn't seem to have a remorseful bone in his body. He will continue to use anyone he thinks will get him what he wants. I am at a total loss. I leave it in your hands."*

Young Henry, having heard the whole argument, went to his mother. His heart was breaking for the person dearest to him. "Don't cry, Mother," he said, kissing her cheek. "Sometimes, Gerald says things he doesn't mean."

Henry didn't believe what he was saying, but he couldn't see his mother suffering. "I'll always take care of you, Mother. You'll see." He pulled her up from the bed. "Let's go to the kitchen. I'll make us a good cup of tea, and we can share the last piece of apple pie."

It was breaking her heart. *This poor, pitiful child! He shouldn't have to try so hard to make things right.* As they sat down to the table, she pulled a chair close to hers. "Come, sit near me," she said. The obedient child moved closer and rested his head on his mother's shoulder.

"Someday, Henry," Elise said, stroking his hair, "you will be a fine man. You'll have a wonderful woman to love you and to share your life. And you will take your own children fishing and camping and to visit their grandmother. It will happen. You'll see."

Henry began fumbling with his necktie. "Girls don't like me, Mother. They say I'm weird. They like Gerald a lot. They're always inviting him to birthday parties, but they never invite me. And, well, Father doesn't like me, either. Why doesn't he? I try hard, but I must have done something very wrong for him to turn me away."

Henry rose, looking like a pathetic, unworthy, waif of a child, begging to be loved. Elise felt a crushing pain like a vise bearing down on her chest.

"Oh, darling boy, don't you know that girls play silly games? They invite Gerald because he flatters them and tells them how beautiful they look. Young girls fall for all that nonsense. But you, dearest," she said, gathering him in her arms, "you do not need to gain attention in that way. It will be your respect for women and your superior intelligence that will one day draw lovely women to you. Not now, Henry. Not now, but someday."

Elise purposely avoided the issue of Henry's feelings about his father. There was nothing she could say or do to make things better.

CHAPTER THREE

"It is a wise father that knows his own child."

"Elise," Henry commanded. I must take an important call. The boys are in the study. Tell them to wait for me. And please, instruct the staff that under no circumstances are we to be disturbed."

The boys took their places in the soft, leather chairs, waiting for their father as instructed. Gerald poked his brother, teasing.

"I think this is it, Henry! It's the big one. I can tell. Father's been fumbling with his necktie all day. It's a dead giveaway. It means he's nervous. And you know what he's nervous about? Only one thing I can think of. He's going to give us the big talk. You know, birds, bees, and birth control."

Henry began shifting from side to side. "Now? You mean, he's going to talk to us about…well, you know."

"I sure do know, brother. I sure do. Little does our father know that I'm way past that – way, way past that! As a matter of fact, I can probably teach him a thing or two." Gerald laughed, pointing to his crotch.

Henry was shocked. "You can't mean…I mean…it can't be! You're only thirteen!"

"Yeah, isn't that great? So, you, my friend, have a lot of catching up to do."

"But who…where…how?" Henry couldn't imagine how his brother had been able to pull it off without anyone finding out.

"God, Henry! You really don't get it, do you? I can see it's gonna be my job to educate you. See, first you got to find somebody who isn't gonna tell the whole damn town. Somebody who isn't crying afterward, like 'Oh, Gerald, do you love me?' And worse, 'Will you respect me after?' he mimicked in a sing-song voice. What a bunch of crap! I, for one, will love and respect any horny broad who'll give me what I want, and I found myself a real honeypot. The only thing she wants from me is sex – and plenty of it!"

Henry's shock turned to a real need to know. "Is it Madeline McDonald? Everybody at school says she's easy. I heard them say she puts out. Is that what they mean?"

"Yeah, stupid. That's what they mean. But that's not who it is. Madeline's just an amateur. You don't think for one tiny minute that your brother would fool around with young stuff that don't know a thing about how to perform!"

"Perform what?" Henry's eyes were wide now, and he could feel himself sweating.

"Good God, my dumb brother! I can't believe we were sprung from the same loins! Perform sex, idiot! Anything your heart desires, my friend. I've had it all – and from the best. Frenchy taught me plenty. I was a little nervous at first, sure, but she helped me get over it real fast."

Henry just shook his head in disbelief. Gerald went on, "Hell, Henry, you sure know a lot about math and manners and the market, but you don't know squat about what really counts. Get with it, brother! Once you get it, you'll never again give a damn about math and the rest. Just go do it, Henry, but get a good one. As a matter of fact, I'll set it up for you."

"Are you going to tell me who it is, Gerald?"

"Okay, but don't go blabbing it to Mom. I know the two of you are thick, but if she finds out she'll insist on sending me to military school, and that would be a disaster." Gerald put his head against the door to see if he could hear his father's footsteps. He spoke quietly.

"It all happened when we were at our other house a few months ago. I was riding my bike about two miles past the crossroads and came to the French house. I…"

"You mean where Eunice French lives? I met her once. But it can't be her! She's so timid and shy."

"You're right. It's not Eunice. I wouldn't give her the time of day. But her mother! Now, that's a different story."

"Her mother!" Henry shouted, in disbelief.

"Shut the hell up, will you! You wanna get us both sent away?"

"But how did it happen? I mean, how did you know…"

"Luck, brother. Just plain old-fashioned luck. I didn't know a thing about her except she'd always smile and wave to me when I rode by. One day, I was riding by her house and I got thirsty. I knew there was a pump in the back yard, so I knocked on the door and asked if I could have a drink. Frenchy was as drunk as a skunk. She told me to come in and she'd give me a cold drink. As she walked past me on her way to the refrigerator, she pressed her big, luscious boobs against me. She started talking about weather and school and all kinds of crap, but I could tell from the minute I walked in she was hot for me."

"How could you tell? Did she say so?" Henry started getting up from his chair. "Ah, you're just making up this whole story. I bet you never…"

Gerald snickered. "So, you think I'm making it up, huh? Well, I don't really give a damn whether you believe me or not. It's your loss. There's a lot more to tell, but if you don't want to hear it…"

Henry refused to show Gerald his naiveté. "Okay, okay. I believe you. What happened then?"

Gerald could tell that he had Henry's complete attention. He took great pleasure in describing all the details. "It didn't take long before that broad had her hands down my pants. Well, you don't think I'd turn it down! I mean up until then, all I ever did was think about it and dream about it. Before you know it, we were rolling around in the sack. Let me tell you, Frenchy was true to her name. I had it all, and I mean all! I was initiated good and proper."

Henry looked away. He still did not understand what his brother was talking about. He'd heard talk from some of the boys at school about "feeling up" some girls, but that's all he knew.

"Did you ever go back?"

Gerald laughed. "Are you kidding me? Would you? Let me tell you that once you've had it, you'll think of nothing else. Father is happy when I get excited about going to our country house on weekends. I'm excited, all right. Real excited!"

Henry heard enough. He forced himself to remain calm, not showing any sign of emotion. He knew how much his brother thrived on delivering something shocking, and he'd be hanged if he'd give him the satisfaction of listening to one more remark. He chastised himself for allowing the conversation to get this far.

"I've heard enough, Gerald, and I don't like what I'm hearing. If you get caught and our parents find out that I know about your visits to that woman, I'd be in big trouble for not telling them. I don't want to hear any more."

Henry was getting worried, not for Gerald, but for the scandal that would be thrust upon the family if it were found out. The French family could and probably would tap into the Merriweather wealth in exchange for keeping quiet. After all, they wouldn't have to be concerned about a tarnished reputation, and they knew the Merriweathers could afford to pay plenty to erase the scandal. The thought prompted a question.

"Aren't you afraid of getting caught? I mean, what if her husband comes home or what if Eunice finds out?"

"Well, it's like this. The husband walked out a while back and Eunice…well, I'll tell you what, Henry, if Eunice happens to walk in on us, I'll…I'll just invite her to join us. Then, when she's well-seasoned, I'll give her to you. Call it a gift."

Henry couldn't believe what he was hearing. How could Gerald ever think that he…

Gerald leaned in closer to his brother and grinned. "Now, wouldn't that be a kick, Henry? What the hell, it would all be nice and cozy – all in the family, you might say. Then, when you finally get to be a man – that is, if you ever do, you'll thank me."

Henry's ire had been growing until he no longer could contain himself. He rose from the chair, put two hands on his brother's shoulders, looked directly into Gerald's devious eyes and said, "You know what, Gerald? You are disgusting. You're worse than disgusting. You are pig dung!"

He grabbed his brother by the hair and lifted his face to meet his own. "If you really want to know the truth, little boy, I've always been jealous of you. Father always favored you, though I cannot even begin to understand why. You get whatever you want because you use people. And when you don't have any use for them, or if they need something from you, you just get rid of them and move along to the next poor victim. You are a pathetic excuse for a human being and this…this Frenchy is too good for you!"

Gerald painted his face with a smirk. "So? So what? I get what I want, while Mother's good little Henry goes on playing with his toys, wishing he could be like me. Only, he's not smart enough! Not smart enough to figure out how to play the game."

He pulled away from Henry's grip and slammed his hand down on the arm of the chair.

"Or…geeze, Henry! I know - you're one of those queers, aren't you? Now I understand why the stable boy is looking so happy these days."

Henry fought to have his voice remain calm. He would not show Gerald any sign of the fury exploding within him. "That doesn't even deserve an answer, Gerald. I don't owe you or anyone an explanation for who I am or what I am. Do I have to treat people like trash to prove I'm a man? And do you know what? I'm glad we had this conversation. It taught me that I don't want to be one bit like you. You treat people like dirt. You may think you're smart, but you're stupid, and some day your selfishness is going to catch up with you. I hope I'm around to see it!"

The boys heard their father's footsteps. They settled back in their chairs, awaiting the talk their father had planned. But Henry already had his lesson. And Gerald didn't need it.

CHAPTER FOUR

"You told a lie. An odious, damned lie…"

The sun was reflecting brightly on the lake, but its warming rays did nothing to stave off the cold of the November day. Henry was the first to speak. "So, Gerald, what is it? We've been together seventeen years, so I know you well enough to understand that you didn't ask me to come out on the lake with you because it's the brotherly thing to do, did you?"

Gerald responded, "No, I didn't. But I could have. I mean, I really like you Henry, and we don't get to spend a lot of time together. We should, though, and I'm gonna see to it that we do in the future. I…"

"Just stop, Gerald! We're not close and we both know it. Now let's just get to what's going on. Are you in trouble again?"

Silence filled the air for a moment. It gave Henry time to conclude that his brother probably was. "Answer me, Gerald. What is it now? Is it big?"

Gerald just looked at him and didn't respond. Henry slammed his fist against the side of the boat. "I knew it! What now? Did you get caught cheating again or is it money trouble? It's the only time you know me."

For the first time, Henry witnessed a serious look on his brother's face.

"No, nothing like that," Gerald responded. "I can only wish it could have been something as simple as that. I could have managed through that kind of thing, but this…"

"So, get on with it. But understand that this time, dear brother, I'm not going to bail you out. I don't care if you do get shipped off to military school instead of to father's grand Alma Mater. Everything is always about you, Gerald, and you don't give a hoot about anybody else. It's time you grew up."

Gerald reached down and retrieved a brilliant red leaf floating on the lake, twirling it around his fingers. "You know, Henry, sometimes I wish I could be like this leaf – just there for everybody to enjoy and admire. No expectations, nothing to think of or worry about."

"Cut it out! Get to the point. This isn't about leaves."

"A minute ago, you said it was always about me. Well, this time it's about you, Henry."

Henry stopped rowing. "About me? How could anything be about me?"

Gerald began tearing the leaf to shreds. "You know how identical we are. Even the house servants can't tell us apart."

"Not *are*, Gerald, *look*. We are identical *looking*. Get on with it. I want to get back."

"Okay, just remember that everything can be fixed."

"Good Lord! Will you get on with it! If you're going to tell me, tell me."

"Okay, here it is. A couple of months ago, right before the Back to School prom, I noticed gorgeous Celine Harding in the hall. I'd been wanting to take her out for a long time, but she's really fussy about who she dates. I knew I didn't have a chance, not with my reputation. So, while we were in English class, I gave Bill Williams a note and asked him to deliver it to her. It was a really nice note about how much I respected her and that I'd be honored to have her go to the prom with me. She wrote back right away and said she was hoping I'd ask her, and that she'd be glad to go."

There was a short pause. "Okay. Is that it? You came here to tell me you took Celine Harding to the prom? I already know that."

"Well…it's not that simple. Actually, I…I kind of… signed *your* name to the note. Celine thought she was responding to you."

Henry turned scarlet. "Damn you, Gerald! Damn you, you did it again! You've used my name in the past to get what you wanted, now this? What kind of a person are you? I've begged you not to do it again and you promised you wouldn't!" Henry had all he could do to keep from pushing his brother into the lake.

"Why do you continue to do this? Do you think I have no limit to what I'll tolerate from you? Well, you're wrong! This time I'm finished. I'm going to Father and tell him what you did. Not that I expect it will do much good. If he had taken a stand with you long ago, we might not now be having this conversation. But, who knows, Father may even have reached his limits with you!"

Gerald buried his head in his hands. "Umm…there's more. I haven't told you the worse part. After the prom, we went back to Celine's house. Her parents were gone for the weekend, and I…well, we had too much to drink and we spent the night in bed."

Everything came spewing out. "I didn't mean for anything to happen, Henry, honest I didn't. But, well… you know."

Henry shot Gerald a look of disgust. "What? You spent the night with her, and she still thinks it was me." Henry was silent for a moment; then said, "That's it! I won't have it, Gerald. I will not have Celine think I could be capable of such behavior. I'm going straight to her house and tell her everything."

"That's not all," said Gerald, "and it's why you can't go to see Celine. See… uh, I called her this morning. She started to cry and told me she's pregnant."

At first, Henry felt like he was drowning. He was sure he'd fallen overboard and was experiencing some kind of blackout. When he came to his senses, he realized this was, indeed, real. His brother had used his name once again and had gotten a girl pregnant.

"And you never told her you lied to her, so she still thinks it was me, right?" Henry shouted.

Gerald raised his voice. "Well, what did you want me to do? I was so shocked by what she was telling me that I didn't know what to do. I know it was wrong, but God, Henry, don't make it such a big deal. I just didn't know how to get out of it."

Henry responded, "That's strange!" You're a master at knowing what to do at exactly the right time. Forgive me if I don't believe you." He turned the motor on full speed and headed to shore.

Gerald kept shouting. "Henry, please don't do this. We have to talk this out. I'm sorry. Honest. I know you want to go straight to Father and tell him the whole thing, but you know that if you do, it'll ruin my chances for Yale. God only knows where I'll end up. Father's been getting tough with me ever since I got drunk and totaled his Mercedes. I'm afraid he'll keep his word and send me off to New York Military Academy."

Gerald was saving the trump card and now was the time to use it. "And you know that Father will tell Mother. You know how sick she is, Henry. Her heart is so bad that a shock like this could kill her! Neither of us would want that, would we?"

Henry kept going, faster now. "You should have thought about Mother while you were doing it, Gerald."

"OK. I deserve that. But, there's a way out. There's something we can do, and nobody will know. Here's my plan. You go to Father and tell him you got a girl in trouble. He's not going to think a thing of it, Henry. In fact, Father will be glad. You know how he is. He already suspects you're queer – something he absolutely detests and will never accept. If he thinks you've got the spunk to get a girl pregnant…well, he'll be thrilled. Trust me, I know Father. I've already spoken to Celine and we came to an understanding. She's agreed to leave town and stay with her cousin in Florida. She has no intention of becoming a mother and wants to give the baby for adoption. She'll never name the father. All this, of course, for a hefty price."

Henry did not want to hear any more but, like it or not, he was in it too deep. "And who do you suppose is going to provide the money for your plan?"

"Father, of course. All you have to do is tell him what happened. He'll take care of everything in minutes."

"How can you be sure he won't tell Mother? She's the one I worry about."

"He won't tell her. He doesn't tell her about lots of things."

"I can't! I won't! You're asking me to admit to something that goes against everything I believe in. No, Gerald! No! All these years I've had to sit by and watch you and Father go off together while I was stuck in my room, studying and wishing I could be you, just once. Now, on top of all of that, you want me to take the heat for you. No, I tell you! I've had enough!"

"What if I told you I'll change. No more wine, women, and song. If you do this and I get to Yale, I promise to buckle down and become a student. I just need a chance, Henry, just one chance."

The boat reached the shore. Henry was the first to climb out. "Who are you kidding, Gerald? You'll never be a student. You don't have it in you. I said no, I mean no!"

Gerald picked up a stone and flung it hard into the lake. "Well, I'll just have to tell Father. I may as well tell Mother, too. She'll have to know."

Henry twisted his brother's shirt collar. "Don't you dare! Don't you dare tell Mother. You know how proper she is. This will kill her."

Gerald punched him in the stomach. "Let me go, you fool! I'm telling you that if you don't agree to this, I will go to Mother. How will it feel for you to be responsible for her death?"

"You would do that? I can't believe even you would stoop so low."

"Watch me, Henry. In fact, I'll visit Mother as soon as we get back. She should be the first to know."

Elise's bedroom suite door was closed, a sign that she was still napping and wished not to be disturbed.

Gerald ignored the signal and knocked. "Mother, I'm sorry to disturb you, but we really should talk."

"Is that you, Henry? Have you come with my tea?"

Gerald opened the door and entered, with Henry following. "No, Mother, it's Gerald, but Henry's right behind me."

Elise was genuinely pleased. "Oh, what a lovely surprise," she said, as Gerald fluffed the pillow behind her. "I never get to see the two of you together any longer. I'm thrilled."

"Gerald sat down at the foot of the bed and took her hand. "Well, Mother, I don't know if you're going to be so thrilled when I tell you what I've come about."

Henry kept poking Gerald hard on his shoulder. He whispered, "Don't you dare!"

Gerald began. "I don't know quite how to tell this to you, Mother. I don't want to upset you, but…"

Henry could not let it happen. His mother meant everything to him, and he couldn't watch her fade at the news. He went over to Elise, kissed her cheek, and gave her a broad smile.

"Oh, that brother of mine!" Henry forced a chuckle. "He worries about you so; you'd think you were made of cotton candy. He won't be able to get it out, so I'll tell you. You know that Father has been able to get Gerald into Yale. What he's trying to say is that he wants to leave immediately after graduation instead of waiting until fall. He says it can give him a real head start so he can study until school begins."

Gerald stepped back. I knew it! I knew Henry would never let his mother suffer. So what if I have to leave early for college? It'll give me more time to party.

Henry continued. "He's so afraid you'll be upset with him leaving early, but I told him I thought you'd be fine with it. You know I'll be here to look after you until school begins in September. What do you think, Mother?"

Elise smiled, relieved. "Why, is that all it is? Naturally, I don't want either of you away from me. I need a little time to get used to the fact that my boys will be going off on their own. I'm proud that you've made such a responsible decision. I think it's a brilliant idea! We can start shopping tomorrow!"

Gerald kissed his mother. "Thanks, Mother. I had a strong feeling you'd agree. Now, we're off to tell Father."

The boys walked down the long corridor towards their father's study. "This is it, Henry," said Gerald. "This is as far as I go. The rest is up to you. Remember what I said. Don't be too serious, and you'll see that Father will make light of the whole thing."

"You know I'm doing this for Mother's sake. You win the match, Gerald, but I promise someday I am going to win the trophy. Don't ever forget this promise!"

Henry Merriweather III was seated at his desk, poring over some old documents when young Henry knocked.

"Henry! How good to see you! How are things at school? I received some bills from Harvard yesterday and paid them, promptly. Happy to do that for you, Son."

"Thank you, Father, but I'm not so sure you're going to be happy when I deliver the news about why I'm here."

"Well, now, Henry. What could be so terrible? Your grades are great. You'll be the class valedictorian, for sure. And some day, you'll take over for me at the bank. I'd say things are just about as good as can be. So, what's the problem?"

"It's girl problems, Father. I kind of…well… I got a girl pregnant."

His father didn't speak for a few moments but continued puffing on his pipe. Finally, he said, "Is the girl going to cause trouble? I mean, you certainly don't plan on marrying her, do you?"

"No, I barely know her. It was just a one-night thing. She's planning to give the child for adoption, but she wants money. Lots of it. She told me she'll have to leave school and go away for a while, and she'll have tons of expenses. She said she'll never disclose the father's name, if I give her enough money to forget the whole thing."

"Are you sure about this, Henry? Sounds like blackmail to me."

"Yes, I suppose it is a kind of blackmail. But I don't see any way out, do you?"

His father did not respond immediately; then said, "No, we don't want the Merriweather name sullied. Your mother would be destroyed." Henry's father leaned forward in his chair, still puffing, and dialed the number of his attorney.

"Tom, it's Henry. We have a little situation here. Nothing big. Just a little… you know, boys will be boys." He went on to describe the entire event. "Meet me here in the morning with the necessary papers. You understand that it must be an ironclad agreement. Then, the girl can come to your office and sign the documents. I think we should offer monthly checks until the child is eighteen. Tell her that if she discloses any part of this, her checks will be discontinued. Make it lucrative enough for her to keep her mouth shut but make it clear that if she thinks she can go on asking for more, the deal is off. Thanks, Tom!"

Gerald was right. If his father was upset, there was no sign of it.

"It's all taken care of. Your mother shall not know." He smiled. "And Henry, I don't want you to be the least concerned over this."

Henry rose from his chair and put his arm around his son's shoulders. "Truth be told, I've been known to have a few…well…experiences in my day, but I was just a bit luckier than you. I very much realize how hard it is for a man to control those urges. Don't ever be ashamed of being a man, son. Next time try to be a little more careful, that's all. You can have whatever you want if you know where to go. Classy, beautiful women who will do anything for a price and not ask questions. If you're interested, I can arrange it."

Henry left his father's study feeling nauseous and wanting to be alone. He flopped across his bed and stayed there for the rest of the afternoon, trying to assimilate all that happened. He lost whatever small amount of respect he had left for his father. It would have been more acceptable if his father displayed rage, but his cavalier attitude about such a serious matter and his complete disregard for Celine left Henry cold. And it seemed to him that his father knew too much about "classy, beautiful women." Could it be…? The idea sickened him.

Henry asked to be excused from dinner that evening. Instead, he built a fire in the patio fireplace, wrapped himself in a woolen blanket, and sat, watching the lingering embers. Elise, thinking Henry must be ill, sent Gerald in search of him.

"Hey," Gerald said, approaching his brother. "Mom wants to know where you are. You sick?"

Henry did not look up but continued to stare at the fire. "Well, yes, I suppose you could say I'm sick. Fact is, I'm sitting here thinking of just how sick I am – of you. I'm trying to come up with an idea to make myself feel better. I think I've finally found the answer."

"Oh, come on, Henry! You're just upset right now. It all worked out okay, didn't it? No one's the wiser."

"That's where you're wrong. I'm the wiser. I wonder if I will ever be able to look at myself in the mirror and not think of how I didn't stand up to you. That pain will never go away. I can't change it, but I can do something to get my life back."

Henry rose and moved close to Gerald so he could look at him directly. "I've decided that you will no longer be my brother. For now, and until you leave in June, I will remain in the house and pretend to be happy. I can do that. I've had a lot of practice. After that, I promise I will never see you or speak to you in any way except at holiday time when I have no choice but to be at home. So, go on your way. Do what you do. Live your life. But do not attempt to contact me in any way or for any reason. I will not be available to you."

"Don't be a fool, Henry! You know father has plans for both of us to work together. We're going to have to begin at the bank in four years. What are you going to do then? Have silent business conversations?"

"I have no idea what will happen between now and then. Maybe things will somehow be different, and father will come to his senses. I certainly hope so. Right now, get out of my sight because if you don't leave, I will."

Part Two

1940 to 1951

Tabitha Whittier

Jed Whittier

CHAPTER FIVE

*"When we're born we cry that we are come to
this great stage of fools."*

"Where is that doctor?" Pastor Jed Whittier bellowed. "Bertha,
come here at once!" The housekeeper ran up the steps and into
the bedroom where Jed's wife, Anna, lay suffering a long and
difficult labor.

"I don't know, suh!" answered the anxious housekeeper. "I sent
my Bill to find him this morning, but the milkman come by and
tol me Doctor Hubbard probly at Colonel Hanson's lunch party,
it bein' New Year's Day and all. 1940! Can you believe it? Well,
Miss Anna, she shoulda gone to the hospital a while ago. Now,
looks like I's gonna have to do it myself."

Anna screamed, "Jed, do something! Lord above, do
something!" Bertha rolled up her sleeves and threw Jed a look
that she meant business.

"I's tellin' you to leave this room, Pastor Jed. I ain't got no time
to deal with the likes of you. Gwan! Bertha done brung many a
chil' and this one's comin' fast now. Git!"

Jed did as he was told. He took his post outside the bedroom
door where he could hear the long, low moans of his wife.
Bertha continued to shout orders. "It's comin' now, Mrs. Anna.
You jes hold tight to that bedpost and push hard. In another
minute you is gonna have a beautiful little girl or boy." Finally,
there was a long scream, followed by a deafening silence; then,
Bertha's loud wail.

"Mr. Jed! Mr. Jed! You needs to come!" Jed pushed his way past
the excited woman to his wife's side. "What's wrong?" he
insisted, fearing the worst.

"Mrs. Anna done fainted, but the baby…the baby…she's gone, Mr. Jed!" Bertha began sobbing. "Lord have mercy," was all she could say as she handed the baby to him.

Jed took the limp, lifeless body of his new daughter into his arms. Somewhere he had read about gently massaging the baby's heart. He wrapped the child in a blanket and rubbed her chest, ever so gently. Then, he began blowing softly into the baby's mouth.

Suddenly, the baby began to cry, flailing her arms and kicking her feet. "Well, now," said Jed, turning to Bertha. "Good thing I knew what to do. You sure are not much good in a crisis, are you?"

Bertha lowered her head. "No, sir, Mr. Jed. You done a fine job, suh, a fine job."

And so, it was that Tabitha Whittier came into the world – a traumatic event for both mother and child. Anna remained in bed, exhausted and pale, while Bertha took over the care of the child.

A few hours after the birth, Doctor Hubbard arrived to examine Anna and the new baby. "You certainly have a beautiful child Jed," he said. This little one had a rough start, but she's fine now."

Before Jed could respond, Doctor Hubbard went on. "Let's step outside for a moment," he said, soberly. "We need to talk."

The two stepped out into the hall. The doctor put his hand on Jed's arm. "Anna's not to have another child, Jed. She wouldn't be able to survive the trauma. Her heart is already weak."

Jed did not know how to respond. After a few moments, he spoke. "I…I don't know what to say. I mean, I don't really care about another child, but…are you trying to tell me that I can't…well…I shouldn't…so what's a man supposed to do, anyway?"

"Do you hear what I'm saying, man? Your wife's heart is very weak. She may not be around to see Tabitha grow to be an adult. Seems to me, especially you being a man of God, you'd be more concerned about Anna than with your own pleasures!"

"I'm sorry, doctor, it's just such a huge shock. Of course, I'm concerned about Anna."

Doctor Hubbard calmed down a bit. "There are methods of birth control, as I am quite certain you know. And…uh…there are other ways of getting close to your wife. I'm sure you understand."

Jed thought about the times he'd been with other women who would do anything, try anything just to be with him. He recalled his first sexual experience – a clumsy attempt behind a bale of hay. It was far from romantic, but it was raw and forbidden. He knew immediately that it was the best thing that had ever happened to him. He knew that he could use his good looks and winsome manner to get more – much, much more. And he did.

"I understand perfectly, Doctor, he said, rubbing his forehead. "But, Anna, well…she believes there is only one way for a man and woman to be together and even that is to be reserved for the procreation of children. She's also very naive about the ways of the world. She doesn't understand that things are different now. Women are beginning to think there's nothing wrong with a good…Oh, pardon me for being so forward."

Doctor Hubbard lit his pipe. "Seems like you know a powerful lot about women, Jed," he said, in a tone that let Jed know he was being properly chastised.

"Well, you understand, Doc. I pride myself on being close to my congregation. Men tell me things."

Doctor Hubbard collected his belongings. "I'm sure they do, Pastor Jed, I'm sure they do. And I'm sure the women do, too."

Jed offered his hand to the doctor. "Thank you, Doctor. You can be sure Anna will be well cared for, and as for myself and my needs…well, I'll just have to pray on it."

The doctor looked directly at Jed. "I have a feeling you will have no problem at all," he said, and turned to leave.

Jed understood that his life was about to change. He hurried out of the house and into the barn to saddle his horse. He needed to feel the sting of the wind against his face. He wanted to keep going and going – out of sight, into nowhere. His thoughts were racing as fast as the horse that carried him. He felt a fleeting sense of compassion for Anna, but it was short lived. He was sorrier for himself. He could never be able to spend his entire life celibate.

So, we can't have any more children. Well, so what! They're nothing but a nuisance anyway. But I'm young! How can a man my age be expected to do without? It isn't right that I should just ignore the urges that take over a man's body. On the other hand, it could turn out to be fine. Anna's not interested anyway. She does it because she feels it's her wifely duty. She never voluntarily approaches me. She'll be happy to be rid of it."

Jed pulled back on the reins and the horse slowed to a trot. His thoughts continued, back to the times when, before they were married, he and Anna discussed the family issue. Anna was adamant about having children. She wanted a big family; he did not. But he wanted Anna. Daughter of a respected Baptist minister, she was quiet and unassuming and well-versed in the bible. He thought her perfect for him and his ambition.

Jed turned the horse around and returned home, satisfied with his decision. It would be best for all of them.

There were times when Jed made a clumsy attempt to be a father. He would occasionally bring Tabitha a lollipop or carry her to church and sit her in the front pew. Anna was forced to admit to herself that her husband could never be the type of father she'd hoped for. She felt that he had little time for anything at all except his congregation. He was at the church all day and, sometimes, well into the night. Anna tried to understand his responsibilities, but she felt isolated and alone. *He is a man of God. Certainly, he must understand how much we need him.* She decided to wait for an opportune moment to approach him.

Anna found just the time when Jed came in, whistling, late one evening, long after Tabitha was put to bed. "Welcome home, darling," she said, smiling. "I made your favorite peanut butter cake and your mamma's chocolate frosting."

Anna pulled up a chair for her husband and placed a large slice of cake before him. "Tell me about your day, dear. You must have been very busy today. It's quarter past ten. You shouldn't work so hard, Jed. What was it tonight – a hospital visit to old Ben?"

Suddenly, Jed's mood shifted, and he shoved the plate onto the floor. "I'm not hungry," he growled, "and why do you insist on questioning me the minute I walk in the door?"

Anna was stunned at Jed's response, but immediately blamed herself for his reaction. *There I go again! Why do I have to spoil everything? He's tired, is all. He just needs to sleep.* She tried to convince herself that it was her fault; that she should just have left him alone.

"I'm sorry, Jed. I shouldn't have. It's just that…" Anna paused, not sure she wanted to go on.

"Well, what is it? I really need to get some sleep."

Anna found the courage to speak. "Jed, is something wrong?" she managed to say. "I've been noticing you're becoming preoccupied and distant lately. And you spend no time with Tabitha. She needs you. We both need you."

Jed was quick to retaliate. He knew if he could turn the conversation around to make his wife appear guilty, he would be home free. "Need me? Why should you need me? You have the girl!"

Anna was shocked. "Why, Jed, how can you be so cruel? Tabitha is only a small child. It's important for her to know how much both of us love her. Since you're not around, I must be the one to spend time with her. But I don't mean to exclude you, dear. I'm so sorry if…"

Anna put her arms around her husband's shoulders. "If I've given you any reason…if I've put you aside, I'm sorry. I'll try to be more mindful of it. But, Jed, you spend so much time away from us."

"You should understand full well what I am called to do. My people need me and appreciate me. I only wish I could say that about my wife – my wife who…oh, never mind!" He stormed out of the room, leaving Anna alone with her only companion, the night.

Anna's fragile heart forced her to spend many hours each day in bed where her greatest fears resided. She knew that she would most likely not live to see Tabitha through her teen years. She felt acutely responsible to see that her daughter be trained properly. Past years proved to Anna that Jed would have no interest in Tabitha's future once she was gone.

She lay back and allowed her thoughts to take over. Tabitha shall be well schooled in the things that will make her happy as well as desirable. I will encourage her to take her schooling away from here – from this backward place that knows only petty gossip and hypocrisy.

Anna turned on the radio, hoping to escape her thoughts, but she could not. I know Jed will want to marry soon after I'm gone. I hope the woman's at least a decent person and not one of those cheap women I've heard he's been seen with. Oh, God, please help my child! Help her to find a good life and a husband who will be faithful and good to her.

Anna insisted that love conquered all. Jesus was love. Jesus could make everything right. At least that's what she'd told Tabitha. For a while, Tabitha believed her mother. But now, now that she was eleven, she wasn't so sure. It seemed to her as though there were secrets in the house. It wasn't shouting; just discussions about things that Tabitha did not understand. She could hear words like "perfume" and "other women."

The confused child prayed to the Jesus that was supposed to fix everything, but after months of praying decided that Jesus must be busy with someone else. She thought it was probably because she'd asked for a new bike for her birthday, so she changed her prayer. *Jesus, if you were going to give me the bike, you can forget it. I'd rather have something else. Please make my parents stop arguing. If you do that for me, I promise to never ask for another thing."*

And there were other things – things that Tabitha needed to know about herself and her own blossoming body. She could tell that her breasts were getting larger and there was hair growing between her legs. She desperately tried to ask her mother about what was happening.

"Mother," she said, "Sara Jane showed me her new bra and said that I should be getting one, too. Do you think so?"

Anna turned to face the window. "I'll see to it that Bertha gets you some new undershirts at the mercantile. It's all you need. Now, please get me some tea."

Tabitha started out of the room; then turned. "Oh, and she also said that her brother told her that she should give a boy just enough to keep him interested, but no more. Enough of what? When?"

Anna was visibly shocked. "Please, Tabitha, go down and fetch my tea. I'm not feeling well." Tabitha felt rejected and alone, but reluctantly returned with her mother's tray. It was obvious that Anna was not going to address the issue.

Tabitha's thoughts turned to Jed. Maybe I should ask my father! He knows about a lot of stuff. I will ask him. Just as soon as I can, I will!

One day, when the bougainvillea was in bloom and the summer full of promise, Anna called Tabitha to her bedside. "You know that Mother is unwell, don't you child?" Tabitha lowered her head. Anna lifted her chin, fighting to hold back emotion. "Now, now, dearest. I plan to be here for a while. I want to watch you grow and graduate and go off with some wonderful young man who is worthy of you."

Tabitha lay alongside her mother, curling up against her, taking in the wonderful scent of Red Rose bath powder she had known since she was a child. "I don't want to go off to school, Mother," she said, forcefully. "I just want to stay here with you."

Anna smiled and held her daughter close. "Well, we'll just have to see about that. Things may change as you grow older. You're a bright girl, Tabitha. One day you may realize that Emporia, Virginia is just not enough for you. After you graduate from college, you may not be satisfied with a life that revolves around Sunday afternoon socials and grange dinners."

Anna wanted to go on. She wanted to confide in Tabitha about so many of the things she suspected about Jed. But it wouldn't be good. After she was gone, there would only be Jed to look after Tabitha. There was no one else. It would be better if her child didn't know.

CHAPTER SIX

"The devil can quote scripture for his purpose."

Jed Whittier took great pride in the numbers that flocked to the Ebenezer Baptist Church to hear him preach. He reveled in watching his audience swoon and beg forgiveness for their sins. It made him feel alive and exhilarated. He rejoiced in having such power. Yes, the affable young preacher certainly had a way with his minions.

Many women, disillusioned, disenchanted, and despondent found the comfort and reassurance they longed for when talking to their handsome pastor. Just being in the presence of this charming man made their bleak lives bearable. Jed was happy to oblige. He would tell each of them what they desperately needed to hear:

"Mrs. Carmody, I hear tell today is your thirty-eighth birthday. I told the choir members they surely must be wrong; that you cannot be a day over twenty-five!"

"Miss Sarah, what makes you even consider going on that diet? Why, any man can see that...well, you just give that some serious thought."

"Mrs. Collins, your husband has a what – a girlfriend? Why, you must be mistaken! I cannot imagine him leaving such a charming, sophisticated woman."

Jed was equally as clever in attending to the needs of the men. He would incorporate one bold message into many of his sermons: "Wives, be subject to your husbands as you are to the Lord God Almighty!"

"Here it is, ladies. Turn to Ephesians, 5:22. Will all of you kind ladies please read what is commanded there?" Jed paused; then continued. "Yes, my dear friends, God has *commanded* you to be subject to your husbands. There doesn't seem to be any confusion about that, does there? Tell me, my dear friends, did I make a mistake? Does it say that you must submit to your husband whenever it is convenient – like when you want a fancy new coat or some new wallpaper for the kitchen?"

The women exchanged glances as Jed went on. "Does it say that your husband must submit to *you*? And does that beautiful passage command that you put your husband first in all things because he is bringing home the bread? No. It does not. We are called upon to understand that the reason a woman must submit to her husband in all things has to do with three little words: *He knows best!* That's all! Now I want you to write those three words on the very front page of your bible."

Jed waited for the women to follow his instruction. He went on, "You see, my good women, God gave men a better understanding of the ways of the world. That is why he made Adam first. You understand that, don't you? When God was satisfied that he had created a perfect human, he sent Eve to take care of Adam's needs."

Pastor Jed began pointing to his audience. "Sarah, Elizabeth, Mary Sue, Florence – do you understand?" The women did not respond but put their heads down.

Jed knew he'd captured the attention of everyone present. He would take his point home. "Ladies...my dear, dear ladies," he said in a more endearing voice, "might I ask you now to please just take out your pens and underline that passage?"

The women were clearly uncomfortable, but if their good pastor felt it was so important, it must be. They began underlining. Their husbands just smiled and underlined, too.

The sermon went on. "This is the word of GOD, my friends! Are you going to argue with the good book and run the risk of burning in hell for all eternity? I surely will not! I do not wish to answer to the Lord on that great judgment day for selfishly going against his word. No, your dear pastor will never risk his salvation!"

Jed paused, putting his hand over his heart. "Now, let us hear the great amen, my friends. Get into it, now! Amen?"

The first response was weak. For a minute, he thought he'd pushed too far. He brought forth his biggest, brightest smile, directing it to the ladies in front. "Oh, come on, now! I need to hear a much better 'amen' from all you lovely ladies! I am just dying to get to those delicious elderberry and shoo fly pies provided by the kind women of the social committee. Now, nice and loud, AMEN?"

"AMEN!" shouted the congregation, smiling. It was over. Jed had satisfied every man in the church. Since it was only the men who voted on a raise in his salary, well… it couldn't hurt.

But the raise was not granted. There were unexpected, costly repairs to be done to the church basement, so the committee decided to put Jed's raise on hold for another year. His bills were mounting. Jed's salary could not match his need for his extravagant social life.

One particularly gloomy evening, Jed decided to take a walk to clear his head. He needed to devise a plan – something that would help him get past the next several months until he received the small payment from his grandfather's trust fund. He felt no remorse or guilt about his extravagance.

Jed's thoughts rankled him as he walked. What's a man supposed to do? It's not like I'm hurting anyone. After all my hard work, and Anna being sick for all these years, I feel entitled to a bit of bourbon and an evening or two with my female friends. And, if the Lord wouldn't want me to enjoy myself, he wouldn't give me these powerful urges.

Jed went on rationalizing and thinking about the female companions in his life. He'd never bothered much with women from his own town; it was too dangerous. There had been two, however. Mabel, from the flower shop and Louanne, the owner of the feed store. They were both married and had no intention of leaving their husbands. It was safer that way. Jed knew his affair with them had to end the night Louanne's husband came in after closing, and he was forced to hide in the loft on top of bags of manure.

The early evening offered no escape from the uncomfortable, sultry day. Jed opened his shirt and continued walking, without direction. He had to come up with something – a way to get the money he needed before Anna – or worse, his congregation – would find out about his financial trouble. He'd already borrowed on the house. Anna had no way of knowing about that. He made certain all the paperwork and bills went to the church office. He'd already sold his grandfather's guns and his grandmother's diamond rings and fine china. There was nothing more to sell. He was desperate.

As he turned the corner onto Sycamore Street, he came upon Claire Beaumont, the church secretary, sweeping her front porch. His first impulse was to walk by quickly. He was in no mood for idle conversation. It was too late. She already spotted him and waved. "Oh, Pastor Jed! My goodness, what are you doing in this neighborhood? Are you on a sick call?"

"No, just walking Miss Claire. Sometimes a person is required to clear his head, don't you agree?"

"Why, yes, of course," Claire replied, more than a little flustered. She never did understand why the mere sight of this man set her to sweating and at a total loss for words. In the interest of being polite she went on, devising the only conversation that made any sense to her.

"It's such an uncomfortable evening, and you have a long walk before you get home. Would you like a glass of lemonade?"

Jed had to admit he needed a break from the heat.

"Well, now, Miss Claire. That would be just the ticket. May I step up to your porch?"

Claire pointed to her father's old rocking chair. "Daddy always loved this chair. Come refresh yourself and I'll get the lemonade."

As Claire went inside, Jed took in his surroundings. It was a decent home. The long porch was freshly painted and the brass door knocker, polished. The front windows were open, and the scent of lemon polish and coconut cake greeted him from inside. As he rocked, Jed closed his eyes, basking in the heady aroma of gardenia and heliotrope, against the cacophony of katydids.

How pleasant this is – peaceful and welcoming. Miss Claire would have made someone a good wife, I'm sure. She's kind and gentle and a great housekeeper. Too bad she's so…

The sound of the front door opening startled him. "Here's the lemonade, Pastor Jed, and I thought you might like to try some of my fresh coconut cake," said Claire, placing a small tray in front of him. Jed drank the lemonade in a few gulps and started on the cake.

"Well, I do declare, Miss Claire, this is so delicious! How is it that your homemaking talents are…oh, forgive me – I shouldn't have said that."

"Wasted, you mean?" Claire turned away. "They're not, really. There's Mother, of course, and Uncle John. They're all I have."

"You don't have to settle for that, you know," said Jed. There's a lot more to life."

Claire rose from her chair and unconsciously pulled down her girdle, a habit that gave away her nervousness. It gave Jed a chance to really examine her body that was covered with a faded housedress, several sizes too big. The dress was long, but the part of her legs that was visible was shapely – firm and nicely curved. The old housedress, ugly shoes, and disheveled hair made for a combination that would attract no man.

Jed decided that he'd spent the required, polite amount of time with Claire and rose to leave. "Thank you, Miss Claire. This refreshing stop was just what I needed. I'm sure I will see you in the office soon. You take care now and save me a piece of that cake!"

Secretly, Claire did not want Jed to leave. The short amount of time she'd spent with him was wonderfully exhilarating. How could he know that…

On his walk home, Jed's thoughts turned to Claire. I wonder. She's got a nice house –paid for, I'm sure, and probably lots of money from all the years she's been alone. She sure doesn't spend it on herself!

He sat down on a bench and tried to digest what he was thinking. I must be crazy! How can I possibly be thinking of making a move on her? It would take everything in me to seduce that unattractive old maid.

He tried to put the thought out of his head, but it kept haunting him as he continued to walk. Still, I'm sure she has money. She also has access to the church funds. I can tell she likes me. I saw her face get red when she served the lemonade and I touched her hand. It's a sure sign. I don't know how, but if I can just get past the looks…Jed challenged the ridiculousness of the situation. Sure, I can do it! Unless I miss my guess, Miss Claire Beaumont is ripe for the picking. I know she won't tell a soul. She'd lose the job she depends on and the respect of the entire town.

For the first time that day, Jed broke out in a broad smile as he began formulating his plans.

CHAPTER SEVEN

"The lady doth protest too much, methinks."

A serious woman sat at her desk poring over church accounts. "This desk is as old and as tired as I am," she said, without anyone to listen. "At least it's worn out from being used, and it has plenty of secrets in its guts. More than I can say!" She gently stroked the top of the desk. "It's okay, my friend. You don't have to feel sorry for me."

No man had ever been interested in Claire and she long ago convinced herself she was perfectly happy without a man. The responsibility of having a husband just would not do. She thought of men as useless creatures that lacked class and decorum. Moreover, they were demanding braggarts who searched for reasons to cheat on their wives. None she knew were worth her spit – none, that is, except for Pastor Jed. Now, here was a real man.

Claire locked the door, removed her blouse, and pinned up her hair against the oppressive heat. She put her head back to allow the air from the small fan to reach her neck. But, when she closed her eyes, it wasn't her work she was thinking of. It was Pastor Jed.

She couldn't remove herself from the scene of his visit with her. She remembered his smile – small and reserved, as though he were carrying a huge weight. She recalled how his hand brushed against hers. Sheer accident, of course, still…She had followed his eyes as he tried to examine the parts of her she kept hidden from view. Were these things just part of her imagination – or were they her wildest dreams come true?

Claire's emotions about Jed were growing with each passing day. Her erotic dreams were a safe place to act upon all the fantasies exploding within her.

There was a secret place in Claire's soul and in her body – a very unsettling, exciting place the lonely woman recognized, but never divulged. She was hungry for passion – the kind of passion that could exist only between two people who wanted it desperately. Each night she would dream about how it would feel to have a man next to her, on top of her, inside her, groaning and begging for her. Each night she would try to paint a face on her fantasy.

Sometimes, her fashioned lover would be dark with blue eyes that would come alive at the sight of her. Another time, her imagination painted a picture of someone older with silver hair that glistened in the moonlight. Some of her visitors were tall and thin; some thick and muscular. All of them adored her and fulfilled her every sexual need, as she did theirs. But always, always, her imagined lovers would disappear not long after she created them. She was left with only one face smiling down at her, again and again. It was Jed Whittier.

The sound of a key in the door startled Claire. She immediately rose to her feet, knocking over the small fan as she did. She grabbed her blouse and made a hurried attempt to put it on, but it was too late. Jed had already let himself in. There was no hint today that this was the man she knew who usually remained at home on Saturdays, preparing his sermon. The tanned, muscular form in front of her in white shorts and tight white shirt was the most handsome man she'd ever seen. She was completely taken in by the bold, masculine scent of his expensive cologne. The flustered woman tried to look away, but Jed made his presence known.

"Why, Miss Claire! What in the world…I didn't expect to find you here! If this isn't the best kind of luck." Jed was certain he would find Claire working on Saturday mornings. It had been her habit ever since he'd known her.

Claire was clearly flustered, as she attempted to button her blouse. "Pastor Jed! I'm so sorry! I…I thought I'd use some free time to work on the books and, well…it's so terribly hot that…" She continued fumbling unsuccessfully at closing her blouse. Jed offered his hands.

"My dear woman, you are working too hard! Just look at those hands – they're so wet it's no wonder you can't get them to work!" He took a clean handkerchief from his pocket and wiped Claire's hands, gently stroking each finger. "You're trembling! My goodness, we can't have that now, can we?"

Jed reached for the top button of Claire's blouse and fastened it, successfully. He had to be careful. *Just enough; not too much. I don't want to scare her away,* he thought. His hands found their way to gently place the button in its proper place. He understood the move to be bold and seductive – but Jed knew very well how far to go with this first encounter. He would stop.

Claire's thoughts were going in so many directions, she was becoming light-headed. Oh, Lord! This can't be! He's touching me! What should I do? I should slap his face and tell him that his actions are forward and inappropriate. I'm not that kind of woman! Then again, he really didn't do anything terrible, did he? He simply buttoned the top button of my blouse because I couldn't do it. Is he being kind, or is he…? And what if Mrs. Carmody should come in to check the choir robes? How would it look?

The telephone rang, removing Claire from the moment. "Don't answer it!" insisted Jed.

Claire looked puzzled. "But, Pastor Jed, it could be…"

"I don't care who it could be right now." he said. "Right now, your comfort is my priority. You need to rest and relax and go off to where it's cool, if only for a couple of hours. And I think I have just the place. Do you believe in providence, Miss Claire?"

Claire began vigorously dusting the desk with the handkerchief. "I'm sure I don't know what you mean. What does providence have to do with this?" she said, rubbing harder.

"Providence. You know, things are providential when they are governed by a force that is greater than any other thought or plan."

Claire thought for a moment. "I suppose so. I suppose it's kind of like when I decided to take the day off because I had a cold, and Mother had her heart attack that very day."

"Exactly! And it is providential that I came here today to pick up the key to the boathouse and found you in such a state. It means that you should listen to what I have to say. You need to go off with me for the day. Come rafting with me, Miss Claire."

Jed walked over to the key holder, removed a large, rusty key and waved it in front of her. "See, this little item is going to provide a day for us the likes of which you've never experienced. Put away those books, my dear! It's much too lovely a day to be wasted in this stale office!"

Claire dropped the handkerchief. "Oh, no, Pastor Jed. I just couldn't! I mean…" She stopped speaking, not prepared to go on.

"Now, Miss Claire, you should start thinking a bit more about yourself. You won't be any use to your good Mama or to me, either, if you collapse from exhaustion! Come on, now, say yes!"

Jed made a motion with his arms as though he were gathering air. "Come to the river with me. I'll introduce you to secret inlets where all manner of wildlife resides – beautiful birds that live only in the marshes, and orchids – beautiful, exotic orchids there for the picking. You'll see strange-looking trees, here in these parts hundreds of years before us, rising high above everything."

Jed knew he had Claire's attention. He would take full advantage. "You and I, Miss Claire; you and I will just drift away and let the raft take us to places that look and feel like paradise. You needn't worry, I'll be sure to get you home in time to give your dear Mamma her dinner."

It all sounded so wonderful, drifting and dreaming with Jed – an opportunity she may never again capture. "But I can't go like this," said Claire, pointing to her skirt and shoes.

"Is that all?" Jed took a stray piece of hair away from Claire's forehead and placed it behind her ear. "Well, my dear woman," he said, moving in closer. "I just happen to have an extra set of clothing in the car. I always carry a spare in case I get wet. Shorts and a shirt. They'll do fine. And, if you feel uncomfortable about leaving here in my clothes, you can change at the gas station and meet me at River's Edge. We'll pick up the raft and set off right away."

Claire began giggling nervously, like a teenager being asked to her first prom. "Well, I suppose I could, but…Pastor Jed, what about Anna? Don't you think you should take her with you instead?"

"Well, bless my soul! Aren't you the sweetest lady to be thinking of my dear Anna! Of course, I'd be taking her with me if I could, but you know how frail she is. She'd never be able to stand up to the trip. Dear wife that she is, she encouraged me to go off and take someone with me."

It wasn't exactly a lie. Anna knew that Jed was unhappy, and she felt as though she was robbing him of his youth and vigor. "Why don't you take some time off, Jed," she said, just yesterday. "You're working night and day, and it just isn't right. I know how much you love the river and, since you don't enjoy taking Tabitha, you might want to ask Amos Johnson's son. I know how fond he is of you."

It was the invitation Jed had been waiting for. He would do just as Anna requested, but his companion would not be Tommy Johnson.

Claire was satisfied. "Well then," she said, giggling, "I suppose we're off!"

Claire did just as Jed suggested. She found a gas station on the other side of the river and changed to the clothing Jed gave her. Claire had never seen herself in such an outfit. Even as a child, her mother dressed her in long, conservative dresses and "sensible" shoes. She often begged to become more modern, especially in high school when the other girls would tease her and call her names. But her parents would not relent, so she spent all her high school days and nights alone, studying and accepting the fact that she was ugly, and that no boy would ever want her.

Now, looking back at her from the mirror was a vision Claire didn't recognize. In front of her was a strange woman – an attractive woman with cheeks the color of ripe peaches; full, lustrous hair, and clear, green, almond-shaped eyes. She thought the shirt and shorts Jed had given her were too tight, and without the girdle she had shoved into her handbag, every curve of her figure showed through. She thought about what her parents would think. *If Father weren't already dead, he'd die now – and Mother with him!* Claire picked up a pair of cheap sandals at the small store connected to the gas station. While she was bending over to put them on, she heard a whistle. She looked up. Standing near her was a young man leering at her.

"Mmm. Want to come see my truck, lady? That's quite a set of tires you're packin' and I could sure use some good tires."

Claire had no idea what the trucker was talking about, but she could tell by the way he looked at her that what he had in mind was something she wanted no part of. She said nothing but left in a hurry. Jed couldn't be left waiting.

As she pulled into the place called River's Edge, Claire noticed that Jed was not yet there. She had no way of knowing that, not wanting to appear anxious, he deliberately planned to be late. *He's changed his mind! Well, who could blame him? I'm sure he has better things to do than to spend the afternoon with me.* She looked at her watch. It was just ten minutes past the arranged time. *I'll just wait a little while longer. Ten more minutes; then I'll go.*

Just short of ten minutes later, Jed arrived. "I'm so sorry, Claire. I somehow lost track of the time," he said, peeling off his shirt. It was then that he got a good look at the woman before him. It couldn't be. This enticing figure could not belong to Claire Beaumont. He followed her ankles to her legs, then to her waist and finally to her breasts. *Good God! I can't believe it! She's built like a ... Oh, I can see this is going to be no problem at all. It may turn out to be fine – just fine. But, slow down, Jed. Take it nice and easy. This might all blow up in your face, and if the congregation were to find out, tar and feathers would be too good for you. Then again, Claire has just as much to lose.*

"Oh, and by the way, may I call you Claire – just for today, mind you. And you can call me Jed. There's no need for propriety while rafting down the river, right?"

Claire was relieved to see him. Her afternoon with him would happen after all. "If you say so… Jed." His name rolled around on her tongue easily, as though it belonged there.

Jed's plan continued to evolve as the pair walked toward the boathouse. Let's see. Late, but not too late. Familiar, but not too familiar. Don't let her know that you've noticed her body. Not right now. Save that for later – maybe not even today. Sit close to her on the raft and see how she reacts to you being so close. If she's receptive, you can give her a small kiss on the cheek and tell her that it's been a long time since you've been close to a desirable woman.

Jed offered Claire his arm as they walked the rocky terrain. His thoughts continued. Tell her you're feeling a bit uncomfortable around her and you don't know why. Mention Anna. You can allude to the fact that you haven't had sex in years, without coming right out and saying it. Women always go for that. Makes them feel less guilty when they finally do it. And, whatever you do, don't talk about money. That won't come for weeks. After she's been with me enough times, she won't be able to say no.

They were approaching the boathouse. Jed opened the door and motioned Claire inside. It was dark and dank. The earthen floor and old blankets on the shelves added to the mustiness. "Let's just get the raft and get out of here," said Jed, untying the knot that held it in place.

They left the boathouse and started down the path toward the river, just as clouds rolled in and darkened the sky. "Damnation!" said Jed. "Looks like we're in for a storm. I know from experience it's not a good thing to be on the river in a storm. We can't chance it. I suppose we should just go back home."

Claire was visibly disappointed. "Storms don't last long around here. Maybe we can wait it out in the boathouse."

Jed agreed. "Okay, but you should know we're not going to be very comfortable in there. There's no place to sit, except for the floor. Are you game?"

"Sure. Maybe we can just put the raft on the floor. It should be some protection, even if it's not comfortable."

"Good idea, Claire. It just might save the day. Let's do it!"

It began raining heavily and the two were soaked by the time they got back to the boathouse. Jed took down some of the musty towels from the shelves.

"Sorry, this is the best I can do. We can try to dry ourselves off a little." He fashioned two pillows from the extra towels and placed them inside the rubber raft. "My lady," he said, smiling, "your castle awaits."

Claire made a feeble attempt to dry herself off; then lay down and put her head back. "Paradise it's not," she said, but it'll do!" They laughed heartily, lying next to one another and talking about their shattered plan.

As Jed lay there, his eyes darted to a high shelf that housed an old jug. "Look there," he said, pointing to the curiosity. "I'll just bet somebody had a good time here. Let's have a look." He retrieved a wooden crate from the corner, used it to reach the jug, and smelled the contents. "Well, well! What have we here? Smells like moonshine to me!" He offered the jug to Claire for her to smell. She jolted back in revulsion.

"Oh, that's awful! Who in the world…"

"You know what I think, Claire? I think the Lord wanted us to find this. Someone was probably in the same fix we're in and left this for us to find."

"But Jed. You know we can't drink spirits. You always tell us we'll burn in hell if we drink!"

"I know…I know. But you are shivering in those wet clothes and there's not much chance we'll get out of here anytime soon. The lord would not look unkindly at us for taking this for medicinal reasons. I'm sure he wouldn't want us catching pneumonia, now would he?"

"I guess you're right," said Claire. "But only a little. I'll take just a little sip."

"Good girl," said Jed, putting the jug up to Claire's lips. She smiled. "It's not bad. It tastes a little like blackberries."

Jed took a few healthy sips and again offered it to Claire. "C'mon. This is going to fix you up real good."

The rain continued to beat against the door of the boathouse, warning the couple to stay inside. But going out was not something they wanted to do anyway. By now, they had emptied the jug and were stretched out, close to one other. Claire felt like nothing she'd ever before experienced. She was, at the same time, numb, giddy, and fearless – feelings that were new and exciting to her. She was a stranger to herself, and it was wonderful. She didn't want to go back to be that old, unhappy, useless Claire. She wanted to be the Claire of excitement, of sensuality, of all the hedonistic pleasures she'd read about but that were forbidden to her. She would be bold. She would never again relive this experience. It was her only chance.

She unpinned her hair and removed her shirt and bra. "I'm cold," she said. "I need you to keep me warm."

Jed tried to contain his shock. *So, this is what the drink does to women. Not so bad. I'll take it.* He moved closer to her, wrapping his arms around her and stroking her back with a towel.

"No," said Claire, "not there. Here." She placed his hands over her breasts. She removed her shorts. "And here," she said, guiding his hands to her place of pleasure. "Do it to me, Jed. Do it all. I've waited so long."

Jed drew back. Things were happening too fast. He was afraid that, once Claire became sober, she'd never again want to be with him. He couldn't risk that. The money was nearly in his hands.

"Oh, my God, Claire! You're driving me crazy! Are you sure? I mean, how could I ever be able to forget you once we've... I couldn't face not being with you ever again. I've waited, too. I've wanted you for so long – all of those Saturday visits to the office; all of the times I hung around after choir practice!" Jed began whispering in Claire's ear, seductively. "And do you think my visit to your house was accidental? No, it was planned because I desperately needed to see you – to be with you for even just a short time. I never dreamed this could happen, and I wouldn't be able to stand it if you left me after we... Are you sure, Claire?"

Claire guided him inside of her. "Don't say any more, Jed. This is sure."

CHAPTER EIGHT

*"Therefore, I lie with her and she with me, and
in our faults by lies we flattered be."*

Jed knew time was running out and he had not yet mentioned the
subject of money. Now would be the time to institute his
clandestine plan. He decided to make a bold move and call
Claire at home, something they'd both agreed would not be safe.

When Claire picked up the phone she heard, "Hey, beautiful,
wanna screw?"

Claire was shocked but titillated. "Jed, are you crazy? Uncle
John is sitting in the kitchen eating his breakfast. If he should…"

"Answer me, Claire, wanna screw?"

Claire whispered, "You know better. Of course I do."

"How much?" said Jed

"You're not making sense," Claire responded, nervously.

"How about tonight. All night, with no chance of anyone
walking in. How about in a real bed? How about dinner and
wine? How about breakfast in bed in the morning?"

Claire chuckled. "Are you hitting the moonshine again?"

"No, beautiful. I have a plan. Tell Uncle John you feel forced to
spend the night with a friend who is ill. I'm going to tell Anna
the same thing. Then you and I are going off to an elegant hotel
in Green Mountain. It's remote so we'll be safe. Meet me at
Hal's diner on route 313 at four and I'll take it from there."

For a minute, there was no response. Finally, Claire said, "I'll be there at four."

Claire was behaving like a giddy schoolgirl as she packed a classy outfit for dinner and splurged at Margo's shop for sexy lingerie and Chanel #5. She didn't understand what Jed had in mind, but she would take full advantage.

At exactly four, Jed appeared at the diner. Claire watched as he went inside to speak to Hal for a minute. When he came out, he opened his car door and motioned her inside; then moved her car to the back of the building, out of sight. Hal came out, gave Claire a leery once-over, waved to Jed, and gave him a thumbs up.

The evening was everything Jed promised it would be. Sex was the priority for hours. Jed saw to it that Claire was completely satisfied even before she had satisfied him. His own gratification was not why he was here tonight.

Claire was glowing as she entered the dining room for dinner. Jed handed the maître d' a large bill, ensuring the best table in the room. Claire noticed that, though the room was comfortably cool, Jed was sweating. She leaned across the table to touch his cheek. "You okay?" she asked, more than a little concerned.

Jed took her hand and kissed it. "Sure," he said, "I'm just sitting here thinking about how beautiful these past weeks have been, and the fact that we'll never be able to do this again."

Claire didn't understand at first. "I know, Jed," she said, reaching for his hand. All of this is more than you can afford. I would never expect you to…"

Now was the moment he was waiting for. "Claire, you know how I feel about you, don't you?"

Claire looked down, unsure of what Jed was saying.

"Look at me, my love," Jed said. "You do know, don't you?"

Claire drank the Drambuie in one fast gulp. "Well, I…I don't know, Jed. You've never said…"

"Words! Women get hung up on them. What I'm trying to say is that I have something to tell you that, regardless of how I feel, I am forced to do. Please try to understand."

"You're not making sense, Jed. What is there to understand?"

Jed got up and helped Claire from her chair. "Not here," he said. I want to hold you now."

Claire was completely taken back. She noticed Jed's demeanor change as they entered their room. He made no attempt to continue with the usual passionate lovemaking. Instead, he lay down on the bed and motioned for Claire to lay next to him.

"Here's what I'm trying to say, Claire. I'm afraid tonight is the last time. That's why I wanted it to be special."

Claire couldn't respond. She was totally shocked and frozen. Finally, she withdrew from his arms and sat upright. "What are you saying, Jed? Why is this the last time. My God, did someone find out?"

Jed shook his head. "No, thank God."

"What can it be?" Claire pleaded. She looked down, her voice quivering. "There's someone else. I knew it would happen. I wondered just how long it would be before you got tired of me. That new young blonde in the choir has a lot of appeal, doesn't she?"

Jed pretended to be angry. "How could you even suggest that I could ever…" He pulled her to him. "You know you're all I want. But it can't be. We're moving, Claire. I've applied for the pastor position at a large congregation in Western Pennsylvania."

Claire was totally shocked. Jed had never mentioned this to her. Why now, so suddenly? She rose, threw on her robe and headed to the bathroom. "Excuse me," was all she could manage to say.

Claire leaned over the sink, feeling ill. She began to cry, then recalled what Jed had once said. 'What I respect about you, Claire, is that you don't get all emotional. I can't stand whiny women.' She splashed her face with cold water, faked a smile, and returned to him. "Well, Jed. I can't say I'm not disappointed. I suppose we just have to be thankful for whatever time we've had. I…I…"

Try as she might, Claire could not contain the tears. She flew into Jed's arms. "Forgive me, Jed," she cried. "I suppose I should be happy for you. I know how much you want a larger parish. It's wrong of me to go on so. I just can't stand the thought of losing you."

Jed released his hold and looked into her eyes. "Do you honestly believe this has to do with ambition, my love?" He kissed her forehead again and again. "Oh, my poor Claire! I would never leave you for such a reason. It's not the larger parish that is intriguing to me. It embarrasses me to discuss this with you, darling, but it's because of finances. I chose a place where I can make enough to support the mounting bills that continue to come in for Anna. I'm in debt, Claire. Serious debt. If I continue to stay here, I will surely lose my home. I can't expect our small parish to support Anna's bills."

"But how can you have afforded all this?" she asked, looking around at the fine surroundings.

"I sold the raft so I could give you a special farewell. I just couldn't tell you this in the boathouse. You are a fine and decent woman, Claire, and I wanted to treat you to what you deserve, if only once. But there's no way out."

Jed instinctively knew the next move would have to come from Claire, and she didn't disappoint him. "Jed, I know you may be upset by what I have to say, but there is a way. I want to help. If

I told you I had a three thousand dollars of my own money, would you accept it?"

Jed held her close. "I couldn't ask you to do that for me, dearest. I could never take advantage of your kindness."

"Consider it done," said Claire, smiling. "You will have the check on Monday."

Jed hung his head. "If it were only that simple," he said. "Fact is, I need more. Much more. Five thousand dollars more. So, you see, there's no solution but to leave."

Claire didn't speak, but Jed could tell she was thinking hard. Finally, she said "I can get it! I know I can. When did you say you'll be getting that check from your grandfather's trust?"

Jed had to come up with a reasonable response. "Three months, maybe four."

"That should be plenty of time. There's money in the church treasury. The auditors just checked the books, so they won't be back for a long time. By that time, you can pay back what you borrowed. No one need know. Consider it an interest free loan."

Jed had no idea how he might finally pay back the money, but he got what he wanted. Time. He would have a couple of months to figure it out. He pulled Claire to him. "Hey, beautiful," he said, seductively. "Wanna screw?"

CHAPTER NINE

"Everyone can master a grief but he that has it."

Eleven-year-old Tabitha knew her mother's days on earth were coming to an end, though it was sooner than either one of them suspected. One dark day, Anna called her to her side, trying to choose words that might make sense to her daughter.

"Dearest," she said, "all of us are put on earth for a time. We don't understand why some of us go before we've had a chance to live a long life but remember it's the order of things. God has a plan that we don't quite understand. I'm sorry you will be cheated of having a mother, but Tabitha…"

Anna pulled her closer. "There is something very important I must tell you. Men are not good alone. They need a companion – someone to look after them. I know your father will no doubt marry soon after I'm gone. Please understand that this is what I want for him. It will be best for you, too. If she's a good person, treat the woman with respect. It's not going to be easy for her, either."

Tabitha just kept shaking her head from side to side, crying. "No! There won't be another mother for me! I don't need another mother. I'm old enough now to take care of myself –and Daddy, too. Bertha will help me! No! Don't ask me to do that!"

Anna pulled back the long strand of hair that had fallen over Tabitha's eyes. "Someday, you'll understand what I'm telling you. Until then, I have plans for you. Go to my closet. On the shelf you will find Grandma's quilt and, under it, a box. Bring it to me."

Tabitha did as she was instructed. "It's pretty, Mamma," she said, through tears, examining a music box in the shape of a piano. "Yes, it is," Anna replied, weakly. "Aunt Mattie left this to me when she died. If you turn it over, you'll find a little button. Press it, and the top will open."

It was a welcome distraction from the grief the girl was experiencing. She pressed the button and it opened, just as her mother said it would. Inside, she found a large wad of money. She had never seen such a large sum of bills.

Anna counted the money over and over, making certain that the entire amount was intact. When she was satisfied, she handed it to Tabitha.

"This is for you, dearest – five thousand dollars for your education. Don't ever, ever part with it. It will do things for you I won't be able to do. Keep it in a safe place and use it only for school. Do not tell your father about this. He's not good with money so he may lose it and you'll never have your education. Promise me!"

Tabitha lowered her head. "I promise, Mama, but…"

Anna leaned back on the bed, totally exhausted. "Now, please find your father. I need him."

Tabitha ran to the church but could not find Jed. The groundskeeper told her that he'd left earlier in the day and didn't say where he was going or when he'd get back. When Tabitha returned home and found Bertha sitting on the steps, crying, she knew.

Two days later, Tabitha sat on the front porch swing, staring at the black-ribboned laurel wreath on the front door. When is it going to come down? I don't want it here! Mamma wouldn't have liked it at all! Mamma loved blue. The bow should be blue!" The heartbroken child went over to the door and began struggling to remove the wreath when Bertha appeared and chastised her.

"Now honey, you can't do that! Your daddy's gonna be real upset with you. You gots to respect the dead! Now, it's time you come inside with Bertha. We is gonna visit your mamma so's you can say goodbye to that beautiful lady."

Bertha put on her funeral hat and removed two pristine handkerchiefs from her deep pocket. "Here," she commanded. "take one. You can cry if you wants to but, honey chil', ain't no reason to cry. You mamma, she's with the Lord and she's happy now. Jes remember that your mamma gonna be at your side. She'll help you when you needs her. I promise, honey."

Tabitha entered the living room, dark now with the shades pulled and the only light coming from tall candles surrounding the coffin. She wanted to run out. She hated the sight of the flickering candles and the sound of sad hymns and the smell of the flowers she once loved. But she knew she'd be punished if her father should find out that she'd left without saying goodbye to her mother.

She took Bertha's hand and shuffled over to the threatening coffin. She was having a hard time trying to put all the pieces together. Tabitha had never seen a dead person. She had been to parish funerals, but only to attend the service and enjoy the big lunch afterwards.

Looking down at the figure of what was once her mother she thought, *Why isn't she smiling? Don't people smile when they're dead? Can she see me from where she is? Does she know I'm here?* Tabitha leaned over to kiss her mother but withdrew at once. Something inside of her was screaming, but there was no sound coming from her. She turned to Bertha.

"I have to go now," she announced, without emotion. I have to feed Kitty. She must be very hungry."

Bertha led Tabitha to her father's side. "Pastor Jed, I knows you is very busy with all these here people, but this child needs you."

Jed waved her away. "Take her to her room, Bertha, her mother is not coming back, and Tabitha is just going to have to find a way to deal with it."

Tabitha did as her father instructed. She went to bed that day and every day after that without being told. And, every day, she screamed inside herself, where no one could hear.

CHAPTER TEN

"The evil men do lives after them."

The new days of spring did not provide Tabitha with the warmth she needed. Bertha fixed her favorite meals, her friends came to call often, and the women of the parish invited her to their homes for homemade ice cream. Even Tommy Ellis, who would ordinarily have nothing to do with her, stopped by every day and offered her a ride on his bike. She was polite to their kind gestures but in the end, refused all of them.

Each day, after school and her daily chores, she would pick up Kitty and go to the dark place under the front porch where no one could find her. The sunless atmosphere and the damp, musty earth matched her mood. She let herself get lost in her thoughts and cry for hours, undisturbed.

Tabitha noticed her father was away most of the time. He had never been home much, but it seemed to her that he was absent more than he was at home. She allowed her thoughts to wander. *I suppose Daddy's just upset. He probably doesn't know much about how to raise a girl on his own. I haven't really been nice to him, and I promised Mama I'd look after him and be close to him. Maybe I should try harder. Maybe we should talk more. I don't know what to talk about, but there must be something.* Tabitha sat up straight and picked up Kitty.

"I can talk to you about anything, Kitty, and I know you're listening, even if you don't have the answers. Maybe I should try to talk to Daddy about school or the church choir or maybe I should suggest that we go to the movies or to the ice cream parlor. I'll try."

Tabitha headed straight for her father's study. It was late afternoon, and she really didn't expect to find him there. She left him a note that said, "Dear Daddy, I think we should try to talk more. I know you are busy, but if you could find the time, we can get together after dinner one day. Let me know, Daddy. I really would like to spend some time with you."

Jed appeared at dinner the next night. "I read your note, child. What is it? I haven't much time," he said, coldly. Tabitha felt like crying, but she needed to go on.

She began pushing her food around on her plate, not looking at her father. "I…I don't know. Sometimes I just want to talk to you. Sometimes it's important and sometimes it's not. I just feel…well, I get lonely for mamma and I thought…" Jed kept looking at his watch, trying to push the conversation forward.

"Oh. That." he said. "Well, you know, Daddies are just not like Mommies. We're just not as good at raising children. Not cut out for it."

Jed took a large sip of coffee but refused Bertha's pecan pie. He had made an appointment in Falls River, an hour's drive away and he surely did not want to keep Mabel waiting. He rose from the table, went to where Tabitha was seated, and kissed her lightly on the forehead. *I may as well try to keep her happy or I'll never get out of here!*

"All right, child," he said. "Let's try for tomorrow after dinner. Meet me in my study. I have only a small amount of time, though. You know, it's the Ladies' Guild Meeting at church."

It was enough to keep Tabitha happy. She went to her room and wrote down all the things she wanted to talk about so that the time they would have together would not be wasted. She wanted to know about things like whether or not there was really a heaven; about what to do when a boy talks to her; about why dancing is evil; and about…oh, yes, she really wanted to know about that bra.

Tabitha kept busy with schoolwork and with writing her questions in the little notebook Sara Jane had given her for her birthday last year. Finally, it was time to meet Jed in his study. At first, Tabitha felt a little awkward; then, she steeled herself. This was her big chance. She wasn't going to let it be destroyed by acting like a child. She knocked on the door gingerly.

"Yes, Tabitha, is that you?"

"It is, Daddy. May I come in?"

Jed responded, "Of course, come in. Remember, we have very little time so let's get to the important concerns first. You've already told me that things are going fine at school, so what can it be?"

Tabitha looked down at the floor and mumbled, "Well, it's just that…well, Sara Jane said I should be wearing a bra." She lifted her head and blurted out the rest. "I tried to speak to Mamma about it once, but she only told me to tell Bertha to buy some new undershirts for me. Now…" Tabitha tried to hide her breasts a bit by slouching. "Well, the undershirts just aren't doing it. I'm, well…I'm…"

Jed knew full well what Tabitha was telling him. He had been noticing his daughter's body changing beautifully in the last months. She was no longer the fragile, gangly little girl that hung around the house in her fluffy robe and old pajamas. She tried to hide the straining buttons on her blouses, and she stopped wearing sweaters all together. Yes, Jed noticed.

"To begin with, Tabitha, I can say with certainty that I'm not a bit surprised that your mother would not talk to you about the bra. Bless her soul, Anna was kind of old-fashioned. She never understood that a person's body is nothing to be ashamed of. Now, what makes you think a bra will fix your problem?" asked Jed, trying to find out how much, if anything, Tabitha knew about the changes she was experiencing.

"I don't really know," Tabitha responded, "but Sara Jane says if I don't wear a bra, the boys will be able to see my…well, my…nipples."

Jed recognized the need to be very contained. "I see," he said, soberly "and do you think Sara Jane is right?"

"I don't know. I don't know why it's so bad for the boys to see nipples. I mean, they must know we have them. And I saw Sara's brother in a bathing suit, and he has nipples, too. So, why is it so bad?"

Jed took some time to answer. He couldn't say what he was thinking – that the sight of a woman's nipples drove him and every other man crazy with desire.

"It's not really bad, Tabitha, but those are things that should be reserved for somebody special. It's kind of like, well, like sharing an ice cream cone with a total stranger. You wouldn't do that, would you?"

Tabitha was surprised at the question. "No, I don't suppose I would."

"But you would share an ice cream cone with me, wouldn't you?"

"Of course, I would! You're my daddy."

Jed smiled and gave Tabitha an affectionate hug, letting his thoughts run wild. I've always wondered what it would be like to have a young girl. This one is so fresh and inexperienced. I'd love to...

"You...uh, you wouldn't let just any boy see your nipples, sweetheart, but you would let me, right?"

Tabitha thought hard. Something inside of her was not feeling quite right, but if her father was saying it, it must be true.

"I...I suppose. I mean, yes, I would."

"Good girl!" Jed walked over and gave her a small kiss on her lips – something he had never done before. "You're getting too big for just a little peck on the forehead," he said. "You're going to be my special girl now, aren't you?"

Tabitha could hardly contain her happiness. Her father had called her his "special girl." She wrapped her arms around Jed and hugged him, tightly.

"I'm so happy we're having this talk, honey," said Jed. It's what we both needed."

Tabitha expected her father to look at his watch, as he always did when they were together. Instead, his voice changed in a way she'd never heard before.

"Now, my sweet, I think it's a good idea for you to get that bra. Get two or three if you like. But first, we need to know about your size. They do come in sizes, you know. I mean, I had to go to the mercantile myself for your dear mother when she became ill. You don't want to go there and act as though you don't know what you're doing, do you?"

"Bertha can probably help me."

"Fah! She didn't before, did she? You don't want her to go on treating you like a child, do you?"

"I guess not. But how do I know what size to get?"

Jed moved closer to Tabitha's body. "Here's how it's done. I put my hands around your breasts and feel them all over. Then, I'll be able to tell just what size you will need."

Tabitha felt uncomfortable. She wanted her father to stop, but she was confused. Something didn't feel right but, what could possibly be wrong? Wasn't this her father who had said he loved her?

Bertha's footsteps coming up the stairs made Jed stop abruptly. He removed his hands and quickly buttoned Tabitha's blouse. "Remember, I love you," he said. "You're my big girl now and big girls never tell about these things – not even to their best friends. If you want to learn about grown up things, you'll have to start behaving like a grown up, so this is our little secret. Promise? Remember, God does not look kindly on those who do not keep promises."

Tabitha wasn't so sure. Something was gnawing at her, but she worked to ignore it. Nothing would take away from the moment she'd waited for. "I promise, Daddy," she said. "I promise I will never, ever tell anyone about our secret."

Jed shoved several bills into Tabitha's hand. "For your bras," he said. "Go right down to the mercantile tomorrow. Make sure you get the prettiest ones you can find. And tomorrow night, after Bertha's gone home, I want you to come in and show me how they fit. Now, kiss your daddy good night."

Tabitha leaned in to kiss Jed on the cheek, but he turned his head and kissed her on the lips again, this time letting the kiss linger just a while longer. "We're going to be really good friends, honey. Maybe I'll even take you to a movie in Forked River on Friday night. Would you like that?"

Tabitha couldn't believe what she was hearing. She had never gone to a movie with her father. He had always considered movies to be evil. But things were different now. Her daddy was changing. He said he loved her. He was really trying to be a better father, so Tabitha decided she would have to do everything she could to make him happy.

Weeks went by. Tabitha began noticing that, try as she might, her father seemed to be unhappy. There were times he didn't eat a bite at dinner. He continued to visit her room but didn't speak much when he did. She blamed herself. *I wonder what I'm doing wrong! Why is he ignoring me? I wonder if it's because he really misses Mamma.* The bewildered girl decided to ask him.

"Daddy, why are you so sad? Are you missing Mamma?"

Jed forced a half smile. "Of course, I miss your mother, Tabitha. I sincerely do. But when Anna continued to be so ill, I decided that she might be better in God's hands than in mine. So, even though I miss her, I know she is where she needs to be. If I seem, well…distant, it's because I'm worried."

Tabitha went over to put her arm around him. She kissed him on the lips, the way he had wanted her to do. "You don't have to be worried, Daddy, she said. I'll always take care of you. I love you."

"It's not that, dear child, it's…never mind, you're too young to have to deal with my problems."

Jed's financial problems were growing as his bills kept mounting. Just today, he received a letter from the bank, threatening foreclosure. In addition, Claire informed him that the auditor would soon be at the church to examine the books. She'd already forged signatures and manipulated accounts as Jed requested but she, too, was becoming sick with worry.

"I'm not too young!" announced Tabitha. "You said so yourself. You said I'm becoming an adult, and that I should learn about adult things. You tell me that every time we…we're together in that special way. I thought you loved me!"

Jed took Tabitha's hand and kissed it. "Come, sit on my lap and give me a hug. I need you."

Tabitha was happy to be close to her father. She put her head on his shoulder, while Jed ran his hands under her blouse. "See, I need you," he said, kissing her on the lips while he fondled her breasts. "It's just that I'm worried about losing you."

"Losing me! That could never happen! What do you mean?"

"Well, dearest, it's like this. You know how ill your mother was for such a long time, right?"

"Yes, I remember," she said, looking away.

"Well, during that time, I had large expenses for her care. I had to borrow money from wherever I could – from insurance policies, from the house mortgage, and I even had to sell valuables to make ends meet. I never wanted your dear mother to know, and I never wanted you to do without. Now, the creditors are after me."

Tabitha put her hands over her mouth in shock. "You mean the people you borrowed from?"

Jed kept wringing his hands. "I'm trying hard to pay them back, but there's not enough money coming in to do that. Soon, they'll put the house up for sale. I need about five thousand dollars in all. I won't have the money I need to take care of you. I'll just have to give you over to your grandmother." Jed faked tears. "I don't want to give you up, but.."

Tabitha interrupted. "Don't you dare! Don't you dare send me with Granny. I want to be with you! I love you! I promise I'll never ask you for a thing. I'll stop eating so much. And I heard Mrs. Foley say she needed someone to help with the children. I can do it, honest! Just don't send me away, Daddy, please!"

This was the right moment. Jed knew about the money Tabitha's mother gave to her – or, he at least, suspected. It happened one night when he was stealing into Tabitha's room. He had to be especially careful, as Bertha was staying the night in a nearby bedroom. He opened the door very quietly. What he saw shocked him. In front of him was Tabitha, sitting on the bed with a huge amount of bills spread out in front of her. His first instinct was to go inside and question her immediately. Instead, he waited. He saw Tabitha get up and retrieve a music box from her nightstand. He recognized it as the one Aunt Mattie had given to Anna years before. He watched as Tabitha stuffed the money into the little drawer, went to her closet, and put it underneath one of her straw hats.

A few days later, when Jed knew Tabitha would be gone for the day, he went to the closet, retrieved the music box, and counted the money – all $5,000.00 of it. He had to have it. He'd find a way.

Jed pulled Tabitha closer to him. "Never mind, sweetheart. Daddy will find a way, I promise. You'll only have to stay with Granny for a few months until…"

Tabitha rose to her feet. "Please, Daddy, please don't send me there! Granny Whittier doesn't like me and… wait! I have an idea. Stay right here. I'll be back in a minute."

In a few short minutes, Tabitha was back, waving something and shouting, "Mamma gave me Aunt Mattie's will money. It's a lot, Daddy – five thousand dollars! Mamma told me not to tell anyone because it's for my college education. She made me promise I'd use the money so I could have a better life. But I can still do that, Daddy, can't I? I mean, you'll pay me back as soon as you can, right?"

Jed hugged her tightly. "Oh, my girl! You would do that for me?" He kept kissing her over and over. "Oh, Tabitha! Thank you so much! Of course I'll pay you back. It may take a little while, but the money will be there when you're ready for college. I promise."

Tabitha sighed in relief. "Thank you, Daddy! Everything's going to be fine now, right?"

"Yes, Tabitha, yes. It'll all be fine now. You'll see. But I think we should add this to our list of grown up secrets, okay?"

"Sure, I promise. I'll never tell."

Jed took his bible, placed it in front of Tabitha and laid her hand on it. "You know, darling, that if you swear on this bible and then break your promise, you will surely burn in the fires of hell for all eternity. You understand that, don't you?"

Tabitha felt uneasy, but she understood that, especially in matters of the bible, her father knew best. "Repeat these words, dearest: I, Tabitha Whittier do promise to God and on my mother's grave that I will never, ever tell about the secrets between my father and me – not about the special way we love each other and not about the money."

Tabitha willingly placed her hand on the bible and recited every word Jed commanded. No one would ever know.

Jed was happier than he had been in a long time. He walked straight down Elm street, stopping at the diner for breakfast, something he hadn't done in a long time. The bank would be his next stop. He was carrying the money Tabitha gave him to pay off all his creditors.

He strolled past the hardware store and the barber shop; then found himself in front of Tessy's travel office and waved at the attractive owner. Tessy had a few years on him, to be sure, but her maturity made her even more seductive. Her hair was still thick and shiny, her waist slim, and her breasts, firm. The way she looked at him, Jed could tell that she, like many of the other women in town, would be his for the asking. But he couldn't be sure that she wouldn't brag about it to all her friends. It would be best to move along.

Tessy wasn't about to let the opportunity go. She flew to the door. "Pastor Jed! What are you doing? Would you be passing me right by without even a how-do-you –do? You get yourself right on in here!"

"Now, that sounds like a real fine invitation, Miss Tessy! But I'm on my way to the bank and…"

"That bank don't close 'til three, you know! Come on in and have yourself a cup of coffee. It's on the house!"

Jed smiled. "Well, Miss Tessy, I suppose I might spare a couple of minutes. Just a few, mind you. I have all kinds of things to do."

Tessy poured the coffee and handed it to Jed. "Black, right?"

"Yes, ma'am. No need for any of that sweet stuff with all of the other sweetness in this room." Jed smiled broadly and took her hand. "How've you been, Tessy? I haven't seen you in church lately."

"Been okay. Just busy. Things are picking up around here. The crops were real good this year, so some of the farmers and mill workers are starting to spend a little money on vacations – something I'm sure you know nothing about. Too bad! You sure deserve a break, and I got some great deals on right now."

Tessy sat back in the chair and put her feet on her desk. "Well, my stars! I just had a thought! You're all by yourself, now that Anna's gone. You must be so lonely and miserable! A nice little vacation would be just the thing!"

Tessy pulled out a few brochures from her desk drawer. "Look what I have – California Wine Region, The Adirondacks, Cape Cod." She tossed them aside. "Nah," she said, "not for you. These are all beautifully quiet, but I do believe you might just be tired of quiet. I mean, you got quiet here, twenty-four hours a day, right?"

Jed threw his hands in the air. "Tessy, you read my mind! I'd love some excitement that doesn't revolve around who won the tractor pulling contest or whose pig got the blue ribbon."

Tessy slapped her knee. "Now you're talking, preacher! I have just the ticket." She pulled out another set of brochures and placed them before Jed. "This is called 'A Trail of Two Cities.' And boy, is it! I did it myself a few months ago. Shopping, theaters, night clubbing, and a stay at the most exclusive hotels in New York and San Fran."

Tessy knew she had to be careful not to offend her prospective customer. "Now, I do realize that the night life wouldn't appeal to you, being in mourning and all, but you might be able to take some trolley rides or go to a nice show. You just can't beat the price!"

Jed flipped through the pages. The longer Tessy kept talking, the more interested he became. California! New York! I've only ever dreamed of those places. But, it's only a dream. I can't possibly...but, with Tabitha's money... I won't be able to pay off the loans, but Harry Sturgis in the credit department at the bank won't turn me down for an extension. I know everything about him and Martha Carter, and if it ever got back to his wife...no, Harry won't turn me down.

Tessy's voice broke through. "If I may be so bold, Pastor Jed, you were the model of patience and goodness with your dear wife until the day she died. Don't you think the good lord would want you to rest and relax so you can continue to be refreshed for your church duties?"

Tessy leaned over and placed her hand on Jed's arm, just short of suggestive. "And wouldn't this just be the greatest way to do that? You gotta think about all of the experiences you'd be able to bring back to that darlin' little girl of yours who has never seen a thing outside this stale old town."

Tessy remembered hearing a few things about the handsome pastor. She didn't know for certain if they were true, but she was willing to gamble. She walked to where Jed was seated and spoke in a near whisper. "I hear tell there are places in the big cities where a man can be entertained to his heart's content! Now, I don't share that with everyone, but for you..."

Jed smiled and traced circles on Tessy's arm. "If you truly believe this would help me in my time of need, dear friend, then I leave it in your hands."

It didn't take Tessy long before she came back with a price. She tossed a few papers in front of Jed. "For you – and only for you, mind you - $4,385.00. That includes everything – air fare, fine hotels, great meals, transportation, and...well, as a favor to you, I'll include a very special kind of private entertainment. But you can't tell anyone about that. I only provide that for certain men I know would appreciate it. Are you in?"

Jed didn't hesitate. He was excited at the prospect of getting out of this small-minded town. He was tired of preaching and having to put up a front before his stuffy congregation. He wanted to see things; do things; be part of things he'd only heard about and read about. He pulled the money out of his pocket and counted it out.

"Here it is, Tess, $4,500.00. I'm giving you a little extra for setting me up with that entertainment. If you do a good job...well, who knows? I may come back to thank you properly."

Tessy laughed. "I'll look forward to that, *Pastor* Jed!"

Part Three

1951 to 1956

Tabitha and Crystal

CHAPTER ELEVEN

"Hasty marriage seldom proveth well."

When Jed returned from his trip he had with him a deep tan, a shirt whose label sported *Brooks Brothers*, match books from *The Gentleman's Club* in L. A. and New York, ashtrays from popular hotels and restaurants, a small black address book, and a new wife.

It all happened so suddenly that even now, Jed wasn't sure it happened at all. He'd met Crystal at a small, dimly lit bar on a damp, chilly night when he was without plans. Crystal was sitting by herself at the bar when Jed arrived. It was crowded, so he pulled up a chair next to her.

Jed glanced over a few times and smiled politely, wondering if this could be his evening's entertainment. The slender, bleached blonde seemed to fit the role, though he thought she wasn't much to look at. He never liked women who felt the need to decorate their faces and, so far as he was concerned, hers was certainly overdone. Jed continued to watch while she lit another cigarette and ordered another drink. He rubbed his chin.

Nah! I don't think so. No class; and if she needs that much paint on her face, she can't be much to look at. I'll wait. Something else is sure to arrive soon. Besides, if I try to get acquainted with her now, she'll be expecting me to buy her drinks all night. I'll just wait a while.

It was when the woman got up and headed toward the ladies' room that he paused to reconsider. Long and slender, she was wearing a very tight, short, black dress and high, high heels that showed off her knockout figure. Jed was mesmerized. Of all the women he'd ever been with – of the assortment of large breasts, rounded back sides, long legs, tucked-in waistlines, none were larger, tighter, longer, or more desirable. He couldn't help but wonder what treasures lay under the façade. His initial disinterest became his greatest curiosity. *Hmm...I wonder.* He tried to think of an approach that might be considered an innocent gesture. When the woman returned to her seat, Jed noticed the small, heart-shaped necklace she was wearing.

"Excuse me, Miss. I couldn't help but notice your locket. It looks so much like a similar one my dear mother wore around her neck every day of her life. She kept a picture of me inside. You must have a picture of your children inside, too."

The woman fondled the necklace nervously. "Oh, no! I don't have children. I'm a single lady! I carry a picture of my parents in here. See?"

She offered the necklace for examination and opened the small heart. Jed took the pendant in his hand, careful to not touch her in any way.

"Well, thank you, dear soul, for sharing that with me. Makes me think you are a person worth knowing in this unfriendly city. I'm Jed Whittier." Jed offered his hand. "And who are you? Do you live here?"

"Well, my proper name is Crystal. My Mama said she knew I would shine someday. Daddy always laughed and said he thought I'd turn out to be a real gem!"

Crystal reached out for Jed's hand and shook it, vigorously. "Nice to meet you, Jed, and I do, I do. Live here, I mean. If you can call it that. My flat is so small and noisy that I sometimes wonder why I stay. Most times it's okay, though. I work in the Lord and Taylor store. Cosmetics. Sometimes they use me as a model in the high fashion department."

Crystal laughed and leaned over so no one else could hear. "Mr. Hugo, he said he was gonna go out on a limb and hire me 'cause of my terrific figure. Then he says, 'We're having a big fashion show for men only. Just promise me you won't talk. Please, do not talk!"

Jed smiled, politely, but Crystal continued laughing. "Well, you know, what would I say anyway? All I know about is Gatlinburg. Tennessee. Boy, would I give anything to live in the country again. Had to move when my daddy died 'cause there wasn't no jobs or nothin."

Jed called to the bartender. "Jack and Coke. Make it a double for this lovely Tennessee passionflower."

Crystal was shocked - and impressed. "Well, if that ain't the cat's pajamas! Jed Whittier, you sure do know a lot about Tennessee! Did you grow up there, too?"

Jed loosened his tie and opened the top button of his shirt. "Pardon me for taking liberties, Crystal. It's just a bit stuffy in here."

Crystal would not let the conversation go. "Did you? Grow up in Tennessee, I mean?"

Jed was not uncomfortable with the question. He thought about the time he'd had a "thing" for Dimples McKenna, the librarian who moved to Emporia from Tennessee. She taught him all she knew about Jack Daniels and Coke, and she certainly lived up to the name of the state flower.

"No, I didn't grow up in Tennessee. I've always lived in Virginia where there's green, green grass and horses aplenty. A lot like Tennessee. I haven't been home in a while, though. I've been here taking care of Auntie Mildred. She lives in Brooklyn and was terribly sick with pneumonia. She's better now, thank the good lord. I just wanted to have the experience of seeing Manhattan before I return home, but I'm a bit homesick and will probably leave soon. I am a Baptist preacher and I really miss my congregation. Then, there's my darling little girl, so alone since her mother passed."

"You're a Baptist preacher? If you don't mind me sayin' so, Jed, I'm more than a little surprised. I mean, word has it that Baptists do not partake. Of the drink, I mean."

Jed took a long swallow of bourbon. "My dear lady, that is absolutely true – most times, that is. But we are permitted to use alcohol for medicinal reasons. Right now, I am sore with sadness. I'm sure the good lord would not mind if I tried to lift my spirits with just a wee bit, don't you agree?"

Crystal shook her head. "Well, if you say it's okay, then I guess it is okay. I don't know nothin' about church stuff. My daddy raised me best he could after Mama died. He wasn't a church goin' guy, but he tried to teach me right. Gave me plenty of good advice, which I carry in my heart."

Crystal picked up her drink and offered a toast. "Well, here's to you, Jed Whittier. Drink up and rid yourself of those awful, sad feelings. Here's to New York and to Virginia and to Tennessee and to my new friend."

The conversation remained easy, and the drinks did their part in making the entire evening a pleasurable one. As the evening wore on, Jed and Crystal became comfortable. Crystal was simple, uncomplicated, refreshing, and easy to talk to. She was certainly a "let down your hair" woman. Jed enjoyed being with her, but "comfortable" was not why he was here. It was time to make a move. He ran his hand up Crystal's arm, stopping just short of suggestive. It was a small, intimate gesture, but one that sent shock waves from her head through her entire body. Crystal had no intention of showing emotion.

Crystal was not naïve about the ways of men. She was used to being the object of the dirty jeers and unsolicited passes but was forced to overlook them if she wanted to remain at her job. She became immune to the sweet talk; the endless lines; the nauseas braggadocio. Only, this one seemed different. Any man that loved his mother and his Aunt Mildred and his little girl and his congregation, well…he was different. And safe.

"You know, Crystal," said Jed as the evening was turning into morning, "I've never seen a real New York City apartment. If you agree, I can deliver you home in a cab and we might perhaps enjoy a cup of coffee together before we call it a day – or a night. We will probably never see one another again, so let's just make this evening last. What do you say?"

There was not a note of hesitation in Crystal's response. Finally, she gave him an affectionate pinch on the cheek. "I say, Amen, preacher! Let's do it!"

Upon entering the apartment, Jed felt a sense of comfort he'd never before experienced. Everything was neat and in proper order. Space was lacking, to be sure, but Crystal used every inch of it smartly, so nothing appeared cluttered or cramped. Jed's eyes immediately found a chair and a little piece of crochet work at the headrest. It reminded him of teatime in his grandmother's parlor. In this tiny room was a small table, set for one. A goldfish and a canary sat, side by side, waiting to be fed. Jed's eyes continued to dart around, looking for a bedroom.

"You need the bathroom, my friend? My stars, don't feel embarrassed! Go through the door to the bedroom and it's just to the left. You gotta go all the way in before you close the door, or you won't be able to. Close the door, I mean. There's two clean towels and a new bar of soap on the shelf. You go right ahead and unwrap that soap 'cause Levine's is having a two-for-one sale on it tomorrow. Would you believe two bars for a quarter? Use all you want and make yourself comfortable."

On his way to the bathroom, Jed made a quick survey of the bedroom. Nice. Clean. Satin coverlet. Of course, those dolls and clowns on the bed don't make for romance, but I'll soon get them out of the way.

When Jed returned, he found coffee brewing and something that smelled like homemade pineapple upside down cake. "Well, Miss Crystal, you are a woman of many talents! Now, I just cannot wait to get to that cake, but first…well, I thought we might relax a bit. I feel a little…well, a little dizzy! I do suppose it's the drink. Not used to it, you know. Is it possible…that is, if you do not think it terribly improper…is it possible for me to lie down on your bed a bit before I return to the hotel? I just don't think I can make it without a brief rest."

"Well, my stars! Imagine you askin' such a question! My daddy always says, 'what are friends for?' You come right on in here with Crystal. She'll take care of what ails you." She took Jed by the hand and led him to the bed, carefully removing the dolls and the clowns, and pulling back the coverlet.

Jed was hoping Crystal would certainly take care of what was ailing him. According to his experienced calculations, he should have her naked and ready to go before the coffee was brewed.

Crystal removed Jed's shoes and rubbed his feet. "Here, now. Daddy always says that if a man's feet hurt, he hurts all over. You just lay back and relax. I'm going to get myself out of these clothes." Jed's eyes followed her as she made her way into the bathroom.

In less than ten minutes Crystal appeared, smelling of Ivory soap and dressed in Howdy Doody pajamas and a knotted pea green bathrobe, her Sunday morning lounge-around-the-apartment outfit. It was immediately apparent to Jed that she was devoid of makeup, and that she was quite attractive without it. She was carrying a tray that held a cup of coffee, a piece of cake, and a plastic rose in a vase.

"Listen," she said, "I hope you don't mind. That tight dress of mine just ain't fittin' for takin' care of you, Jed – and you do need takin' care of! I'll just bet you ain't had no cake and coffee delivered to your bed in a long time, right?"

Jed made a feeble attempt to respond. He'd never, ever had cake and coffee delivered to his bed. He'd never had someone remove his shoes or rub his feet, even as a child. He thought about the times when he cried for someone to reach out to him. He took Crystal's hand.

"You're so right, Crystal. I ain't had no cake and coffee delivered to my bed. Thank you." He devoured the luscious cake and perfect coffee and lay back, enjoying a contentment he hadn't felt in a very long time.

Jed fluffed the pillow next to him, motioning for Crystal to join him. The two talked for hours. Finally, Jed took Crystal into his arms. He felt her warmth against him, and he wanted more. He removed his shirt. "Let me feel you, Crystal. Let me know who you really are. I want…"

Crystal suddenly became serious. "I know. You want to make love to me. Is that what you want? I could tell from the minute your hand found my arm at the bar."

"Yes, I do. But it's not what you think. Sure, I have to admit I'm on fire for that beautiful body of yours. Who wouldn't be? I'm sure you know that from all…"

"All what, Jed?" Crystal sat upright. "You think I've had a lot of men, don't you? You think I'm just playin' them all – sit at the bar, flirt a little, get a guy to buy you drinks, and pay him off in the sack later. Is that what you think?"

"I…uh…I've known women to do it. I mean, they confess to me that they tease guys and cause them to stray. You can't blame me for thinking…"

"Thinkin' I'm that kind of woman?" Furious, Crystal bolted out of bed. Pointing a finger at him, she continued her tirade. "Now you just listen here, Pastor Jed Whittier from Virginia. You may believe that the only state in the union that has any virgins left is your little ol' Virginia. You may further believe that New York City houses only loose women – women on the prowl, women who have an A tattooed on their chest! Well, my friend, you are dead wrong. You are especially wrong about me, Crystal. Sure, I go out to bars now and then. It beats hangin' around this lousy apartment! And I know I don't dress like them southern belles with their crinolines and their cute little flat shoes. Well, they don't have to buy samples like I do."

Crystal picked up a stuffed clown and threw it at Jed. "You can buy me a drink, but you can't buy my virginity – and I ain't about to lose it to you or to any other guy who's expecting to carry it around like a trophy! My daddy always said, 'Why buy the cow when you can get the milk for free.' Well, this here cow is not givin' out with any milk any time soon. My bull's eye comes with a gold ring!"

Jed was shocked. He had clearly set off a nerve in Crystal – one that was raw and hurting. "I'm so sorry, Crystal. I didn't mean to insult you. It's just that…"

Crystal stood with her hands on her hips, as Jed continued. "I know a lot of women, Crystal – single, married, sixty or sixteen. They all have a thing for me. I know, you probably think I'm a pompous bastard – yes, I'll say it – bastard! But, I'm not, really. Just like you, with all the beautiful pieces put together nicely, the lord has seen fit to make me attractive to women."

Jed rose from the bed, went to the mirror and began combing his hair. "I can hardly believe it, but they tell me I'm handsome and personable and, Lord help me, sexy. Would you believe that they…you know… offer themselves to me? But I would never think of going against the good book. It is spelled out in Corinthians, 6:9. 'Do you not know that wrongdoers will not enter the kingdom of God.' I cannot and will not be taken in by the evil temptresses that make men stray. There's too much at stake."

Crystal thought about that for a moment. She admired the fact that Jed detested wrongdoing. Anyway, what was so wrong about being attracted to a man? Like the other women Jed spoke about, Crystal was fully aware that Jed was extremely handsome and personable and, yes, sexy. She took in his desirable, muscular body, his long arms that could envelope the whole of her, and his penetrating green eyes that worked to discover her every part. Yes, she'd noticed, and she wanted him as desperately as he wanted her. But Crystal was a clever woman. She knew what she wanted, and she knew what she had to do to get it.

"So, why am I so different? Why do you want to make love to me?" Won't you burn in hell for that like the bible says?"

Jed was ready for the question. "But we, dear friend, are not wrongdoers. We are two people who met and became immediately attracted to one another. You are not a temptress. You are a decent woman, and I am most properly attracted to you. The bible implores us: 'Let my beloved come to his garden and eat its choicest fruits.' Now, I am inviting you, dear Crystal, into this garden that is perfect and beautiful, and designed by a creator who wishes for us to enjoy all its choicest, ripest, and most luscious fruits. The sin is in turning away from it."

Crystal felt herself weakening, but she had to be true to her belief. No ring; no fling. It always worked for her.

"So, tell me Jed, why me? I mean, there must be plenty of other women out there who would give anything to have you make love to them. Is it because I'm just here – convenient, you might say?"

"I won't lie, Crystal. I can walk out that door this very night and find some very attractive company. Now, *that* would be wrong. I suppose it's because you're kind of different. Maybe it's because you don't put on airs. I hate that. Maybe it's this cozy flat that is so like you – warm and comfortable and dependable. Or, just maybe it's because I yearn for the mothering I've never had. I don't know. I only know you reach me in a way I've never before experienced. That's why I want you, Crystal. Do you believe that?"

Crystal put her hands to her side. Her voice changed. "Yes, I think I do. I believe it because I want to believe it. But, what does it matter? In a couple of hours, you'll be going back to

Virginia and I'll be going back to Lord and Taylor. See? It don't matter."

The words were coming from Jed before he could understand everything he was saying. "Marry me, Crystal. I know it's crazy! We've known each other for only a few short hours, but I know it's right. Marry me because it's honest and decent and good."

Jed held Crystal's face in his hands and looked directly into her eyes. "I'll come and get you in a few months, after I've had time to prepare our home. I have so much to do there, but it will be worth it knowing you'll be waiting for me. You can help me with my sweet daughter. She needs a mother, and I can tell you'd be a good one. I don't have much to offer right now, but soon I'll move along to a larger parish where I can make a good living. You'll see. You won't regret it! We'll be married just as soon as possible, but until then, come to me now. I need you."

Crystal sat down on the bed, shocked by the proposal. "But…but you haven't even said you love me, Jed. How can you –you don't really know me."

Jed pulled her close. "What does it matter – hours or months or minutes. Love happens. Come here and I'll show you just how much I love you." He reached over and began pulling off Crystal's top.

"Stop!" she cried. "You better listen to what I'm telling you or you can just leave now."

Jed felt as though he would explode. "Stop! What do you mean, stop? Please, Crystal, please! It'll only be a few months before we're married. Why do we have to stop now?"

Crystal was adamant. "I told you, didn't I? Daddy said…"

Jed was tired and defeated. Maybe it wouldn't be such a bad idea to stop the pretense and marry her after all. He knew it wasn't about love. He hadn't loved Anna or Claire, either. He wasn't sure he'd ever loved anyone, not even his own daughter. He wasn't sure he even knew what love was. This was a matter of expediency. He would be too busy to take care of Tabitha and his congregation would not take kindly to his sending the child off to live with her granny. Besides, Crystal hinted that her father had left enough money for her to be "comfortable" and, if she had money of her own, well, it wouldn't be such a bad arrangement after all.

Jed put his arms around Crystal. "Okay! You win. Your daddy wins, too. I suppose we just do the wedding. I'll pick you up tomorrow morning at nine. Be ready. We'll be off for City Hall."

Jed hailed a cab and directed the driver to one of the places Tessy recommended. Felicia was waiting for him. He would have to wait for Crystal, but in the meantime, well, there was no need to do without.

CHAPTER TWELVE

"Love all, trust a few, do wrong to none."

Tabitha's special day began when Jed called to say he would be arriving home with a surprise. She remained upstairs all morning, primping. She purchased shiny new blue buttons at the mercantile and carefully sewed them down the front of an old white top. She spent an hour in the tub using the last of the rose-scented bubble bath her mother had once given her, and she begged Bertha for a lemon so she could squeeze the juice over her hair to make it shine. All the while, she kept wondering about the surprise.

I'm sure it's for me! What else could it be? I wonder if Daddy is bringing me some real perfume from New York? No, I don't think so. He went there on a conference. I'm sure he had no time to shop. Still… Exciting thoughts flitted from one desirable treat to another – candy, beads, her first pair of nylon stockings. Finally, around dinner time, Tabitha heard her father's car pull up. She took one last look in the mirror, twirled some stray hairs around her finger, and ran down the steps and into her father's arms. Jed, unresponsive, pushed her away.

"Well, here's my little Tabitha. Don't you look cute, dearest? And how have you been? Have you been listening to Bertha, child?" Tabitha withdrew, not understanding the stranger before her. This man didn't sound at all like the father that held her close and told her about being so grown up and beautiful. This man called her "child" and said she looked "cute." Something wasn't right. Tabitha once again threw her arms around him, searching for the father she'd known and loved. Again, Jed refused her advances.

"Now, dearest, remember that I told you I have a surprise for you. Before I tell you about it, you must understand that I expect you to be a lady – a gracious, welcoming young lady and not a bratty child."

Tabitha had no idea what her father was talking about. Jed took her by the hand and led her to the car. He opened the car door and offered his other hand to Crystal. "This, Tabitha, is your new mother. I expect you to greet her properly and to welcome her into our home."

Tabitha froze, shocked. Surely it must be a mistake – some terrible, ugly joke. Standing in front of her was a woman, the likes of which Tabitha had never seen. Unlike the conservative women in Emporia who never wore bright colors, especially yellow, the creature in front of her wore a tight yellow dress that appeared to be painted on her curvaceous figure. Her high-heeled shoes and belt were of black patent, and her cascading yellow plastic earrings, shining brightly in the southern sun, gave the appearance of fireworks on the Fourth of July.

The bewildered child could not find her voice. Crystal was the first to move. She tried to take Tabitha's hand, but the hand was limp and cold. "Hello, Tabitha. I'm sorry we have to meet like this. I expected Jed to tell you about us when he called you, but I see now that he did not. Oh, men! They just don't understand these things."

Tabitha released herself from Jed's grip and tore into the house, up the stairs and into her bedroom, locking the door behind her. Jed ran after her. "Tabitha, you come out here! I will not tolerate this kind of rudeness. Crystal is now your mother – and you may as well get used to it because she is here to stay. Now, are you going to come out or do I have to break down this door? You know I will!"

Tabitha did understand that Jed was quite capable of rage. She'd seen evidence of it only a few times, but she knew she never wanted to see it again. She opened the door, tears rolling down her face.

"How could you?" she cried. "How could bring home this…this *stranger* with Mamma being gone such a short time? And anyway, you told me that I was the only one you needed! I hate you! And I hate her, too! She'll never be my mother. Never!"

Jed put his hand up as if to strike her but pulled back. He calmed down and announced, "Dinner will be ready at the usual time. You will be there and you will eat your meal and drink your milk and talk to my dear wife and your new mother because if you do not…if you do not, I promise you will not like the consequences."

Tabitha looked into Jed's eyes which she no longer considered beautiful. "You can't hurt me. You can beat me. You can send me to live with mean old granny. You can take away my cat. But nothing – nothing will ever make me call that woman 'mother.' And, from this day forward you will never be my daddy again."

The fury was building in Jed, but he knew he held the trump card. "Well, well. So, you think there's nothing that can hurt you? You're so wrong. If you do not conduct yourself in the manner that is expected in this house, you can say goodbye to your mother's money. You'll never see it again and with it, will go every hope of you going off to college."

Jed reached to turn his daughter's head. "As I say, I shall expect you and your best manners at dinner."

In the deepest part of him, Jed was happy for the incident. He knew Tabitha would never accept Crystal, giving him the fortuitous opportunity to be off the hook for paying back the money he owed his daughter, money he didn't have and didn't expect to have.

Never in her life had Tabitha felt such hate. She was defeated. She remembered her mother's plans for the money and how Anna instructed her to never tell anyone about it. But she had. She had given it to her father as an act of love and faith. He promised to repay it all, but there was never even the slightest attempt. Still, she could not give up hope. It was all she had left.

The unhappy girl would force herself to remain and count the years before she would be out of the place she'd once called "home."

As the days passed, Tabitha quietly did as she was told – all except for communicating with Crystal. Her conversations were clipped and guarded. Crystal had a talk with Jed and asked him to be patient with the girl – that it was much too soon to expect Tabitha to come around. At the same time, Jed was busy, preparing a new bedroom for him and his new bride.

He wanted a place apart – not the frilly, proper room where he once slept in twin beds with Anna. Instead, he decided to redecorate the rooms on the third floor. In earlier years, those two rooms were used only for storage. Now, it would be like a secret hiding place where he might execute all the fantasies he'd dreamed about.

His new wife was nothing at all like Anna, who rarely allowed sex. Crystal was every man's dream – teasing, flirting, taunting. He loved it. He knew he didn't love *her*, but as far as he was concerned, love was overrated.

He sent Bertha to Greene's Department Store to buy satin sheets and flowers and perfume and candles – lots of candles. "Put it on the tick!" he instructed.

Bertha shook her head and grumbled to herself, "Lordy, you'd think the queen herself was comin'. What's all this carrying on fo?" But the woman inside of her knew. *Mr. Jed musta got himself a real firecracker! Uh huh! That's what it takes to be treated like a queen. You gots to be a real firecracker under them satin sheets! Ain't that just like a man! All the scrubbin' and bakin' and cleanin' ain't gonna do it! Firecrackers is what does it."*

That afternoon, when Tabitha returned from school, Bertha decided to have a talk with her. It was clear the child was unhappy. She was pale and thin; not the affectionate, lively girl Bertha had reared for eleven years.

"Now, you set down, honey," she said. "We is gonna have a talk." Tabitha was expecting it. "There's no used you mopin' around this house. Yo mommy is gone. Ain't nothing you gonna do about that. She's lookin' down on you and what she sees she don't like. Miss Anna done tol' you like she tol' me. She say someday Mr. Jed be bringing home a new wife. She say he gonna need a woman, and Tabitha gonna need a mother. Please, try to understand, baby."

Tabitha slammed down the spoon she was holding. "Well, I don't understand! What am I supposed to do? How do you expect me to feel good about this? Can anybody tell me that?"

Bertha just hugged and rocked her, singing as she did. Tabitha began to cry again. "You just cry, child. Go ahead. Then, when you's finished, Bertha has a plan."

Tabitha wiped her nose on her sleeve and took a sip of tea. "What plan? What are you talking about?"

"Well, you know how much ladies like afternoon tea – like we're havin' now. I think it's time you done something nice for Miss Crystal. Miss Crystal, she ain't so bad. She always nice to me, tellin' me what a good meal I made or how nice I fix my hair. Yes'm, Miss Crystal really nice – much too nice for the likes of that…" Bertha realized she was in dangerous territory. She found a special piece of fine linen and took out the best teacup.

"We is gonna fix a nice tray and you is gonna take it upstairs to her. She's resting in her room. Put some of these here cookies on it and a few sprigs of those yellow buttercups from out by the shed. Ain't nothin' like flowers. Go ahead, now!"

Tabitha thought about it for a minute. She wasn't sure she wanted to do this, but if Anna thought it best, perhaps she should give it a try. She wouldn't have to talk to Crystal; just deliver the tray, along with a polite greeting, and leave.

Frightened and nervous, Tabitha climbed the steps, taking care to not spill the tea. As she approached, she saw the bedroom door was slightly ajar. She put down the tray. As she prepared to knock, she heard giggling and strange sounds coming from within. She pushed the door open just a bit, only to discover her father and Crystal rolling around on the bed, naked. *What are they doing? Why don't they have clothes on? Why are they making noise?*

After a minute or so, the giggling stopped. Tabitha had a full view of her father's naked body. Oh, my good lord! His thing is standing up straight. It looks like…yes, he is…he is going to put it into Crystal's privacy! Why does he want to do that? Why isn't she pushing him away? Mamma said it's wrong to let a man see your privacy. He must be hurting her, but she doesn't seem to mind. In fact, she's pulling him closer, like she likes it!"

Tabitha continued to watch, mesmerized. Finally, the event ended in loud moans. Jed lay back, exhausted, as Tabitha listened to the conversation afterward. "Jed," said Crystal, pulling on his ear, "you can't tell me you haven't been around the block a few times! You drive me crazy!"

"Well, darlin'," said Jed, proudly, "the good lord has generously endowed me with the equipment known to give pleasure. But, how about you? When I took you that first night, I knew you were not lying. You were a virgin, for sure. But, where did your experience come from? I mean, you certainly know what it takes to keep a man happy!"

"Hmm," said Crystal. "My daddy always said that a man wants a lady on his arm and, if you'll pardon the expression, a whore in bed. My daddy didn't pull no punches when he educated me. He didn't have no fancy words or scientific explanations, but he showed me pictures in magazines. He told me it's okay to be good to your husband, but not to anyone else."

Jed began stroking Crystal's breasts. "Next time you talk to your daddy, you thank him for me!"

Tabitha felt dizzy. Everything around her began to spin. Her hands were sweating, and her heart was pounding. She felt as though she might vomit. Frantic, she picked up the tray, struggling to return to the kitchen and Bertha.

"Why, child," said Bertha, "didn't you do what we talked about? How come nothin' on this tray is touched. And you looks like you just seen a ghost. What's goin' on?"

"M…Miss Crystal was busy. I didn't want to disturb her."

Satisfied, Bertha went on with her work. But Tabitha was not satisfied. In fact, she was sick inside and out. There was so much she didn't understand; so much she needed to know. Somehow, she had to find out about what was happening in that bedroom. She was sure Bertha wouldn't know and she surely would not make the mistake of going to her father. That left only one person. Much as she hated to do it, she'd have to find out from Crystal, but she would have to wait. The time had to be just right.

The opportunity presented itself when Tabitha hadn't expected it. One summer day, Crystal announced she was planning a shopping trip to Harrison. Jed had to fake being unhappy about it but, in truth, he was happy to have the opportunity to be in touch with Claire. She had been neglected far too long.

"Jed, darlin'" said Crystal, "I'm planning this trip so that Tabitha and I can get to know each other better. I mean, she's okay with me – polite and everything, but she's nearly a teenager and I'm sure she has questions. Maybe I can get her to trust me. And, she needs clothes, Jed. Her blouses are all too tight, and she's still wearing those awful dresses. If she goes to high school like that, the other girls will tease her! I'm sure she'd like some pretty underclothes. I can teach her how to put it all together."

The mention of Tabitha's underclothing sent shock waves through Jed. Suppose Tabitha should tell Crystal about the bras and about how the two of them had been together. Crystal would leave on the next train, to be sure, but not before she'd tell the whole congregation.

Jed had to think fast. "Crystal, there's something I haven't told you about Tabitha. I was hoping it might never come up, but now I feel certain it will. I must tell you that…that Tabitha hasn't been herself since Anna died."

"Well, that's to be expected, Jed. What young girl…"

Jed put his head down. "What I mean is that…well, that Tabitha makes up stories. Dr. Miles said he is sure the shock of losing her mother was too much for her. She finds comfort in fabricating all kinds of stories. Sometimes, they're just little exaggerations. Once, she said she inherited a lot of money from her mother. We all know that isn't true. Anna didn't have a thing. I suppose it was Tabitha's way of saying how much her mother loved her."

Crystal sat for a moment, pondering what she'd just heard. "Wow! I can see this mothering thing is going to be much more than I expected. I'm not sure I know how to handle it, but…" Crystal got up and put her arms around Jed's neck. "We're in this together, Jed, and I'll try to work it out. I suppose that, for now, the best thing for me is to be patient and to not put stock in what she says. In time, I know she'll come to trust me. Once she does, the problem might disappear. Meanwhile, we need to go shopping."

Jed gave Crystal a quick kiss. He reached into his wallet and retrieved a twenty-dollar bill. "This should do it," he said.

Crystal took the wallet from him and removed three more twenties. "No," she said." *This* should do it!"

CHAPTER THIRTEEN

This is the short and the long of it.

"Come on, honey!" Crystal was yelling up the steps to Tabitha. "We should get on the road early. We're gonna have a great time shopping. Crystal's gonna see that you have every little thing you need, and then some!"

Tabitha wasn't excited about the prospect of going to Harrison. Yes, she did need some new clothes, but if Crystal had to pick them out, well, it just wouldn't work. She would have to give it some thought. *Maybe, if I'm nice to Crystal, she might allow me to select my own school clothes. And, she's the only one I can ask about what Robbie told me. Robbie said there are things I absolutely need to know.*

Yesterday, Tabitha was waiting in Sara Jane's living room while her friend finished the after-dinner chores. Robbie walked in and sat down. She liked Robbie. He was always kind to her, especially since her mother died. He'd always told her that he'd be her big brother and that she could count on him to help her.

"So, how's it going, Tabby? I haven't seen you in a while. What's going on in your life these days? How's school? Any boyfriends yet?"

"School's okay, I guess." Tabitha responded, pinching her lip. "Except for the dumb boys. I don't even want a boyfriend. All the boys in my class start giggling and pointing when I pass by, and they say things."

"What kind of things? Are they mean to you?"

"I don't know. No. Well, maybe. I don't know."

"Tell me what they say to you. If you're feeling uncomfortable, it must be something you don't like."

"Well, Sam asked me if I wanted to see his penis. Then, the other boys laughed and said, 'what penis?' Then they all laughed really hard. I…I just don't know…Robbie, what's a penis?"

Rob was not ready for this question. He'd never even discussed it with Sara Jane, but he was sure his mother did.

"A penis? Well, a penis is something boys have, and girls don't. It's what makes them different."

Tabitha wouldn't give up. "Where is it? What does it do?"

The room was silent for a minute; then Robbie went on. "Uh, well, Tab, I just don't feel I should be the one to talk to you about this. Didn't your mother ever talk to you about sex?"

"What's that?"

"Oh. I suppose she didn't. She should have, Tab. You're nearly twelve, and I can see that you're…" Rob got up and began to pace. "There's Crystal, of course. Can you talk to her?"

"No, I hate her! She's a crazy woman! She's not at all like my mother was. Mamma was all soft and gentle and sweet. Crystal has a really big voice and always wears tight clothes. And my father is always kissing her and touching her and…well…doing things to her that I never saw him do with my mother. It's disgusting!"

Rob needed to know more. "What kinds of things?"

"I don't know. I saw it happen, though. I saw the two of them in bed. I don't know what they were doing, but I bet it's something to do with what the boys in my class are whispering about."

Rob's curiosity turned to shock. If this poor child had witnessed what he believed she did, she needed to talk to someone right away. She was already on her way to becoming a desirable young lady and it wouldn't be long before a boy might…

"You really should talk to Crystal, Tabby. I know, she's not your mother. Remember, your mother didn't explain things you need to know. Kids never like their new stepmoms. They're just mad that she's here and their mom isn't. But, in time, you might grow to like her a little. It won't be like it was with your mom, but it'll be okay. And, I have a feeling she'll set you straight. She won't lie to you. You should ask her all about what you just told me. It isn't good for you to be in the dark about what's happening with your body right now. Go ahead. Give her a chance."

So, that's how it began and now Tabitha was going off to Harrison to find out about that thing Robbie called "sex."

The trip was long and boring, and there was evidence of an impending storm. Crystal just went on and on, but Tabitha was not at all interested in small talk. She propped her coat against the window, pretending to be asleep. It was late afternoon before Crystal suggested to stop for food.

"I'm getting hungry, Tabitha, and you must be famished! What say we stop at a diner and get us a good supper. You can help me order since I don't know nothin' about the food of the south. Sound like a good idea?"

" Yes," Tabitha muttered." She had to admit, she was famished. "Can I have a hamburger and some french fries?"

"Go ahead, honey! Enjoy yourself. You can have whatever you want tonight and for the rest of the trip, 'cause when we get home, you and me is going on a diet. I've been packin' on a few pounds myself lately. Those hoecakes! And that pecan pie with homemade ice cream! I ain't never had such luscious treats, but I can feel the pounds going directly to my hips. Jed hasn't mentioned it, but I feel it coming. Every once in a while, I catch him starin' at my…you know, "derriere." He must be wondering if all that baggage belongs to the slender woman he married."

"Why should he care about such a dumb thing? Why should a man care about whether a woman is skinny or fat? That's not why he married you." The truth remained that Tabitha didn't have any idea why Jed married Crystal or, to be more precise, why Crystal married Jed.

"Well, now, my sweet child. I see you have a lot to learn about me and I know I have a whole lot to learn about you, too. What do you say we make a pact – a kind of promise that we we'll be completely honest with each other. I'll answer all your questions best I can. I won't lie. Then, if you want to – and only if you want to – you can fill me in on what's been happening with you. Fair enough?"

Tabitha remembered all that Robbie told her. He was right. Crystal would tell her everything she wanted to know, and she wouldn't lie. First off, Tabitha needed to find out about that bedroom scene. She might tell Crystal about what the boys said, but she wasn't sure yet. She would need time to know her better. Then, there was that business about her father and how he always came into her room at night after her mother died. Something inside of her told her that what Jed was doing was very bad, but she couldn't ask anyone. She had sworn on the bible and she could never break that promise and risk going to hell forever.

"Fair enough," she responded. "So, what's a derriere?"

Crystal chuckled. "Well, it's your rear end."

"What's a rear end?"

"It's…it's… Ah, shucks! Come here, baby, and turn around."

Tabitha did as she was told. Crystal patted her gently. This, honey, is your 'derriere.' It's a fancy word for rear end. Guys have other names for it sometimes. They don't like it if it gets all saggy and out of shape. That's why we have to go on a diet. We don't want our men to look elsewhere."

Tabitha flopped back down and took a long swallow of chocolate milk. "Who cares about that stuff anyway. I don't."

Crystal removed the glass from her hand. "Look at me, honey. You might not care at this very moment, but you will. And so will all of the other girls, and the boys who right now only think about how far they can kick that football. It'll happen, and you'll be happy that Crystal taught you to eat only one hoecake. Now, let's pay the check and get out of here. I was planning to go on, but I'm too tired and it's starting to rain heavy. I think we should hole up in that motel across the street for the night."

"Two hours is all." The burly, grey-haired man in the plaid shirt gave the clerk seven dollars and the clerk handed him a key.

"You say two hours and two hours it is. Don't be late. It's Friday night and there will be other regulars right behind you."

Tabitha nudged Crystal as she signed the register. "Crystal, why did that man pay for only two hours? I thought you got the room for the whole night. I mean, I'm really tired and two hours' worth of sleep just won't be enough for me."

"It's okay, honey. We're gonna be able to sleep as long as you like. That man isn't planning to stay for the night. He'll do his business and be out of here."

"What do you mean? What business?"

"I'll tell you about it later. Right now, let's just get a hot shower and go to bed. There's plenty of time tomorrow."

The room was dark and musty, but the two just looked forward to getting a good night's sleep and going off early in the morning. "You go ahead, Tabby, you can use the bathroom first."

Tabitha collected what she needed and headed for the bathroom.

It wasn't long before Crystal heard her shout. "Crystal, I forgot my pajamas. Would you please bring them to me?"

"Okay, honey, but I'm not sure where they are. Why don't you just come out and get them?"

"I can't. I don't have any clothes on."

Crystal shook her head in disbelief. "Okay, but I don't know why you got such a problem with it. I ain't gonna see anything new! I got the same thing."

"Please, Crystal! Don't make me come out. Just hand me my bag and I'll find them myself. Please!"

"Okay, honey, you don't have to come out until you're dressed."

Tabitha did as she was told; then lay on the bed and waited for Crystal to finish. She felt sleepy, but she knew this would be the only opportunity she'd have to really talk. Crystal finally finished her nightly ritual, turned out the light, and got into the other bed.

"I'm bushed, aren't you? Let's just get a good night's sleep. Goodnight, honey, and God bless you." Suddenly, she flicked on the light again. "Why, I'm so sorry, Crystal plum forgot that you are a good Christian child who says her night prayers. Now, I don't hold to that kind of prayin', but I should. See! You can teach me things and I'll teach you things. Deal?"

"Well, it's not such a big thing. I always just ask God to take care of my mamma and to make me a good girl like Mamma said. I don't know if I'm good or not. I don't think I am. I did something…" Tabitha stopped short. She could not bring herself to discuss the secret.

"You sweet child," said Crystal, "of course you're good. I bet you never done a bad thing in your entire life. Your mamma would be proud of you."

"Have you?" Tabitha saw this as an opportunity to get to that bedroom business. "Been bad, I mean?"

"Hmm. Now, let me think here. Yes, I suppose I have been once or twice when I was your age. Once I used my church money to buy some Tangee. That's pretty bad. Another time I skipped school for a few days. My parents never did find out about it, but the bad feeling I had never quite left me. I learned to never do that again. See, honey, the good lord seen fit to give us that bad feeling, a conscience we call it, to keep us from doing things that aren't right."

Tabitha thought she should stop, but there was too much at stake. She had to find out. "Were you doing something bad when you were doing that thing with my father?" There. It was out.

"What thing is that, honey?" Crystal took a moment to pull back. "Oh, you mean when we had that little glass of wine after dinner yesterday? Why, that's not bad, honey. Poor Jed has to take it for medicinal reasons and I just keep him company."

"No, I don't mean about the wine. I mean about how the two of you were rolling around in bed and that disgusting thing my father was doing to you. Once, when Mamma and I were at the fair, I saw two horses doing something like that. When I asked Mamma about it, she said it was okay if horses do it because they want to get a new baby, but that it's disgusting if people do it when they don't want a baby. Do you and my father want a new baby? Is that how babies get here?"

Crystal was shocked and silent. Oh, my good God! The child must have seen us! She doesn't know the first thing about sex, and this is the way she had to find out about it. Damn that Jed, anyway! I kept tellin' him it wasn't safe to keep that door unlocked. Now, what do I do? What can I possibly tell her?"

Crystal rose to her feet and pretended to have the need to go to the bathroom. It was all too much. It wasn't as though she had experience in child rearing. This was thrust upon her and she realized the answers she would give the girl right now could possibly set her up for a lifetime.

She thought about something her daddy once told her: "When someone's asking you questions and you don't have the answers, just turn things around and start asking questions of your own. It'll make the other person feel important and they'll forget what they asked you." It was worth a try.

Crystal returned to the room and sat at the foot of Tabitha's bed. "So, honey, do you think what you saw is bad?"

"Yes, I do. I think Mamma was right. It's disgusting!"

"What exactly did you see?"

"I saw my father put his thing into your privacy! That's what I saw! And you didn't even try to stop him. Why didn't you? Why did you let him do that to you? Now you're going to have a baby!"

Tabitha stuffed her face into a pillow and began to cry. Crystal picked her head up, gently. "Okay, I get it. I understand why you're upset, but honey, you're wrong. I mean, you're wrong about the baby. There won't be a baby. Not now, not ever. Your daddy…well, he don't want no more children. He says he's got too much work to do in the church."

Tabitha continued sobbing and Crystal continued holding her and rocking her gently. "Precious," she said, "we have lots of work to do. There's plenty you don't know, so I suppose we're going to have to start from the very beginning. I never bargained for this when I married your daddy. I suppose I thought Anna would have taken care of it. Did your mother tell you anything at all about your body and what's happening to it?"

Tabitha wiped her tears and sat upright. "She did tell me something right before she died, but I didn't understand it. She said that someday soon I would see blood on my panties and when I do, I should tell Bertha and she would take care of things. But it never happened."

Crystal couldn't believe what she was hearing. What mother would allow her child to be so confused and upset over something that was such a natural and beautiful part of being female. Anna might have been a "saintly" woman but, as far as Crystal was concerned, she'd missed her mark at raising her daughter. It was at that moment that Crystal decided she would never, ever allow this beautiful child to be so ignorant and unhappy again. She took Tabitha's face in her hands and looked directly into her eyes.

"Beginning right now, child, you and I are going to have a very special relationship. I know I can never be like your mother, but I really want to try hard to be the next thing to your real mother. We have lots to talk about. I think we should start with this."

Crystal rooted through her bag until she found her stash of sanitary pads and laid them out for examination. "These, honey, are for your period which will be coming very soon, I suspect. They are used to collect the blood that will leave your body during a certain time, every month. It's what makes a woman a woman, and…

The two women talked for hours. There was so much to explain, and Crystal had to make sure that what she was telling the child was exactly right. Finally, she took a deep breath. "Well, now, I think we've covered just about everything. Remember, sweetheart, girls have a vagina and boys have a penis. Some boys will want to put their penis into your vagina. They will want to feel your body all over. They'll tell you that they love you and that you'll do it if you love them. But, do not let them touch your body, Tabitha, no matter what they say." Tabitha gasped, covering her mouth and turning her back to Crystal.

"Don't be embarrassed, Tabby. You need to hear it all. As I said, having a man touch you, or demanding to get inside you when you are not married is wrong. Lovemaking is the one precious thing that is saved for marriage and, if you give it away before you're married, no man will ever want to marry you."

Tabitha covered her face with her hands to try to hide the tears that were welling up. Crystal went on. "Intercourse is not a bad thing; it's a wonderful way the good lord gave us of showing how much a married man and a woman care for one another. You can have a baby if you want one but, if you don't want one right then, it's okay to enjoy it anyway."

"So, you were enjoying it when I saw you?"

"Yes, honey, we were. I love your daddy very much and I don't want him lookin' to do it with somebody else. Sometimes, people do that. They have intercourse with somebody else – somebody that isn't who they married. It's very bad, Tabitha. You must never do that, and you must do everything you can to stop your husband from doing it."

"How can you stop it?"

"Well, honey, I suppose I shouldn't be sayin' this, but I promised to be honest. My daddy always said that there's two things a man wants and only two: good sex and good food – in that order. Give it to him and you're set for life."

Crystal stopped fussing with her hair rollers and sat for a moment. "But you know, I do wonder sometimes. I wonder why it's always about keeping a man happy. What about us women? Most women want romance, too. They want to feel loved because of who they are and not for what they can give to a man. They want flowers for no special reason and a guy who helps with the dishes. Most of all, they want a man who will be happy to be true to them."

"So, is my father like that?" asked Tabitha.

Crystal made a move to turn out the light. She didn't quite know how to respond. If she were truthful, she would have to say that Jed was only affectionate when there was something in it for him. She'd have to confess that she never felt she was the only one, and that, in his sleep, he'd called out for "Claire."

Tabitha got up and gave Crystal a brief hug. "I know I'm going to have lots more questions, but at least I don't feel so stupid anymore. And...well...thanks. I really needed to hear what you told me. It couldn't have been easy for you to do that."

It took Tabitha a long time to get to sleep, even though she was exhausted. One nagging thought consumed her. *My father touched my body. No man will ever want to marry me.*

CHAPTER FOURTEEN

*"Lord, Lord, how subject we old men are to this
vice of lying."*

Jed Whittier sat on the front porch, rocking, and enjoying a
rather large glass of bourbon. Crystal appeared, taking the glass
from him and replacing it with lemonade. "What in tarnation are
you doing, Crystal?" he said, clearly annoyed.

"Now, Jed, you promised you were going to cut down. You're
drinkin' a lot more lately, and it's not good – not for you, not for
me, not for Tabitha, and not for all of those people you said
would be condemned for it! You got to stop!"

"Huh! You want me to stop. How can I? You're all driving me
crazy. That daughter of mine barely speaks to me. When you're
not around she stays in her room. And, you're not the woman I
married, Crystal. I'm lucky if I get to have sex with you twice a
week. It's not good, I tell you. It's just not healthy. A man..."

Crystal interrupted. "I know, Jed. You remind me quite often
that a man has needs. Well, this may come as a bit of a surprise
to you but so does a woman."

Jed got up from the chair, grabbed Crystal, and pressed himself
into her. "Well, then," he whispered in her ear, "what's the
problem? Let's take care of each other's needs."

"That's not what I mean, Jed. The needs I'm talkin' about are
different. You don't do things for me anymore like you used to.
When we was first married, I'd find little presents like perfume
or jewelry under my pillow. Sometimes you'd take me Jekyll
Island for a whole weekend. You'd bring me breakfast in bed.
You made me feel like I was important to you. What happened,
Jed? Why did everything change?"

Jed knew why things changed. It had to do with Clem Harris from church. Clem finally noticed Claire Beaumont. It happened during the time that Jed and Claire were deep into their intense affair. Jed convinced Claire she was beautiful and desirable. His words got her to believing that she could be attractive to men – so attractive that she changed her dowdy wardrobe and unappealing hair style. Frumpy housedresses were replaced with short skirts and tight, low-cut blouses.

She learned to walk in high heels and splurged on henna rinse for her hair. She found placement for her mother in a nursing facility and began inviting men into her home. And into her bed.

Clem Harris took full advantage. Once he had a taste of what Claire was like, he wanted her all to himself. He finally proposed. Hurt and upset over Jed's new marriage, Claire readily agreed. But, before she did, she felt she had to confess to Clem about the entire sordid affair she'd had with Jed. She even disclosed what happened to the church funds and how Jed duped her into borrowing the money.

Clem confronted Jed and said that he would keep his mouth shut about it if Jed would never again try to contact Claire. Jed would be forced to hire a new church secretary, and Clem insisted on a full accounting of the church books every month. Clem also said that, if Jed were ever caught with any woman beside his lawful wife, he would make certain the entire congregation would run him straight out of town.

Jed knew he had no choice but to agree. The people of his congregation still admired him greatly, and he had no intention of moving to another place and starting over. But he sorely missed Claire. He'd always believed that one woman was not enough for any man. He insisted that a man should have diversion; new and exciting things to keep him going. Claire provided all of that for him. Devoid of that kind of excitement, Jed became increasingly irritable and sullen.

"Did you hear me, Jed? Why did things change?"

Jed wasn't prepared for the question. "I…uh… I don't know, Crystal. Things bother me."

"Well, tell me, Jed. I'm your wife and I think I should know. Give me a chance."

Jed began pacing. "Well," he said. He had to measure his words. He couldn't think of a thing to blame it on. Crystal had been a great partner to him and a good mother to Tabitha. Then, out of the corner of his eye he caught sight of the new television set in the living room.

"If you really want to know, it's that…that box! I didn't want to bring it into this house, Crystal. You know I didn't. But you insisted and look what's happening. There's a young dude swinging his hips and singing some kind of crazy songs about jail that make women swoon. It'll be the ruination of mankind!"

Crystal laughed. "Oh, you mean Elvis? Elvis don't do no harm."

"No harm, you say? You're going to allow Tabitha to watch that rot? And what about that crazy bandleader that carries that ugly dog around? His wife hardly has any clothes on! And did you know he's been married five times, Crystal? Five times!"

"I think he's kind of cute. He plays happy music that makes people smile, Jed. I think we could all do with more of that. Nobody smiles around here. And anyway, we can't keep Tabby from watching TV. In a couple of months, she'll be off to college and on her own. We won't be able to follow her or make decisions for her then."

The tone of Jed's voice was evidence of his increasing ire. "You and your high ideas! What makes you think Tabitha is going off to college? And, by God, woman, who do you think is going to pay for it? I can tell you I'm not. Not one red cent, Crystal! She's going to get married, and I say the sooner the better. I know she's smart and all that, but not one of the girls in her graduating class is going off to college. Why should she be different?"

Crystal let Jed have his say. She had plenty to say herself, but she was waiting for just the right time. She just let him go on.

"It doesn't pay, Crystal. Educating women is a waste of time and money. Tabitha sure is pretty, so I know she's going to have no trouble getting one of those handsome bucks in town."

Jed tapped his forehead. "I know! I'll talk to Herb Collins that owns the ribbon factory. There's good money in ribbon and Herb has three sons. Maybe I can call in some of the favors he owes me. By this time next year, Tabitha will be baking bread and working at getting pregnant. Yes, I'll talk to Herb tomorrow."

It was Crystal's moment. Her voice remained calm and reserved, but forceful. "No, you won't, Jed."

Jed turned and looked directly at his wife. "What did you say? Did I hear you say no?"

"Yes, you did. And, I never said no to you before. Never. But this time, I'm stickin' to my guns. No. You will not talk to Herb. You will not see Tabitha married and pregnant. Do you understand? No. Not over my dead body."

Jed was shocked. The look on Crystal's face made it clear to him that she meant every word. He'd never before seen such resolve. "What are you saying? You dare go against me when you know what the bible says about obeying your husband!"

Crystal smiled. "Oh, would those words be found in the same passage that talks about drinking? Hmm. Isaiah, I think. Or stealing? Exodus. And the Ten Commandments? Don't make me laugh, Jed."

Jed raised his hand in fury. Crystal didn't flinch. "If it makes you feel better to strike me, go ahead. You're not gonna feel good when I tell you everything else I know about you. I didn't want to do this, but if it means getting Tabitha to college, by God I will."

The expression on Crystal's face spoke more of hurt than of anger. "I know all about the women, Jed. I know you've been cheatin' on me for years. I don't know who or how. It don't matter, but a woman knows. Men should be more careful. They leave all kinds of telltale signs – you know, things like late night phone calls, new clothes and cologne and lipstick stains on their collars. Sure, I know. But I also know it has nothing to do with me. It's just that damned ego of yours feelin' like you were created to take care of all the hens in the henhouse. Didn't mean I wasn't hurt, though. Hurt to the core."

Jed's face turned red with rage. "Woman, you are totally exasperating! How dare you accuse me, a man of God, of breaking my vows? How dare you? You must be crazy!"

Crystal remained calm and committed. "Yes, I was crazy – once. I was crazy in love with you. You sold me a bill of goods and I bought it. But, I'm not crazy anymore, Jed. I've become very smart. Smart enough to know that it won't be long before the rooster's gonna lose his crow."

Jed got up to leave, but Crystal pointed to the chair. "There's more. You better sit down while I tell you exactly why Tabby will be off for college and how she's gonna do it."

Jed rolled his eyes and flopped back into the chair. Crystal continued, "You won't fight me on this. You won't say a word, because I know about the money you stole from her. Tabitha told me all about the inheritance she gave you that you never paid back. How could you? How could you have spent that money, knowing full well that it was Anna's dying wish that her daughter be educated. Anna must have been a smart lady. She wanted her daughter away from you and this place!"

"It's a lie! Tabitha gave me the money because, if she hadn't, I'd have lost the house over all the medical bills. I know she would have wanted…"

"No! Don't hand me that! Anna would have wanted her daughter to have a better life than she had in this house with the likes of you! And you lied to your poor daughter during a time she needed to trust you. That poor child was so upset, she told me all about it."

Jed rose, walked over to Crystal and put his finger deep into her breast. "Don't be so dramatic, Crystal. It doesn't become you. Stay with what you know. Stay in bed."

The strong words cut through every part of Crystal's being, but her resolve was stronger. "You can call me stupid, Jed. You can say I'm crude and that I have no class, and you may be right. But don't ever mess with my determination. Tabitha *will* go to college. I'll see to it. You may not have the money, but I do. I have some money stashed in a bank account in New York City in my name only. When my daddy gave it to me, he said I should keep it for myself and that I should not tell anyone, even my husband about it. He said that a woman should have money put aside. My daddy was a right smart man!"

"So, what are you going to do? You going to leave me? Hah! There's plenty of women around. Women who would be real happy to treat me the way a man deserves to be treated."

"You're right, they would. You can fill them with fancy words and fancy trinkets, and they'll stay with you as long as it takes for the fake gold on the cheap bracelets to turn green. That's when they'll find out who you really are. But you can always move along to the next one, Jed. Women the world over are just as stupid as I was. But, as I said, your crow won't last forever."

Crystal rose to go into the house. "No, I'm not going to leave. With the money I'll be using for Tabitha, I won't be able to go anywhere. But I promise, Jed, someday I'll get far away from you and all of the other hypocrites in this town, who have every bible passage memorized when it comes to condemning someone else, but who think it don't apply them."

"Go ahead! See if I care!" Jed shouted, smashing the glass he was holding.

Crystal returned inside, satisfied. "Bertha, please set tea for Tabby and me. We got lots to talk about!"

CHAPTER FIFTEEN

"Merrily, merrily shall I live now under the blossom that hangs on the bow."

Jed always stopped for the mail before returning home, but today Crystal was first in line when the post office opened. Behind the counter, her friend, Irene, was waiting. Teasing, she waved an important-looking letter.

"Is someone I know waiting for this little old piece of paper?"

Crystal tried to grab it from her. "C'mon, Irene! You know how long I've waited for this! Give it to me!"

Irene smiled and handed it over. "Here," she said. "I sure hope it's good news." Crystal smiled and blessed herself. "I know it is. I just know it! This is my Tabby's ticket to a better life." Crystal couldn't wait to open the letter. It read:

Dear Mr. and Mrs. Whittier:

It is our pleasure to inform you that your daughter, Tabitha Whittier has been accepted...

Crystal didn't read another word. She screamed and danced around the room.

"There *is* a God!" she yelled and gave Irene a big hug. "Oh, Irene, to think my daughter is going to a fine school where my best friend, Helen...well, Sister Veronica will be taking care of her! It just doesn't get any better!"

On her way home, Crystal thought back on how she and Helen had been best friends for all the years of their childhood. They were inseparable "tomboys" during early years. Later, when teenage boys entered the picture, they planned how they would have a double wedding, live next to one another, and have babies at the same time. It was during their senior year of high school that things changed.

One day, while walking home from a movie, Helen made the announcement, straight out and without hesitation or warning. "I'm going to enter the convent, Crystal. I don't expect you to understand, so just don't say anything right now. I've made up my mind."

Crystal recalled how betrayed and alone she felt. But, when she came to her senses, she realized that her special, loving friend was truly cut out to be in the service of God. Though she felt happy for her, Crystal still missed her presence, even though they remained in touch.

While Crystal lived in Manhattan, she would visit Helen frequently. Each time she left the convent, it was with such a sense of peace that she often wondered if she should have followed her friend. The thought was fleeting. She soon realized that convent life of total commitment and obedience was not for her.

Crystal was convinced that Tabitha would be happy at the college where Helen was now teaching. It was a beautiful place; a safe dwelling where she might walk through the gardens, study by the lake, and spend time with good friends.

Tabitha was in the kitchen with Bertha when Crystal came flying in. "Get packed! We're off for a great weekend. First, my sweet, we are off to see Sister Veronica and the college you'll be going attending in the fall. Then, it's New York City! Crystal is gonna spend the entire summer making new clothes for you. Nothing ordinary for my Tabby! We're gonna pound the sidewalks of the garment district to find great fabrics, buttons, and trim. Most of the girls at that college come from families of means, but no one will ever guess that you…well, that we are not so blessed."

Bertha hugged her charge and waltzed her around the room. "You is goin' to college! My baby's goin' to college, just like her mamma said. Thank you, Lord. Thank you for Anna." Then, she turned to Crystal and drew her close to them. "And, thank you Lord, for this good woman. Our baby has been blessed with two good women."

Tabitha put her arm around Bertha. "I've been blessed with three good women, Bertha. Don't you ever forget that! I'm going to miss you both, but I promised my mother I'd do this. You'll both come to visit, won't you?"

Crystal replied, "Of course we will, honey. But for now, let's just get going. We have a lot to do this weekend!"

Crystal and Tabitha were speechless as Sister Veronica showed them around. Their senses were bombarded with the sights, the sounds, even the smells of the campus. Small groups of girls were sitting on marble steps at the entrance to the lagoon, singing. Some were riding bike paths through fragrant pine trails or toting books on their way to the library. Still others were leaving campus through the huge set of iron gates.

"Where are they going?" asked Tabitha, mesmerized by what she was seeing.

Sister Veronica smiled. "Well, my best guess is that they might be on their way into town. No busses here, and the girls are not allowed their own cars until senior year. They must walk. It's a bit of a hike, but it's good for them. Keeps them trim. They might be going shopping or to a movie." She looked at her watch. "Hmm. No time for a movie. They are required to be back by five for dinner."

Tabitha began twirling her hair, a sure sign of the nervousness she was experiencing. Sister Veronica continued. "You might think the rules here are quite stringent. Girls are not allowed to miss meals or to be late for them and, if they go off campus, they must sign out. We must always know where our girls are. We feel it is for their own protection."

Tabitha was wide-eyed. "What happens if you break any of the rules?"

Sister Veronica smiled. "If you break rules, you must face consequences. Sometimes, that just means you must stay on campus for the whole weekend. If it's a serious infraction, like drinking, you might be forced to go before the Student Government, and the officers will decide your fate."

"Can you be…expelled?"

"Sure. But it seldom happens. Most girls are here because they have the desire to be educated, and they love where they are. You will never need to worry about being expelled. From what I already see, we're going to be proud to have you with us. The sisters here are committed to your entire welfare. After you get to know us, you'll find we're just women like you. We're here for you to lean on and to share your secrets, if you wish. It's not only our job, it's our desire."

Sister Veronica was expecting Tabitha to get to the question of boys. When none came, she took it upon herself to broach the subject. "We see to it that our girls have a social life. You will be allowed to date on the weekend, but you must abide by the time rule. If you're late you won't be able to get into your dorm without calling the sister in charge. We also have plenty of dances here, and there are proms in New York City at the Biltmore Hotel. Our girls love that. Of course, they are chaperoned. Some of our girls meet boys through roommates or friends and go off to visit them at West Point or Fordham or other colleges and universities. None of the girls seem to lack for boyfriends, and I'm quite certain you won't, either."

Tabitha turned away, but Sister Veronica continued. "Yes, we want you to have fun. But, first and foremost, you must maintain good grades. Much will be expected of you. This is a liberal arts school so, along with the courses in your chosen field of study, you must fulfill requirements in the arts. You will be expected to familiarize yourself with the world of literature, art, and classical music. You will follow rules of etiquette, grace, and dress.

Finally, you will be expected to present yourself in a fashion that is befitting a graduate of this institution, whether you decide to teach, enter the world of business, or devote your life to motherhood."

Tabitha felt a little sick to her stomach. She turned to Crystal. "I don't know, Crystal. I just don't know if I can do this. It seems like an awful lot and I'm not at all prepared for it. Maybe I should just…"

Crystal interrupted. "Should just what? Just go back? You wouldn't only be going back, Tabby, you would be going backwards. Is that what you want for yourself?"

"I guess not. It's just that I'm really scared. And what if the other girls don't like me?"

Sister Veronica intervened. "You won't have a bit of trouble with the other girls, Tabitha, trust me. And, if things get you down and you aren't able to go home to Virginia, you have another home right here.''

Sister pointed to the chapel. "I know you are not of the Catholic faith, but you will be asked to attend chapel services just like the other girls. We think your spiritual life is just as important as your academic life. It doesn't matter what faith you are. Catholic, Protestant, Jew are all represented here. The only thing God wants is that you open your heart and allow him in. The Holy Spirit will guide you."

Sister Veronica put her arm around Tabitha. "And, if He's busy with someone else, I'm available at any time. I want to be a kind of mother to you in Crystal's absence. It's the least I can do for leaving her without notice!"

Crystal poked her friend and laughed. The three stood under the huge beech tree against the afternoon sun. Sister Veronica motioned to the door of an imposing mansion. "You'll live here during your senior year. Our girls love it! So, come on in and look around. If you look past the marble staircase and the jade fireplace and the exquisite artwork, you just may find some ice cream in the kitchen freezer. I'm dying for a root beer float. What do you say?"

CHAPTER SIXTEEN

"A hit, a very palpable hit."

High School graduation was over. Tabitha felt relieved, but anxious. Now that she would not be in school for the summer, she would be forced to be in the company of her father. There were times she yearned to tell Crystal about what he had done to her, but just could not force herself to reveal the truth. There was that promise on the bible.

Tabitha retreated to her alone place under the porch. She picked up Kitty, found her favorite corner, and began talking to her mother. *Mamma, Bertha told me you'll always be with me. If you're listening, please help me. I'll be going away soon. I don't want to take the bad secret with me, but I don't know what to do. If I tell Crystal, she will want to leave my father. Where could she go without money? What can I do?*

Tabitha waited awhile, convinced that she would hear her mother's voice. The only voice she heard was Bertha's, shouting "Miss Tabitha! You come on in for dinner now. Bertha done made your favorite fried chicken."

She picked up Kitty, held her close and said, "As if fried chicken could do it, Kitty. I guess Mamma didn't hear me."

The miserable young girl went inside and took her place beside her father. He began, "Lord, let us give thanks for the bounty we enjoy. Remind those who come to this table with a long face that they are exceedingly blessed to have such an attentive, generous father."

Tabitha busied herself by helping Crystal in whatever way she could. Midsummer was unbearably hot, so she purchased a used fan from Jake's and set it up in Crystal's sewing room. She made pitchers of cold lemonade with ice cubes made from Kool Aid. She pinned Crystal's hair up and put cold compresses on the back of her neck. Still, there was no respite from the southern heat as Crystal worked diligently on Tabitha's wardrobe.

By the last week of summer, Crystal took a huge sigh and announced. "We made it! We're finished!" The two women danced around the room until Crystal was too weary to go on. "Tomorrow is the fashion show, darling. I've invited Bertha and Sara Jane and her mother, and Aunt Hattie, and old Mrs. Burns and the Hanson twins from the drug store. We'll serve iced tea, and I'll have Bertha make some of those cookies you like. You go to bed now, honey, and I'll clean up this mess."

Tabitha touched Crystal's arm. "No, you should rest. I'll clean up. And, Crystal…I need to tell you that…that I like you very much. You're becoming a real mother to me. Thank you."

Crystal couldn't speak through the tears she felt. "Don't you know you were my child from the first day I saw you? Come here, sweet." Tabitha flew into her arms and, for the first time in a very long time, felt wonderfully warm and safe.

The aroma of pecan jumble cookies wakened Tabitha early the next morning. She ran down to the kitchen, still in her pajamas. "Bertha, what will I ever do without my favorite cookies?" she asked, devouring three of them.

"Don't you worry none, chil', Bertha's gonna send them to you. And I's gonna save all the best pecans from my tree so's I can make you that shortbread you love. Don't you fret about that. But now, we gots to get the parlor ready. Won't be long before your guests arrive."

Tabitha busied herself about the room, arranging chairs and fussing over Anna's pretty napkins and special glasses. Finally, everything was ready. She took her leave and returned to her bedroom, making a mental note about makeup. *Finally! Crystal said I'm allowed to wear Tangee today. My father will be furious, but who cares. I may even wear some of that lovely cologne Aunt Hattie gave me for graduation. She said to save it for special occasions, and today is it!*

The guests began to arrive promptly at one o'clock. Crystal arranged it so that all of Tabitha's new wardrobe would be hung on a makeshift rack in the morning room. It wouldn't take long for Tabitha to change from one outfit to another. The Hansen twins could take turns playing the piano while she was changing.

When all the guests were seated, Crystal spoke: "My dear friends, you are in for a real treat. This delightful young lady will be off for college soon and, since you won't be there to see her new wardrobe, we are bringing it to you. Now, let's begin."

Tabitha opened the door and walked through the room while Crystal continued: "Our first outfit is typical of what the young college student of today is wearing. The plaid woolen skirt is box-pleated, and Tabitha sure is thin enough to wear it. Notice the large pin that seems to keep it all together. It's just for decoration, but it is a fun accent. Notice the sweater. The collar was made from the same fabric as the skirt." Tabitha swirled around, allowing time for the women to finger a fabric that was foreign to them.

"Seems hot!" said Sara Jane, fanning herself.

"Yep! It's hot for here, all right. But Tabitha's gonna need something warm for northern winters. Next outfit, please."

Tabitha was pulling at the hangers. "Let's do the suit. It's one of my favorites!" As she viewed herself in the mirror, she once again took time to admire Crystal's careful tailoring. She knew she looked great in the creation. She was confident as she once again entered the room.

"Now, here's a little number that's gonna make people sit up and take notice. This short, bolero jacket is flattering to just about any figure, especially with the darts at the (excuse me) bust. Don't you agree that it's sensational on Tabitha?

And so it went for the next hour: more skirts, a raincoat, a few tea dresses. Finally, it was time to show the evening gowns. When Tabitha entered, wearing the copy of Coco Chanel, everyone gasped. The taffeta seemed to pull in light from different directions. Depending on how she turned, the full skirt was purple; then red; then a blend of the two. The shoulders were bare, and at the waist lay a huge handmade flower of the same fabric.

For a moment, no one spoke. Aunt Hattie was the first. "Isn't it a bit...well...revealing? I have to say that I do not think that Anna would..."

Crystal spoke up. "There is nothing vulgar or revealing about this dress, Aunt Hattie. Bare shoulders are nothing to be ashamed of. What counts is how a woman acts in a dress like this and I know our Tabby is gonna be a proper lady – just what Anna would want for her."

"It's absolutely beautiful, Crystal," said Sara Jane's mother. "I only wish I could be as talented as you are so Sara Jane could look as smart. I think you deserve a round of applause."

Everyone in the room rose to their feet and applauded, heartily.

Part Four

1956 to 1960

Tabitha and Henry

CHAPTER SEVENTEEN

"Life's uncertain voyage."

Tabitha's freshman year was without incident. Her days were full, acclimating and embracing an entirely different way of life. In Emporia, she only had Sara Jane and her cat as companions. Her father demanded absolute quiet inside the house, especially at the dinner table.

It was different here. She loved the sound of her dorm mates who happily chatted about boyfriends, joined in with the latest songs, or traded sweaters for the weekend. She was happy for them, but she wasn't ready to join them.

Tabitha was heavy in thought as she made her way to her room. *I love being here, but I still feel like I don't belong. Why can't I feel like the other girls who get excited over joining the debate club or going home with friends on the weekend.*

Two of her classmates walked by and shouted, "Hey, Tab, we're on way to sign up for glee club. Wanna join us? It'll be fun, especially when we perform at St. Pete's or St. Joe's."

"I...uh...I really can't. Logic and philosophy are giving me a real problem, so I have to use any free time to study." She waved to them and said, "Thanks for asking, though."

Dumb me! That's what I mean. Why couldn't I just have said yes. She continued walking and chastising herself until she arrived at her room.

As she entered, Tabitha noticed a note on her dresser.

Tabitha,

Please join me this evening for tea. I shall be in my room after dinner and evening prayer.

Sister Veronica

Tabitha fingered the note nervously. She had seen Sister on many occasions but never had she been invited for private tea.

Must be urgent. It can't be anything about Crystal. I've just spoken to her. My grades are good; even more than good. I don't think I've offended anyone. What could be so urgent or so private?

At 7:00 sharp, Tabitha was at Sister Veronica's door. "Sister, may I enter?" she said, softly.

"Come in, Tabitha. I'm waiting for you."

The young girl had never been inside the private quarters of a nun. The first thing she noticed was that everything was so pristine – no tablets or pens lying around, no radio playing, no family pictures. Just a framed photograph of Saint Francis and a crucifix on a polished nightstand. The room smelled sweet and clean, like the Jean Nate often sent by Crystal.

Sister Veronica gave Tabitha a quick hug and pointed to the only chair in the room. "Have a seat. I'm going to sit on the bed after I pour our tea."

Tabitha obeyed and sat, hands folded, nervously awaiting what Sister Veronica had to say.

The nun was quick to pick up on her nervousness. "Tabby, relax! You and I are just going to have little chat. We haven't done that in a while and I thought it might be time."

Tabitha unfolded her hands and put her head back. "Oh! I thought for sure you were going to tell me that I'd done something wrong. That's not it, is it?"

"Oh, my, no! You've been an exemplary student and a beautiful asset to this college. It's just that…well, I've been going through the room requests for next year and I see that you've asked for a private room. Are you having a problem with your roommate?"

Tabitha was quick to answer. "No, Sister. Not at all. Mary Ann has been great. I just want to be alone, is all. I need privacy when I study."

"Yes, I've noticed you're pulling away more and more. Soon, you will be starting your second year here and, though you don't seem to be terribly dissatisfied, you also do not take part in any of our fun activities. I haven't seen you at a tea dance or a prom. You haven't joined clubs or groups. The biggest thing is that you seem to be spending more and more time in the chapel."

Tabitha got up and walked over to the large window. "Look at that. It's still light outside. Summer is nearly here," she said, hoping Sister would change the subject.

"What is it, Tabby? What's bothering you so much that you can't talk about it?" Sister asked, compassionately.

Tabitha did not look directly at Sister Veronica but continued to stare out the window. "I…I want to become a Catholic, Sister. Then, I plan to become a nun."

Sister Veronica had been through this in the past with young women who were having a difficult time finding direction. But this was different. There was more to this than Tabitha was telling her, and the astute nun felt the need to find out exactly what it was. She knew she would have to tread lightly. She walked over to Tabitha and placed her hand on the nervous girl's shoulder.

"Oh, I see. You wish to become one of us. My, this comes as quite a shock. Does Crystal know?"

"No, no! I haven't told anyone. I have it all worked out. I plan to do what it takes to convert, and as soon as that happens, I will ask to enter the convent."

"And what made you decide to do this, child? When did you reach this conclusion?"

"I don't know. It's just that I see how it is with you and the other sisters. You seem to have such peace here. You do your work every day. You eat and pray together like it's a real home. Most of all, you take care of one another."

Sister Veronica spoke tenderly, guarding her words. "Yes, Tabitha. We do all those things. The sisters here and in other convents care very deeply. We work at helping one another because we realize we are doing God's work. But there is much that is not readily visible to those on the outside; times when we have short tempers, or go through menopause, or have terrible cramps."

Sister Veronica motioned to Tabitha to sit down. "There are also times when we wonder what it's like to have a good man beside us and children pulling at our skirts. When things get especially difficult, we cry into our pillows and wonder why we elected to follow this lifestyle. Some of us make it; some don't. Those of us who remain understand that, though we have dark days sometimes, things would be much darker if we didn't follow our hearts."

Tabitha was shocked. "Is that true, Sister? Are nuns like that, or are you just trying to talk me out of it?"

"Every word is true, dear. And, if I thought for a minute you had a true vocation, I would embrace your decision and work as hard as I could to help you. But…"

"But you don't think I do, do you?

"No, I don't. You're too sad. A girl about to enter the convent is happy. I've seen girls enter for many different reasons. Some are trying to run away from an unfortunate home situation or a man who rejected them. Others are deeply wounded and want to just feel better. They think the convent is a safe escape from the ills of the world. Still others, and I hope I'm one of them, have a true calling and pray to live happily and die happily within convent walls."

Sister Veronica looked directly at Tabitha, lifting her chin. "What I do think is that there is something very wrong and you're not willing or ready to discuss it with me. I don't want to push it. Frankly, I may not be the one you should tell. If you wish, you can give me the name of another sister you trust, or you might wish to take advantage of our counseling services. Would that appeal to you?"

Tabitha began to feel the tears; but worked to ignore them. "No, not really."

"Well, then, what can we do?" Sister Veronica began rubbing her upper lip – something she did whenever she was deep in thought.

The room was silent for a bit. Finally, Sister Veronica said, "You know, there might be something!" She began fingering the small crucifix she wore at her side. "I think you need some experience in the world outside these walls. It seems all you've done is to trade the cloistered environment of your small, unsophisticated hometown for yet another kind of cloistered environment here. That's not good. It doesn't make for good decision making, does it?"

Tabitha frowned. "I'm not sure what you mean."

"I mean that in the morning I'm going to put a call in to Mr. Feldman in New York. Crystal and I are good friends of Solly and Rachel Feldman. We worked for them for a time, while we were doing our New York thing. Solly owns a shop in the garment district, and I know he'd just love to have your help on weekends. Work with him awhile. Learn the trade. Find your way around town. Enjoy the sights and sound of the city. Give yourself until graduation. The experience can't hurt, and I'm sure you can use the money. After that, if you find you are still bent on following the religious life, I will help however I can. I promise."

Sister Veronica began pacing. "Yes, that's it. It will be a great experience for you. You'll have your normal routine during the week. On Fridays, when most girls are leaving for home, you'll take the train to the city. You can help Rachel prepare for Seder on Friday and work in Solly's shop on Saturday. I know Solly will insist you take some free time to go for a walk or do some shopping. On Sunday, you'll no doubt work in the shop again; then take the 5 o'clock train from the city and be back here for 7 o'clock curfew. The Feldmans will love it and, unless I miss my guess, you'll love it, too. What do you think?"

Tabitha put her head back and closed her eyes. "Oh, Sister. I don't know. I've never been to the city on my own – never even *seen* a city! I wouldn't know my way around, and to stay with strangers…"

"From the instant you meet Solly and his wife you'll be family. They're wonderful people and they'll take care of you like you were their own. Meanwhile, my dear, think about what I said. Sooner or later you are going to have to face your problems head on. Now would be a good time. Why carry that burden to your new adventure?"

CHAPTER EIGHTEEN

"Fortune is merry and in this mood will give us anything."

Tabitha found a cab, all the while clutching the money Sister Veronica gave her to pay for it. She arrived at the Feldmans where she entered the front hall and walked up the steep steps to a door that said 23A. It wasn't long before a comely, smiling woman greeted her.

"So, come in! You must be Tabitha." Mrs. Feldman gave her a hug and pulled her inside. "Solly, she's here! Tabitha is here. Come see!"

The man that walked into the room was not as Tabitha pictured him. In her imagination, she made him out to be a tall, well-dressed man who wore onyx cufflinks and shiny shoes. In front of her stood a short, stout man with a beard who wore strange-looking clothing and a hat that covered only half his head.

"Well, so this is Crystal's Tabitha she speaks about all the time. Maziltoff, Tabitha, come in! We're getting ready for Sabbath, but we have some time before it begins. Let's all have a cup of tea and some of Rachel's rugelach. We'll get to know each other."

Tabitha shifted in her chair. The Feldmans seemed to go on and on, wanting to know everything about her – where she was from, what happened to her mother, how she ended up with Sister Veronica, how she got on with Crystal. Then Solly mentioned her father. His questions about her father served only to drag up the pain she had been harboring every day.

"My father is a Baptist minister. He has a small congregation in our town," was all she could manage to say.

Solly slapped his hand against his cheek. "Your father is a Baptist and you go to a Catholic school and now you will be living in the house of Jews. Oy!"

Tabitha didn't share the humor, but she was quick to respond. "Yes, it should be quite an experience."

She didn't tell the Feldmans that Sister Veronica was a shrewd individual who sensed there was something very wrong. She didn't tell them about how she was planning to eventually become a Catholic and enter the convent. She didn't tell them that her decision would be based on how she could make reparation for the disgusting sin she committed because she wanted her father to love her. She didn't tell them that her heart was so broken that, regardless of Sister Veronica's kindness in sending her here, it would never mend. She didn't say that right at this moment she was feeling faint and didn't really want to be in this strange place at all.

It was Mrs. Feldman who sensed Tabitha's discomfort. "Come, my dear. You should eat. Sit!"

The tea and cookies were welcome and comforting. "Thank you, Mrs. Feldman, the cookies are really great," she said.

"Oy, so formal she is!" Mrs. Feldman took Tabitha's hand. "Darling, you're going to be with us for a while and that makes you family. Please. Call me Rachel, and this poor excuse for a prince charming is Solly."

Tabitha cringed. She expected Mr. Feldman to bristle at the insult. Instead he leaned over, gave his wife an affectionate peck on the cheek and responded, "But this prince gave you two beautiful children, right?"

Rachel pinched her husband's cheek. "Of course right," she giggled.

The two smiled knowingly at each other. It wasn't long before Tabitha found herself smiling, too. She felt relieved to be in the company of such a warm, loving couple. She looked forward to hearing more about her new job and her new environment.

Rachel took her hand. "I want to know all about you. We'll have plenty of time to talk later, but first we have things to do. Come, I'll show you around. It's almost Sabbath." They went into the small kitchen.

"You're going to have to learn about our Sabbath rules – well, not rules exactly. Let's just say it's a way of life. You go to a Catholic school, right? You have traditions and rules, right? When you don't eat meat on Friday, it's because your religion tells you it's wrong. Our rules may seem a little strange to you, but we believe they are God's commands. For you, it will be just a matter of helping us in the shop and at home so we can better follow those commands."

Rachel led Tabitha into the bedroom that was to be hers. "This was once my daughter's room, but she's married now and moved uptown. Iris and her family come for Sabbath every week. She should be here soon with Michael and the baby. We still have some time before sundown, and I know Solly wants to show you around the shop. You will work there on Saturdays when the shop is closed. There's plenty to do with the displays and the inventory and the books. Solly will show you."

Tabitha's head was reeling. Everything was so strange and overwhelming. She'd felt this way only one time before, when she first met Sister Veronica, but this was worse – much worse. Everything was so strange. Rachel said she would be family, but Tabitha wasn't sure she wanted to be. *I think I should call Sister Veronica and tell her that it's just not going to work. I'll never get used to this!*

Tabitha was on the verge of tears when the apartment was suddenly full of happy noise. Rachel came in to get her. "Tabitha, this is my Iris. Her husband is Michael and the baby is Ruben. You'll be seeing a lot of them."

Tabitha put out her hand in a polite gesture, but Iris ignored it and, instead, gave her a warm hug. It was immediately obvious that she was no more than a couple of years older than Tabitha.

"Shabbat Shalom," said Iris. Her hug felt warm and sincere.

Rachel intervened. "You can return the greeting if you wish, Tabitha. It's not so hard, but don't feel like you must. Just be yourself. It works a lot better."

Rachel turned to her daughter. "Iris, Papa must show Tabitha around the shop now. You'll talk later."

It was a small shop. Tabitha found she had to squeeze her body between bolts of cloth to make a path. The old wooden cupboards housed a dizzying display of sundries – needles, thread, pins of all sizes, trim of all shapes and colors, all jammed together with no sense of order.

"I know," Solly said, as if reading her mind. "Not good, right?"

Tabitha smiled, timidly. "I guess it's not so bad."

"My Rachel, she's a good cook, a good wife, and a good mother. But she is a terrible helper in the shop. She doesn't know from organization. That's going to be your job. The shop is closed on Saturday, so you'll have all day to yourself in here. Maybe you can make a better mess?"

Tabitha thought she might like the challenge, and the thought of being alone appealed to her. "Yes, I think I might be able to make a better mess. I'll start tomorrow."

"Good! You'll stay in the shop until three. After that, you'll close the shop and go out. Go shopping. Take in a movie or go for a long walk. Enjoy yourself. It's easy to get around in this city and you'll learn fast."

Solly took out a small wad of bills from his pocket. He handed Tabitha five dollars. "Here." he said, "It's just a little something in case you want a treat to go with your coffee. Sister Veronica said I don't have to pay you much. I don't know what "much" is, but I'll be fair. Crystal will tell you. I'll be fair."

Solly shoved the bills into Tabitha's hand "Now, Rachel will be screaming for us any minute and we can't be late for Sabbath. Come. You'll join us."

Tabitha found her place at the table and sat respectfully watching, trying to assimilate everything she was witnessing. Rachel lit the candles, the signal for Sabbath to begin. The men adjusted their caps, and Solly began to pray over the wine. Everyone at the table seemed involved in that special moment of prayer and kinship. Even the baby sat, patiently waiting for the prayers to come to an end. After everyone said the "amen" the mood turned less serious, leading to a great deal of happy talking and eating.

The jovial din, the sights and sounds and smells of the apartment made Tabitha begin to feel more at home, but she was exhausted. It was a lot to take in. She excused herself early, said goodnight, and flopped across the comfortable bed.

I wish someone could help me explain how I feel. I don't know what to think! Growing up in Emporia, it was quiet all the time. Father was busy doing whatever he does, and Mother was too sick to hold much of conversation. The only one I had to talk to was Bertha. She couldn't explain the ways of the world to me because her world consisted of a square mile. The best thing that happened to me was when Crystal sent me to be with Sister Veronica. I love it there! I think I never want to leave those beautiful surroundings where I sit down to a white tablecloth every night and afternoon teas on Sundays.

Tabitha rolled over, facing the window and a flashing neon sign from across the street.

But here I am with the Feldmans and a different kind of life. It's all so strange to me! I still don't know if I can do this.

Tears rolled down her face, but Tabitha wasn't sure if they were tears of loneliness or unhappiness or just plain exhaustion. She also recognized that the tears could possibly be coming from that dark place in her soul that never, ever forgot what her father had done to her; the enormous, unrelenting pain she carried with her every day.

When Tabitha woke the next morning, the apartment was quiet. She threw on a robe and tiptoed into the kitchen, where she found a note saying that the Feldmans had gone to temple, that she should help herself for breakfast, and to please start the stew and set the table for Sabbath. Next to the note was the key to the shop.

Tabitha showered and dressed. The stew would be a challenge, but Rachel left explicit directions. Beef, beans, barley and water all mixed together and placed on a cookie sheet over a very low flame. It should be finished by the time the Feldman's returned. She finished washing the dishes; then headed downstairs, happy to be occupied.

As she entered the shop, Tabitha set her sights on where she would begin. She decided it would be the back room. She would move everything to the front, mop the dusty floor, and rearrange the many bolts of material. At first, she thought it best to sort according to fabric, but finally decided things would be better organized if she would put color families together.

It wasn't long before she noticed something more pressing and urgent. The display window was dingy and in need of a wash. There were bolts of fabric piled high, with no semblance of order or reason, and dust covered everything. Many people walked by the shop, but no one even bothered to look inside.

Tabitha bristled. No wonder no one wants to come into this shop. I wouldn't either! I think my first job should be to make this window more appealing to people on the street.

She rolled up her sleeves and tied back her hair with a rubber band. She removed everything from the window and started scrubbing. By the end of the day, the floor of the window display and the window itself were sparkling clean. She'd found a lovely antique chair in the back room that she scrubbed and polished. It was perfect for showing off the exquisite, iridescent pink taffeta she'd draped around it.

On the seat of the chair, Tabitha placed a beaded handbag at just the right angle so the sun could capture the small crystals and make them dance. She retrieved a pair of long, white gloves from the glove box in the corner and lay them at just the right angle, next to the purse. In another box she found a couple of white silk gardenias that, she decided, were still in decent shape. She wired them together and made a pink grosgrain bow to hide the wire. Finally, she smiled, satisfied with what she'd done. *Simple and elegant. Crystal said that's the key to most things.*

The old clock was chiming six when Tabitha finally sat down. It had been a good day. She began to discover that she had talent. She prayed Mr. Feldman would like what she did, but even if he didn't, she did. Mostly, Tabitha realized that she had not been the least bit unhappy all day. *I think I finally get it! Being creative and keeping busy is just what I need. Maybe that's why Sister sent me here. Oh, God, let Solly like what I've done. I want to stay!*

Tabitha went upstairs at six to have dinner with the family. They were happy to see her and asked about her day. "Oh, said Tabitha, it was fine. I spent the time becoming acquainted with the shop and doing a few little things. I hope you don't mind, but I've moved some things."

Solly laughed. "Moved some things, did you? And who would notice? Thank you, Tabitha. Thank you for moving some things, my child. I'm sure it's fine."

Everyone laughed and enjoyed the rest of the evening together. It was about eight o'clock when Iris began to gather her family's belongings. "Ruben has to get to bed. It's nice to have you with us, Tabitha. I hope we haven't overwhelmed you too much. I look forward to spending time with you again next week."

Tabitha gave Iris a hug. "Yes, you will see me next week and, if your father likes what I did downstairs, I'll be here until I get the shop where I'd like it to be. I hope we can become good friends, Iris."

Solly could hardly believe his eyes when he entered the shop next day. "Oy, Tabitha, it's a miracle! Already it's a miracle! The window…it's a miracle!"

Tabitha smiled. "You like it then?"

"Like it? I tell you again, it's a miracle! You did all of this in one day?"

"Yes," said Tabitha. "I did, and I enjoyed it. Actually, I can't wait to get started on the back room next week."

Solly put his arm on her shoulder in a fatherly gesture. "So, you are sure it isn't too much for you?"

"No, not too much, Solly," Tabitha replied. "I can handle it."

Solly rubbed his chin as he continued to gaze at Tabitha. "Such an idea I have!" He sat down in the small chair behind the cash register and went on rubbing his chin. "You know, your talent is wasted upstairs. I can see that. I will talk to Rachel about the Sabbath work. I'll make her understand that you should only work here, in the shop."

"Oh, I don't know…will Rachel be angry?"

"My Rachel? Angry? No, Rachel doesn't get angry. Maybe a little…annoyed, you know, and that she does every day! But I'll explain to her. The way I see it is that your work will bring in more customers, which means there will be more money, and then Rachel can hire a new helper upstairs."

Tabitha gave Solly a slight hug. "Oh, thank you, Solly! I'd like nothing better than to have the time to make this shop special."

Solly's manner became a bit more serious. "So, tell me. Did you go for a walk or for coffee across the street?"

Tabitha didn't respond. Solly waved his finger at her. "Not good, my child. The experience you will have here will not only be about work, right?"

Rachel entered the shop from the inside staircase. "Of course, right!" she quipped. She turned to Tabitha and took her hand. "Solly is right. If you are going to stay here and help with the shop, then I insist you take a regular lunch break and go for a walk. There is so much to see! You should find out how others live. It will open your eyes."

Rachel pointed her finger at Solly. "And you, old man! You're taking this girl away from my kitchen?"

"Well, I just thought…"

Rachel smiled. "This time you thought right. This girl has an eye that will pay the bills. She should not be making the stew and baking the challah. She'll work only in the shop."

Solly hugged them both. "Oy, women! Such a thing!"

Tabitha returned to school, happy to continue working on her term paper. It would take up most of her time before she would return to New York. Sister Veronica was on retreat, so Tabitha wasn't able to thank her for insisting she have the experience.

She did call Crystal, keeping her abreast of all that was happening with the Feldmans.

"Oh, honey," Chrystal said, "I wish I was there! I'd love to get back to working with material and buttons! Oh, how I envy you!"

Tabitha realized she should stop talking about her grand experience. Crystal seemed lonely and in need of something in her dreary life.

"Oh, I'm sorry, Crystal. I didn't mean to go on so. How are you? I hope you're finding something to keep you busy. You have such talent! Maybe you should think about opening a shop of your own."

"Well, honey, you know that's not possible. Jed wouldn't want me doing that. He wants me at home, morning, noon, and night. I don't know why. He's never around."

Tabitha could only imagine where her father would be. She felt sad for the woman who had done so much for her. She finally understood that she had come to think of Crystal as her true mother.

"Crystal," she said, "Do you mind…that is…don't you think it's about time I called you Mamma?" There was not even a pause. Crystal could barely speak. She tried to control her voice. "Why, honey, I prayed and prayed this day would come. I would be so proud to be your mamma, and you know I couldn't love you any more if you were my own."

"I know, Mamma," said Tabitha, "and I am going to work as hard as I can to come home to spend time with you. I know I haven't been home since I started school, three years ago. You know I miss you, but Solly counts on me working in the shop summers and I really could use the money. I don't expect you to…"

Crystal interrupted. "Oh, honey, you've got it all wrong! I try to send you a few dollars when I can, but I do understand about you needing extra money. Solly really needs you and there's nothing here for you in this tired old town. You do what you think is right for you."

Tabitha decided that what was right for her was to not be anywhere near her father. She would continue to study and work so she could save enough money to someday send for Crystal.

The conversation ended with love and promises. Tabitha recognized the need to go home, if only to collect her belongings and end all that was left of her life in Emporia, Virginia.

During the weeks that followed, Tabitha continued her work at the Feldman's. Though she'd been excused from Sabbath duty, she voluntarily performed the weekend tasks in the kitchen before going to work in the shop. Nothing seemed like work to her. Under Rachel's excellent tutelage, she became an expert on making challah, preparing stew, and seeing that everything was ready for dinner. She enjoyed shopping for ingredients and learned the art of haggling with the butchers.

"You call that beef?" she'd say. "Bernbaum's is cheaper by thirteen cents a pound, and better, too. And take your finger off the scale when you weigh!"

CHAPTER NINETEEN

"It is meant that noble minds keep ever with their likes."

The change of season was approaching and there seemed to be no end to busy in the shop. Tailors arrived from opening until closing. Prospective debutantes came with their seamstresses, poring over silks and lace for their exquisite, one-of-a kind ball gowns. Wealthy Manhattan matrons sent their personal dressmakers in search of the finest fabrics for their new seasonal wardrobe. Word had gotten around that, despite the size and less than desirable location, *Solly's* was now carrying exquisite merchandise. Solly had long ago given Tabitha a substantial raise and was talking about opening another shop.

"So, you'll get your degree and after you'll come by us," said Solly, smiling broadly. "With your talent and my looks, the whole town will come."

Tabitha laughed out loud. "It's a good thing I have talent, Solly. I don't share your good looks."

Solly turned suddenly serious. "Oy, you really don't know how beautiful you are, do you? Men come and men go in the shop. I see them. Do you think they are all after wool or gabardine? No, no, my pet. They want to buy your attention. But I'm thinking it's not for sale. So again I say, come with us, meet a good man who will work alongside you and together we'll all be happy. Right?"

Tabitha just smiled. There was no use arguing with Solly. "Of course right!" she replied. She'd learned that from Rachel. "Tell them they're right," Rachel said, "then go off and do what you want and make believe it was their idea. Works every time."

Tabitha had not given any thought to what she would do after graduation. She continued to see her future only through a dark cloud. She kept praying for the darkness to pass, and the sun to shine.

It was the kind of day that kept the tourists out of the city. New Yorkers loved it. Incessant rain pounded the sidewalks and allowed for the natives to have their way, ducking into local bars or coffee shops, looking for familiar faces. Tabitha longed for just this sort of day. She would be able to devote most of her time to completing orders and checking books. But, as soon as she sat down, she heard the familiar tinkle of the old doorbell. She threw her pencil down, wondering if it were just someone wanting to get out of the rain.

A young man entered the shop, removed his hat, and shook it vigorously. Tabitha bristled and rushed to cover an expensive bolt of brocade she knew would be stained by the water. The young man, recognizing what he'd done, immediately pulled back.

"Oh, how clumsy of me! I'm terribly sorry. Have I caused a problem?" He fumbled in his coat pocket and retrieved his wallet. "Here," he said, handing Tabitha a crisp one-hundred-dollar bill. This should cover the entire bolt."

Tabitha responded, examining the fabric. "It seems to be okay, and even if it were not, I couldn't take this money. What you did was not deliberate. It was a normal reaction. No harm done."

"You're very kind," responded the young man, not looking at Tabitha. She could tell immediately from his red face that he must be painfully shy and uncomfortable.

"Come," she said, pointing to the small table and set of chairs she had set up for prospective customers. "Let me have your coat and take a seat. You should have a cup of hot tea. While you're enjoying the tea, you can tell me how I might help you today." She quickly added, "Unless, of course, you just came in to get out of the rain."

"Oh, no, I actually need a bit of help. I wonder if you might do me a favor." The young man handed Tabitha an engraved card that identified him.

Henry Merriweather IV

Merriweather Banks

Assistant to the President

Tabitha felt she should probably be impressed, but elitism was not part of who she was.

"So, Mr. Merriweather, I am Tabitha Whittier. No title. Just a college student working for a few bucks. How can I help you? If I'm correct, you have your own tailor so I hardly know what I can do for you."

"You can actually do me a huge service," replied Henry, looking down at the old hardwood floor and blushing again. "I...I seem to have lost a button from my jacket. That is, I'm on my way to a very important meeting with my father. He will surely notice the missing button and he'll...well, he wouldn't like it. Do you have a close match you can sew on for me? I'll pay you well."

Tabitha felt uncomfortable about the mention of money again. "I think I have a close match. If your father doesn't examine it too closely, you'll get away with it." She began searching through the thread. "I'll have it done in no time and please, let's not mention money again. Let's just say it's a pleasure to accommodate someone in distress."

The teeming rain added to the coziness of the shop. Tabitha noticed that the flush in Henry's cheeks was gone; that he had leaned back comfortably and was intent on their animated conversation. She set to work while he took in the surroundings.

Henry had only experienced these kinds of shops from the outside and they usually looked dingy and in need of sprucing. This room was warm and inviting. He wondered if Tabitha had anything to do with it. She appeared to be out of place here. She seemed to him a refined young woman; one whose life's work might be in art restoration or research. Art was his passion, and Henry had to admit that he was already fantasizing about her. *I know it's not possible, but I wonder how I might have her become interested in me. I'd love to take her to the opera, or art exhibits, or to have her just as a friend to talk to.*" Suddenly, Henry realized he never thought about a girl in that way. The idea caused his heart to race.

Tabitha broke the reverie. "So, do you live in the city?"

"I maintain a residence on 82nd St. It's near the Metropolitan Art Museum and not far from Mother…I mean, home. It works for me. I spend a great deal of time taking in the exhibits and listening to the lectures. It's a treasure right in my backyard, so to speak. Do you go there?"

Tabitha sighed. "Heavens, no, but I wish I could. I don't know much about art and artists, but I really need to learn more. I'll be taking a course on the impressionists next semester."

"How many more years do you have?" "

"Just one. You must be finished with school, though."

Henry nodded. "Yes, I got my degree early because my father wanted me at the bank as soon as possible. I'm going for my master's at Fordham. Business, of course, but I would have opted for art history. There was no use discussing it with father. He said all artists are…oh, sorry…forget I said that."

Henry got up from the chair and looked out the window. "No sign of it stopping anytime soon." He was happy that the teeming rain might keep him a prisoner for a while longer.

Tabitha finished sewing on the button and began pressing the jacket, all the while thinking. I wonder if it would work for me. He seems like a nice enough guy. If he could help me when I'm in town, things will go a lot smoother for me next semester.

"May I call you Henry?" she asked, handing him his jacket. "I think we know one another well enough for that, don't you?" Henry blushed again.

"Oh, of course. I would love it…Tabitha. But please, I just wouldn't feel right if I didn't pay you."

Tabitha continued speaking as she retrieved Henry's raincoat. "Let's just say it's good business." Then, unlike her, she added, "You know, there is something you might do. I know how busy you must be, but if you could find some time on Saturdays I might be able to break away for an hour or two, and we could go to the museum and hang out with the impressionists. It would give me a jump start on my art courses for next semester."

"I would be honored, Tabitha. As a matter of fact, I was planning on going there tomorrow. There's an Edward Hopper exhibit, and he's one of my favorites. Would you like to join me?" Gerald immediately thought about the propriety of the invitation. He did not want to appear presumptuous. "Or next Saturday," he added, quickly. "We can go next Saturday, if you prefer."

"Not at all. I can do it tomorrow. I'll look forward to it." She walked over to Gerald and whispered in his ear, trying to add a bit of levity to the otherwise serious tone of the conversation. "You won't tell anybody, will you? I have to confess I have no idea who Edward Hopper is."

Henry's smile lit his face. It was then Tabitha found him to be far more attractive than she originally thought.

"See, I knew I'd find a smile in there somewhere," she teased. I'll be ready at four tomorrow. Meanwhile, practice. Smiling, I mean."

"So, how was business today?" asked Iris, motioning Tabitha into the kitchen. "Papa says things are going really well since you've been with us. I'm so happy, my dear friend."

Iris took Tabitha's hand. "We've been together for a couple of years now. We *are* dear friends, aren't we, Tabby?" said Iris, moving closer.

"Of course, Iris. More than friends. Like sisters, really. I've always dreamed of having a sister, and now I do. You'll always be that to me."

Iris was waiting for this moment. She was trying to find the right time to approach Tabitha and she felt now was just that time. Her face lit up.

"Sisters share things, don't they?"

"Sure! I don't have much that you could want but anything…"

"Not that kind of sharing. I mean, sharing ideas, sharing secrets, sharing even the most private thoughts. That says we trust each other. Remember when I told you about how I find Michael's lovemaking just routine? There's no spark; no passion – just obligation. I told you that I sometimes fantasize about making love to sexy Samuel from the delicatessen."

Iris put her head back and laughed. "I can't have Samuel and I'm sure that, once I got a taste of him, I'd run back to Michael. Samuel probably picks his teeth or passes gas or something. But just for one short minute, Samuel is perfect, and I am beautiful, and we're locked in each other's embrace. See, it takes me somewhere else. Somewhere where I'm not cleaning Ruben's vomit, or making soup, or scrubbing the toilet. With Samuel I feel desirable, loved, and appreciated if only for a few fleeting seconds. Do you remember that conversation?"

"Of course, I do. I remember being kind of shocked that you would think enough of me to tell me something so private."

"See, that's what I mean, Tabby. It's that kind of thing. It's sharing even the ugliest part of yourself with someone you trust. I know there's nothing you can do about how I feel, but it's good to get it out. Even if you think I'm crazy; even if you think I'm an evil woman; even if you tell Mamma, I have to take that chance. It's what sisters do."

Tabitha squeezed Iris's hand. "Thank you for making me your sister. I don't think you're crazy or evil at all! You're just…well, just you."

Iris gave Tabitha a kiss on the cheek. "I just want you to know that if ever there's anything you want to tell me, I'll be around and I won't think you're crazy or evil, either."

This could be the time Tabitha was waiting for. She looked away. "Well, there is something…"

"I knew it. I could tell. I've been waiting all this time for you to let it out. Tell me, honey, what is it? What's causing you to withdraw; to have nightmares; to be distant and sad. You need to get rid of it."

Tabitha paused for a couple of minutes; then picked up a book. "I…I have to study now," she announced.

Iris threw her hands in the air. "Study! See, that's what you do. You study. Oy, Tabitha! Don't you ever want to be in someone's arms and have him close to you? Don't you yearn for his kisses and his touch? Don't you ever wonder what it's like to make passionate love to that man?"

Tabitha threw the book on the table. "You don't understand me. I don't understand me!" I've been a mess since I was eleven years old!" Tabitha flew into her room and flung herself across the bed.

Iris was not about to let it go. "Is it that bad? My God, Tabby!" She put her arms around her miserable friend and held her close. "Go ahead. Cry. Cry all you want. I won't ask you again. I'm sorry. I only thought…"

Tabitha sat up. "You did the right thing, Iris, honestly. It's just me. The words won't come out. Something happened a long time ago and it was my fault. I can't forget it and I don't want to. I know someday God will punish me for my sin. I'm afraid. I'm so afraid! I'm tired of carrying this around, but I don't know where to go with it!"

"Well, maybe someday you'll let me know what is so terrible. I can't help you until you do, but what I can do is make a great egg cream." Iris yelled, "Mamma did Saul deliver the setzer yet?"

Rachel yelled back, "Twenty- five years Saul delivers seltzer on Friday, so why should today be different? And make one for me, too!"

Iris escorted Tabitha to the kitchen table. "You, my friend, need a tasty treat right now and, while you are drinking, I will tell you about a wonderful man – a stranger who does not know you and will never judge what you think you may have done."

Tabitha wiped her eyes and blew her nose. "Who is it?"

"Rabbi Kadish. There can be none better. He is a learned man. He has many degrees, but his real brilliance is in the way he handles people. He is filled with compassion and understanding. He will welcome you and, after you spend some time with him, you will think of him as your own brother. Please, Tabitha, try."

"But, I'm not a Jew," Tabitha lamented.

"It doesn't matter. Our rabbi is here for anyone. Think it over for a bit. I'll be waiting for your decision tomorrow. Meanwhile, drink up. I'll make us another round."

The limousine arrived promptly at four. Henry Merriweather stepped out to assist Tabitha into the back seat and took his place beside her. He was impeccably groomed, but Tabitha was quick to notice that he was not up to the latest fashion for young men. His dark, navy suit, starched white shirt, and striped bow tie made him look much older than his years. Tabitha noticed he had the habit of adjusting his necktie.

Henry moved close to the door, assuring a proper distance between them. "Thank you for being prompt," he said, opening the conversation.

Tabitha smiled. "The nuns taught us well. If we're late for curfew or meals we're disciplined. Sometimes that could mean staying on campus while our friends are off to an afternoon movie."

"That seems a bit harsh," Henry said. Then he recalled the times his father severely disciplined him for a similar infraction. "Is that the worst of it?"

"Sometimes we're not allowed to go home for the weekend."

"Have you ever had your weekend privileges taken away?"

"No, but even if I had, it wouldn't matter. I live too far away to even think about going home. Also, I don't date so there would be no reason for me being late."

Henry could hardly believe what he was hearing. She doesn't date! She's beautiful and intelligent – the epitome of everything a man could want. Hmm. Catholic school surrounded by nuns. I wonder. He had to know. "Tabitha, are you…are you perhaps planning to become a sister?"

Tabitha took a minute to choose the words. "Well, I can't say the thought hasn't crossed my mind. It's too soon for me to make such an important decision. Let's just say that I am never more comfortable than when I am with the sisters. It's so peaceful there."

Henry recognized the sickening feeling in his stomach. He wanted to say, *"No! Don't do it! You can't even think of leaving me and I can't let you go!"* But he knew it was too soon. He would be chasing Tabitha away. He would have to take his time winning over the young lady who had already captured his heart. It would have to be done in small steps, but he would do it. Tabitha Whittier was worth it.

Before Tabitha knew it, she was standing in front of the Seurat Henry spoke of. Henry beamed with excitement. "I wanted you to see this before we go upstairs to the Hopper because it's on loan and won't be here long. It's a great example of pointillism. The technique is one that you should familiarize yourself with. I happen to think the pointillists were brilliant."

Henry pointed to several areas of the painting. "Each tiny dot of his work draws you into the big picture. If you examine this work closely, it appears to be a series of unrelated dots. But step back and you will be able to see how, with color, light, and form the artist connected the dots to bring forth a beautiful message. That's what art is you know. It's provoking feelings and telling a tale without uttering a word."

Tabitha stood, mesmerized, staring at the painting. Finally, she said, "I see what you mean. This is the way life happens, isn't it? One tiny dot at a time."

"How astute you are! Yes, life is about connecting the dots. We can paint it beautiful by bringing in light and color, or we can paint it dismal and gray and find ourselves being swallowed by darkness."

Henry pointed to a different angle. "It's easier for the artist. He can control the light with even a single stroke. We often live in darkness because we don't know how or where to find the light."

Tabitha thought it to be a profound statement, especially from someone so young. Henry took her arm. "Now let's get to the Hopper exhibit. You'll see it's quite different."

As they exited the elevator, Henry continued. "The Seurat no doubt made you feel good. The impressionists are brilliant, but..." He led her into a separate room. "This is Edward Hopper's work. I'm not going to tell you what I think about these. I'd like to hear how you feel after you've had a chance to examine them. Let's not talk while we're in here. You can tell me about it afterward."

It wasn't long before Tabitha understood what Henry told her. She felt strange – a feeling that defied description. She couldn't wait to leave the gallery.

Finally, Henry spoke. "I'm anxious to hear what you have to say. Tell me."

Tabitha seemed to look past him and said, "I don't know, Henry. How can I say I don't like this artist? He certainly is a master at painting a story with light. But his subjects! They seem depressed and lonely. I can't say the paintings make me feel good. It's almost as though…"

Tabitha felt like she could be the subject of one of the paintings. The Hopper paintings were instrumental in resurrecting the depression and aloneness she was trying to forget.

"I'm sorry for being such a bore. It might be difficult for you to understand."

Henry did understand. He understood the utter misery he felt when his father continually put him aside.

"You'd be surprised," was all he managed to say.

Tabitha had to admit that she was enjoying her time with Henry. She understood and respected his perceptive thinking. She was already feeling better than she had in years. Still, what Rachel told her about visiting the rabbi stayed with her and she couldn't wait to get home to deliver her decision. It was made when Henry said, "We often live in darkness because we don't know how or where to find the light." Tabitha was tired of the darkness. She would visit Rabbi Kadish as soon as he would have her.

CHAPTER TWENTY

"Fire that's closest keeps burns most of all."

Rabbi Kadish's office was not at all what Tabitha expected. She thought she'd find objects of religious significance, but all she found was a few books with what she believed was Hebrew lettering. The rest of the room was cozy – a desk, two comfortable-looking chairs, and some crude paintings.

"Ah, I see you are admiring my children's work," said Rabbi Kadish as he entered. The man was younger than Tabitha guessed he would be, probably no more than forty. "That's a gorilla, in case you haven't figured it out," he said smiling. His amiable manner immediately put Tabitha at ease.

"Well, now that you mention it," she responded, "I must say I see a resemblance."

"Well, now, Tabitha Whittier, that is the only gorilla in this room, and he's harmless. So, you're safe. Please make yourself comfortable. Take the big chair. I seem to have better success with that one."

Tabitha noticed a box of tissues discretely placed on the small table beside the chair. She wondered how many persons made use of those tissues. A visual image raced through her mind. *One tissue, a small problem like a fight with a mother-in-law. Two tissues, a larger problem – arguments over money, maybe. Three tissues, big, big problems.* She thought she would more than likely be three or more. Rabbi Kadish caught her staring at the box.

"The chair is a recliner. Kick off your shoes, put up your feet and let's begin." Tabitha leaned back in the chair with an eye on the door.

"It's okay, Tabitha. Be assured that you can leave at any time. I usually like to do hour sessions, but we might want to do more – or less. It all depends on you."

Rabbi Kadish sensed her extreme anxiety. "You know what I'd like to do? Let's play a little game. It may seem a bit juvenile to you but bear with me. Iris didn't tell me much about you, except that you are a college student and you're from the south. The little game allows me to understand items which may be essential to why you are here. Okay with you?"

Tabitha nodded; then took a sip of water from the glass beside her.

"Good. I'm going to say a name or mention a place. If it's something that brings you joy when you think about it, just smile. If it is something that causes you pain or anxiety, don't smile. It's really simple. Ready?"

"I…I suppose so. Go ahead."

"Let's start with flowers." Tabitha recalled the flowers in the room where her mother's body lay. She did not smile.

"Chocolate pie." She smiled.

"Bicycles." She smiled. The Rabbi went on: bubble gum, best friends, purple ink, cozy pajamas, school – she smiled at all of them. Then, Rabbi Kadish said, "Mother." Tabitha didn't smile. He went on.

"Father." Tabitha did not smile. Instead, she hit the side of the chair with her fist.

"Alright, Tabitha, I think we may be getting to a sensitive issue. Would you like to take a break? We can continue another time."

Tabitha knew that if she left now, she might never return. "No! I want to go on."

"Then, let's talk about your mother first. Why does the mention of your mother's name make you unhappy?"

"Because she died. She left me when I was just eleven. I needed her so much. She was sick for a long time and finally, one day, she just let her life slip away. She shouldn't have let that happen. She should have cared more about me."

"Do you feel your mother was responsible for causing her own death?"

"I guess. In a way. I think if things were better between her and my father, she might have fought harder. I know she was sick, but she was also very unhappy. I don't think she even tried. She should have confronted my father or…or left him. I would have been far better off if she'd left him, believe me."

"Do you know why she was so unhappy?"

"I didn't know then. But I know now – now that I know why some men stay out late or come home smelling like perfume. They whisper on the phone and begin to bring their wives gold bracelets or fancy earrings that they would never have spent money on. They are horrible, ugly, cheating, monsters that think only of themselves and not a whit about the damage they are inflicting on their wives and children!" Tabitha's face turned red and she began twisting knots in the tissue she was holding.

The moment Rabbi Kadish was anticipating was before him. He understood that if he were to say the wrong thing, look the wrong way, make the wrong gesture, Tabitha might leave and never come back. He didn't say anything for a few moments but stood up and went to the window.

"My goodness, it's getting dark. We've skipped tea! That will never do. Would you like to end the session now? I know you're on a tight schedule and the Feldmans will be waiting."

"No, not until I tell you everything. It's taken me years to do this and I'm afraid if I leave, I'll never come back. I want to be better, Rabbi. I want to smile again – really smile. I can't go on like this!"

"Then we'll just have tea here. You know, I sometimes I like to slip a tad of sherry into my tea. It's just the ticket. Would you like to try some?"

After several sips of the warm, comforting brew, Rabbi Kadish began again.

"So, my dear, it seems clear to me that your problem is mainly with your father. Or is there someone or something else?"

"No, you're right. My problem is with my father, but it's mostly with me."

"Oh, how so?"

Tabitha got up and began pacing. "Oh, God, this is so hard!"

Rabbi Kadish pointed to the door. "See that door? You cannot imagine how many injured souls have walked in and out of it. I think I've heard every conceivable shocking story and tried to mend every broken heart. Sometimes, I succeed pretty quickly. Other times, well, it takes a while longer. Just as I begin to feel good about someone, things go back to square one and the person is banging on my door once again. It's all part of being human, Tabitha. If we don't work together to discover the cause of your grief, you will carry this burden for the rest of your life. You will be continually ill in your soul and I won't feel good about it, either. So, as hard as it is for you, it is for me, too."

His words were sobering. Tabitha lay back in the chair. "Alright, I'll tell you. But can you turn around and not look at me?"

"No, I don't think so. It's just you and me, Tabitha, and you're pouring out your soul to me, Rabbi Kadish. You need to look at me or you will only talk to my back which, by the way, won't respond."

"Oh, God!" Tabitha cried. Finally, the words poured out. Tabitha had rehearsed and rehearsed how she would say them, but it didn't matter now. The words spewed forth like the vomit that rids the body of all manner of sickening things.

"My father fondled me over and over when I was just eleven. I let it happen and I didn't tell anyone! All I wanted was for him to love me!"

Tabitha began to sob and didn't stop for a very long time. Rabbi Kadish let her go. Finally, she cried, "Please help me! What was wrong with me? Why did I let him continue? I should have known better. I hate him…and I especially hate me!"

The rabbi sat and waited for Tabitha to let out all the pain and tears. Finally, he said, "So, my dear, you have finally let it go. This is the first step. It's all we need for the moment. I think you should go home and rest. For now, the most important thing to take with you is that *you* are in no way responsible for what was done to you. You were eleven years old. You had neither the emotional maturity nor the sexual sophistication to put a stop to his advances. Your father knew exactly what he was doing. He knew full well that it was a crime, but his selfishness got in the way and he continued to harm you. Do you understand?"

Tabitha reached for a tissue, but the box was empty. "See," said Rabbi Kadish, "there can be no more tears. I cannot accommodate them!"

He took Tabitha's arm and led her to the door. "Our next meeting will deal with trying to understand your demons. Only then can you be rid of them. From what you've told me, we should be meeting now on a regular basis. It won't be easy. There will be more pain and more dreadful memories. I'll bring in a fresh supply of tissues, just in case. Can you prepare yourself for that?"

"I…I suppose so. I know I want to."

"Good for you. Next week, then. And Tabitha, go out and have some fun. You're in a perfect place to do that."

The next weeks went by quickly. Each week Tabitha would remain with the Feldman's and go with Henry to the Metropolitan.

There was so much to do to get ready for finals, and Tabitha wanted to study the new patterns and styles for the fall season. She couldn't believe how many months of preparation were necessary in running a successful garment operation.

One Thursday evening at school she heard a shout from the end of the hall. "Hey, Tab, there's a guy on the phone for you. Says his name is Henry."

At the announcement, the girls in the dorm left their rooms and gathered around Tabitha. "You little sneak! You never told us you were seeing someone. Is he cute? Are we going to meet him?"

Tabitha tried to silence them. "He's a friend, that's all. He's teaching me about the impressionists. Honest!"

"Sure, we know, and he's making quite an impression on you, right? Tell all!"

"Leave, please," said Tabitha. "There's nothing to tell," she said, shaking her head and picking up the phone.

"Tabitha, it's Henry. I just wanted to tell you that there is a special Matisse lecture this weekend. The museum will be very crowded, so I think we should go early on Saturday."

Tabitha had to think. There was much to do in the shop. Rabbi Kadish was kind enough to put aside some time for her after Sabbath on Saturday night. Still, she could work in the shop early morning, then meet with Henry around noon, and see the rabbi in the evening. It could work.

"Alright, Henry. You're very kind to do this." Henry did not even hint that this would be special for him; that the days dragged by until he could make this call; that Tabitha suddenly meant everything to him.

As the conversation ended, Tabitha noticed Sister Veronica standing with her hands on her hips, smiling broadly. "So?" she asked.

"So, what?" said Tabitha, shyly. "There's nothing to tell. Henry is just a guy that's helping me with my art courses. You know, we talk about Hopper and Matisse and stuff. We're just good friends!"

Sister Veronica waved to her from a distance and shouted, "That's what they all say!"

The museum was crowded, as Henry expected. "I'm happy we were able to get here early. Let's go directly to the lecture and then…where would you like to dine tonight?"

Tabitha should have expected the invitation, but it escaped her. She couldn't bring herself to tell Henry about her sessions with Rabbi Kadish. "Oh, I can't tonight, Henry. I have so much work in the shop and then there is food to prepare for tomorrow's dinner, and Iris wanted…"

"Oh," said Henry. "I'm sorry. I suppose I didn't ask you properly. Of course, you must be busy. Perhaps another time."

Henry felt he was crossing boundaries he had no business crossing. Why should he think Tabitha would want more than just a casual meeting? He was not the kind of man women swooned over. He wasn't Gerald. He was smart and dependable, but he was not Gerald. He was sensitive and accommodating, but he was not Gerald. The feeling of excitement and anticipation abandoned him.

"Well, we'd better move along," he said, turning from her and leading the way to the second floor. They worked their way around the rooms that housed the paintings. Henry was cordial and amiable, but Tabitha noticed a change from his former demeanor.

"Are you alright, Henry?" she said, touching his arm. Henry pulled back. "Oh, yes. I'm fine. I just want to get through this in a hurry as you have so much to do."

"I didn't mean…I'm sorry, Henry. I think I've offended you with my prattle about all the work I have. It's not fair to you. You've been so great and I'm learning so much. Please don't take offense."

"I'm not offended, Tabitha. I do wish we could have a bit more time together, but it's fine, really." Henry smiled and whispered," As a matter of fact, it will give me time to call Marjorie."

He was lying, of course. There was no Marjorie. Henry turned toward one of the paintings. "You know, the school year will be over soon and I feel I've given you a start on what you will need to know. I think I must call an end to our time together. It's been fun, and I hope you've learned a lot, but I really must devote more time to Marjorie."

Henry turned and put out his hand, "Thank you. You've been a really good student. I've enjoyed your company and I hope our paths will someday cross again."

Tabitha was shocked. "But…"

"You have my card. If you are looking for a job after you graduate, give me a call. There are all kinds of opportunities at the bank and we might be able to work out something for you."

It was Henry's way of leaving a door open that he could not bear to close.

Tabitha did not understand any of it. It was all so abrupt and unfeeling – not at all like the Henry she knew and admired. There had been nothing even the slightest bit romantic between them, but to lose Henry as a friend was almost unthinkable.

"Please don't do this," she said. "I can't imagine losing your friendship. I'm sure Marjorie won't mind if you call me now and then, will she?"

"I don't think so, but you know how women are. Jealous to the core. I know I'll want to know how your course is going, so I may call you in the fall sometime. Goodbye Tabitha."

CHAPTER TWENTY-ONE

*Do you know I am woman? When I think I must
speak.*

The warm spring evening was perfect. The window of Tabitha's
bedroom opened to the roof of the third floor. It was an ideal
spot to meditate on an evening filled with the scent of new earth
and blooming wegelia. Tabitha could feel the night arrive and
envelop her in its welcoming embrace as she stepped outside
carefully and sat down. She lay back and allowed the night to
have its way, realizing that she might never again have this
experience. So enraptured she was, that she did not hear Sister
Veronica entering her room.

"Well, well," Sister Veronica poked her head through the
window. "I see you've discovered my favorite spot! Move over.
I'm coming out," she said.

Tabitha's voice revealed the panic she was experiencing. "Oh,
Sister, I am so sorry! I'll come in right away. I just…"

Sister Veronica pulled up her habit and squeezed through the
window. "I told you I was coming out and that's what I'm doing.
What you don't know is that this was my room when I was a
student here. I spent a lot of time on this roof, and I miss it. Now,
move over!"

The two sat for a long time, chatting, laughing, and just being
friends. Finally, the conversation turned serious. "Tabitha," said
Sister Victoria, "I am so happy you're better. Whatever it was
that was bothering you was leaving you crippled. I think you're
finally ready to move along. Any more thought of entering the
convent?"

Tabitha had a strong feeling the question was coming. "I don't know, Sister. On a night like tonight, feeling the powerful presence of God, I want to spend the rest of my life with him. But…"

"Let me guess," said Sister Veronica, "you want a home and children and a man to love."

Tabitha looked off to the distance. "You may be right. I don't know for sure."

"Is there a guy in your life? Henry maybe?"

"Not exactly. I like Henry and I can't even conceive of not having him as a friend, but…"

"But there's something missing, right?"

"Kind of. I mean, he's sweet and kind and very much a gentleman. But he's so, well, reserved or something. It almost seems as though he's from another century. If he only could be a little less serious and a bit more…I don't know…fun, I suppose. I've been so lacking for fun that I just can't wait to find it. I just can't explain it. Every woman wants romance, I think. You know, the little things that make a woman happy. I don't exactly know what that is, but I suppose I'll know it if I find it. I just want to feel like I'm worthy. Like some guy is going to go out of his way to make me happy. Do you know what I mean, Sister?"

Sister Veronica's voice gave away her thoughts "I surely do. Sometimes you young women believe that we nuns couldn't possibly know a thing about men. I daresay that most of us have had a serious love connection before we entered."

"So, what was it that made you decide to choose the convent? I mean, if you love someone, wouldn't you want to be with him, work for him, have a family with him?"

Sister Veronica thought a moment before answering. She knew her response would be an important consideration. Then she said, softly, "Ah, but I didn't go the other way. I went the right way, for me. I am with my love every moment. As I am pulling weeds in the garden, visiting nursing home patients, or teaching in the classroom, I am doing God's work. And, as for children, I have had hundreds through the years." She gave Tabitha's hand a squeeze. "You being one."

Sister Veronica got up and brushed the roof debris from her habit. "So now, I must go. If Mother Superior finds us, we'll both be in trouble. Think about our little talk. Hope it helps."

The two climbed back into the room. As Sister Victoria opened the door to leave, she turned back and, with a huge smile said, "I probably shouldn't be giving this away just yet, but I think the news should help give you direction. You will be graduating Summa! I am so proud of you."

Part Five

1960

Tabitha and Rabbi Kadish

CHAPTER TWENTY-TWO

"Mine eyes are full of tears; my heart full of grief."

Though Tabitha was anxious to see Rabbi Kadish, her parting with Henry made her feel unhappy. The rabbi noticed.

"You're particularly sad today, Tabitha. I don't blame you for feeling upset over the fact that I couldn't see you last time, but I was really sick."

"Oh, no! I'm happy you're well now. I guess I'm just a little tired."

"Alright then. Let's begin. During our last session you left me with something very important to think about. You said that what happened between you and your father was your fault. You said you should have known better and that you can't now forgive yourself. Is that correct?"

Tabitha put her head down. "Yes, I should have known better."

"Well, let's just take one thing at a time. Did you invite your father to do what he did?"

"Oh, no! No!" Tabitha cried.

"Did you make him believe that you liked it?"

"I...I don't know. I don't remember. All I wanted was for him to say he loved me."

"And you thought that by allowing him to continue he would one day say that he loved you."

"Yes, I suppose so. My father hardly ever talked to me, except when he wanted my money."

"Money? You never told me about that."

"He needed a lot of money because of my mother's medical expenses. He said I would have to go to live with old granny and he would sell the house."

"And you became frightened and upset."

"Yes. My granny is really nasty, and I felt sorry for my father, so I gave him the inheritance money that my mother gave to me for my education."

"And did you feel that if you would give him the money he might finally love you?"

Tabitha shook her head, crying into her tissue. "I was desperate for someone to show me affection. Any kind of affection, I guess."

"Do you know the difference between love and affection and just sexual gratification?"

"I don't know. Not with a man. I mean, I know Crystal loves me and the Feldman's have a real affection toward me. But the sexual business…no. I've never experienced it."

"But you know about sex?"

"I know what I saw, and what Crystal told me after that."

Rabbi Kadish sat back and crossed his legs. "Tell me about it."

Tabitha pulled the box of tissues closer. "It was right after my father brought Chrystal home. I didn't like her one bit. Bertha said I had to be nice to her and sent me upstairs to bring Crystal some tea. When I got near the bedroom, I noticed the door was open slightly. I heard sounds from inside, so I looked into the room. What I saw was something I didn't understand. My father was on top of Crystal, jumping up and down on her. I thought he was hurting her because she was moaning a lot. But he was moaning, too. Then, he moaned really loud and stopped. I was thinking of going inside to see if anyone was hurt, but then my father slumped over and smiled. Crystal was smiling, too."

"So, what did you think was happening in there?"

"I had absolutely no idea."

"Did you ever try to find out?"

"Not for a while. But then, when Crystal and I went off to Harrison, I asked her. That was when I found out everything about sex."

"Have you ever dreamed of having a man have sex with you?"

"No, but I often dream about my father doing those things to me."

"Tell me about it."

Tabitha rose and began pacing and crying harder. "I…I can't!"

"It's alright. Take a few deep breaths and a sip of water. If you don't want to continue now, we'll let it go. But we are making strides, Tabitha. It would be a shame to stop now. We're right on the brink. If you can get past this painful event, we might be able to move to healing."

Tabitha sat down again and began. "I'll try. In my dream, my father comes into my room and pulls back the covers. He begins stroking me like he always did. Then, he gets on top of me. He's doing something that makes me cry, but all he does is laugh louder and louder and louder and says 'Daddy's little girl! Tabitha is Daddy's little girl!' He keeps laughing until I wake up."

Rabbi Kadish stopped for a bit; then cleared his throat. "You must be upset when you wake up."

"Yes, very upset. I'm usually sick to my stomach and have a difficult time getting through my first class. Sister Veronica noticed. She has no idea what I'm going through. She thinks it's because I'm worried about entering the convent."

Rabbi Kadish walked Tabitha to the door. "My dear, you've had enough for one day. You've worked very hard through this and you deserve now to go to the Feldman's where you can share some family time. Are you alright?"

Tabitha did not respond for a few moments. "I suppose so. I just feel very lonely right now."

"I understand. You need someone who will just give you a big hug and some sincere reassurance. Is there someone who might be able to do that?"

Tabitha thought about Henry and how he had suddenly abandoned her. "No, no one," she said, as she began to leave.

"Look at me, Tabitha," said Rabbi Kadish. "Believe what I'm telling you. There will be someone someday soon. You have made a wonderful beginning in bringing forth the things that are keeping you a prisoner. Soon, I suspect very soon, you will be free. Meanwhile, we will continue to work. I'd like to get you ready for that trip home before graduation. See you next week."

Tabitha was surprised that week when the phone rang in her dorm and Sister Veronica answered and handed it to her. "Crystal?" Tabitha asked.

The nun smiled, knowingly. "No, it's Henry." Tabitha grabbed the phone, but hardly knew what to say.

"Hello, Henry. Why are you calling?" From the tone of her voice, Henry could tell he had made a mistake. He'd tried not to call her but gave in to an impulse.

"Oh, I…I…how are you?"

"I'm alright. Studying and working." There was a telling pause. "And how is Marjorie?"

Henry was not prepared for the question. His response surprised him. "Marjorie is, well… Marjorie is a figment of my imagination. There. I said it."

"What? That doesn't sound like you, Henry."

"You don't know me well, I think," he answered. "When I was little and very unhappy, I used to make up friends that would come whenever I needed them. Freddy was my car friend, Bobby was my horse friend, and Carl was my very best friend who came when I was sad. I liked Carl a lot."

"And Marjorie? What kind of friend was Marjorie?" Tabitha teased.

"Let's just call her a convenient friend. She was always available to get me out of a jam. Look, Tabitha, do you have any time tomorrow? I'd like to explain."

Tabitha wasn't sure she wanted to return to a relationship with Henry but convinced herself that it wasn't a relationship. It was just two friends sharing coffee. She'd missed that.

"Meet me at the Coffee Café across the street from the shop. We'll talk."

Henry was elated. Maybe there was hope, after all. He would have to find the right words, and he wasn't really good at it, but he'd find a way.

The coffee shop was especially crowded. Tabitha sat, thinking about how she'd met Henry during this kind of rain. A button! He came into the shop for a button. I sewed it on, and Henry ended up teaching me about art. I remember Sister Claudia talking about symbiotic relationships in class. Maybe it's that, but it's nothing more. I certainly miss his friendship, but I don't want him to think I'm really interested. I hope he feels the same way."

As Tabitha sat over her coffee, she looked around to see if she might find someone that would exemplify the kind of man she wanted in her life. *Look at me! I've never before looked at a man, much less dreamed about what my ideal man might be.* She turned to face the gentleman standing at the door. He was tall and distinguished, graying a bit at the temples. He smiled at her, exposing perfectly formed teeth and a few crow's feet wrinkles right where they should be.

Tabitha could feel herself blushing. The man got up and began walking toward her but instead, leaned over and greeted the striking young lady at the next table.

How stupid I am she thought. To think he might actually be smiling at me. Look at her!

The young woman turned the heads of everyone in the coffee shop. There was something about her that exuded charm and elegance and sophistication. Tabitha examined the look she wore; simple black sheath of good wool and stunning black patent shoes and handbag. The only adornment was a single strand of perfectly matched pearls and small pearl earrings. Tabitha could tell by her walk and demeanor that the young woman radiated the self-confidence she herself lacked but hoped she might someday own. Her thoughts raced. *That woman is attractive, but you couldn't call her beautiful. But, she has an aura about her that commands attention. I wonder…*

"So, young lady, what's bringing about that dreamy look that I don't see very often?" Henry startled her. He leaned over to give her a slight peck on the cheek.

"Hello, Henry! It's good to see you. Did you have to take a late lunch to see me?"

"Not really. My father is away so I don't feel as driven."

"Great. Would you mind very much if we just go for a walk through the park?"

"Of course. I'll get a cab and after our walk we can do dinner at… there I go again, making plans. I'm sorry, Tabitha. We'll just go for a walk."

Henry hailed a cab. "Drop us off at the east end of the park."

It was the usual Friday traffic mess, but Henry was glad for the opportunity to chat.

"Did you mind that I called you, Tabitha?" he said, not looking at her.

"Not really. I mean, I was surprised. I thought I'd offended you and that I'd never see you again."

"I wasn't really offended – just disappointed, I suppose." Henry moved away from her and looked out the window. "I'm not good at this, Tabitha. What I mean is, I don't really know what to do when I'm in the company of a lovely woman. I don't want to put you off. I really value your friendship, but I don't know what to do to have us remain friends. If I can't take you to dinner or a show or for a carriage ride, what can I do? Would you like us to be just telephone or letter friends?"

Tabitha sunk back in the seat. She felt sorry for Henry. He was so uncomfortable. She couldn't just come right out and tell him that she was afraid he'd eventually want more.

"I can't blame you for feeling the way you do, Henry. You're such a good person and I don't want to lead you on." The thought of the convent suddenly came to her. "I don't know where I'm headed. There's a good possibility I'll become a nun.

Then again, if Crystal should become ill, I may have to go home to look after her. Then, there's my career. I have no idea where that might take me. I just don't want one more distraction in the mix. Can you understand?"

Henry didn't buy it. He recognized that these were just excuses. If she had truly wanted him, she would stop at nothing. But he was not about to give her up, on any level.

"I understand. Tell you what. You call the shots. When you feel like doing something or just talking, give me a call."

Tabitha felt safe now. These were terms she could accept. Then, she remembered what Rabbi Kadish once told her about needing a hug. She turned to Henry. "As a matter of fact, there is something you can do. I need a hug. Just a nice, friendly hug. Can you do that?"

Henry slid across the seat, put his arms around her shoulders and let them linger for a short minute. "Like this?" he said, being careful to not get closer.

"That's great, Henry. It's just right," said Tabitha, leaning her head on his shoulder. "The rabbi was right. Everyone needs a human connection."

Henry didn't understand what Tabitha was talking about, but he didn't care. He felt wonderful. He was also in need of the human connection he missed for so long.

Suddenly, Henry pulled away. "Pull up in front of that bank, driver." It startled Tabitha. "What's going on? Why are we stopping here?"

"I've been wanting to show you something. Please understand, though, it's not meant to impress you. It's just that you've often asked what I do, so I thought I might show you." Henry pointed to the top floors of the building. "My office is on the 22nd floor."

Tabitha's eyes went immediately to the large brass letters that read *Merriweather Bank.*

"Wait a second! Merriweather. That's *your* name!" she said, putting her hand over her mouth.

"Yes. It's my family's business. At the moment, I'm my father's assistant. He'll be retiring soon, so he's training me to take over."

"But you're so…"

"So young? Yes, I suppose I am," Henry said, looking pitifully sad. "Too young, actually. My father has been grooming me to take over from the day I was born. He would hear of nothing else. So, here I am."

"Is it what you wanted for yourself?"

"Myself? Are you kidding? It's far from what I would have chosen to do. If I could follow my passion it would be in the art field."

"Why do you feel compelled to obey? Couldn't you take a stand?"

"No, there's only my brother and me and my brother is father's golden boy. He's off the hook." Henry sighed a deep, pensive sigh. "Hey, it's okay, Tabitha. Honest. It has its compensations, to be sure."

"And what would they be?"

Henry smiled and signaled the driver to continue. "Well, how I see it is that if my father wasn't so fastidious about a missing button, I would never have met you. That's compensation enough."

"Thanks, Henry. Telling me about your father couldn't have been easy. Maybe someday I'll tell you about mine. Not yet, though. Not just yet."

Henry took Tabitha's hand. "It's easy talking to you, Tabitha. You're the only one I've ever opened up to. And now, there's just one more thing."

Tabitha reached over to straighten Henry's tie. "And what would that be, my friend?"

"You'll be graduating soon. I won't ask what you plan to do after graduation. You might go back to Virginia, or you may find a job that will take you even farther away. It may be your heart's desire to enter the convent. I just want to tell you, Tabitha, that if you love the city as much as I do, you might consider staying here and working for us. I know you would be a great asset."

The statement sent Tabitha reeling. "Oh, Henry, please…I mean…well, my degree will have nothing to do with finance. I'd get fired the first day!"

Henry laughed. "What I have in mind is something that is foreign right now but, if you get in on the ground floor, you can be successfully educated. By the time you graduate, all the departments in the bank will be computerized. You'd learn on the job. If it doesn't suit you, you can move along to something that does. There's a lot of opportunity to advance. Just think about it when it's time to make decisions. Whatever you do, Tabitha, wherever you go, I want my best friend in my life."

CHAPTER TWENTY-THREE

Desperate times breed desperate measures."

As was her usual habit, Tabitha sank into the deep, comfortable chair across from Rabbi Kadish. Seder was over, but the lingering aroma of chicken soup and challah still permeated the room.

"It's really wonderful of you to see me on a Saturday night, Rabbi. I'm sorry to be such a bother."

"It's an important issue, my dear, and tonight can be an important night. How better to serve God?"

The rabbi set some candles on the table and around the room. "I want to try something, my dear, but I don't want you to feel in any way uncomfortable or threatened. With your permission, I'm going to light the candles and turn out the lights. I want you to concentrate only on the candles and their warmth. You should feel a sense of comfort drifting into your being, giving you strength and encouragement. Is that alright?"

"It's fine. I'm ready."

The rabbi began. "Tabitha, the last time we spoke you told me some pretty awful things about what your father was doing to you when you were such a young girl. You also confessed to feeling guilty about not stopping him. Is that correct?"

Tabitha let the flickering candle flame find her soul. "Yes. That's what happened."

"Alright. We've talked a lot about you. Now it's time to talk about your father."

"What do you mean? I've already told you all there is to tell."

"Yes, I suppose you've told me much of what I needed to know. Enough for me to want to know more. Since our last talk, I've spent a great deal of time trying to put the pieces together. From all that you and my experience have told me, I believe I can safely conclude that your father could be a narcissistic sociopath."

Tabitha sat upright. "A what? What's that?"

"I'm sure you know enough about psychology to know that there are certain...well, let's call them "aberrant" human behaviors. It means that, for whatever reason, certain people operate in a way that is outside the norm. Sometimes, their behavior is perceived as being nothing more than a bit weird. At times, however, the unacceptable behavior is such that it can cause severe pain and even danger to those with whom the person comes in contact. Often. the pain that is inflicted is most damaging to those with whom they are close – even their own families. These mentally ill people have no consideration for others and will happily take advantage of them. They may understand just how much they've hurt someone, but they just don't care. Unfortunately, your father could be one of these persons."

Tabitha began biting her nails. "Are you saying that my father is mentally imbalanced?"

"I don't know him at all, so I cannot give you a definitive answer, but from what you're telling me he exhibits all the signs. What I'm afraid of is, the older he gets, the more he will be forced into proving to himself that he can still be the biggest and the best. He needs treatment, but the problem with the narcissist is that he will never agree to treatment because in his mind, he is not wrong. He's a master manipulator who believes he has the answer to everything. It's easy to understand how he drew you in. You were starving for attention and affection. He made you believe what you were doing with him was perfectly normal; a kind of special, loving pact between father and daughter."

Tabitha wanted to stop. She couldn't face revisiting the whole ugly mess. But she came to understand that Rabbi Kadish was safe. He wouldn't want to cause her any unnecessary pain. She had to do this. If she wanted to get better, she would be forced to go on.

"So, are you saying that everything he was telling me was a lie? He said he loved me. He told me that's what people do who love one another. I didn't know…"

The tears came without invitation. Rabbi Kadish let Tabitha cry for a while. "It's okay, Tabitha. It's cleansing to have a good cry every now and then."

After a few minutes, Tabitha tried to compose herself. She was embarrassed that she had shown such emotion, but the man sitting across from her had such compassion in his eyes that she soon got over her discomfort. She looked at him directly.

"Are you telling me there's nothing I can do; that I should just try to get over it and move along? Because if that's the case, we should just stop right here. I've been trying to move along. All I'm doing is putting one foot in front of the other. But nothing changes. I'm still stuck."

"That's a perfectly understandable place to be, my dear. Those of us who are trained know that this is quite common – that sometimes people freeze and cannot move past the hurt."

The rabbi rose, walked to the window and smiled. "Typical Saturday night. There are people scurrying off to meet someone for a night on the town; Catholics on their way to St. Patrick's, actors on their way to makeup, shoppers hoping to find that ultimate bargain, children on their way to the hospital to be at the bedside of a dying parent. Some are happy; some are miserable; some are at a place in between. Where would you be, Tabitha?"

"What do you mean?"

"Would you be with the happy ones?"

"Of course not!"

"Then can we assume that you would be with the very sad?"

Tabitha took her time about answering. Finally, she said, "I...I don't know. I'm not *always* sad, but I'm not happy, either."

"So, do you think it's safe to say that we might be able to get you to a point where you might enjoy true happiness?"

"If you can find a way..."

"No, dear young lady. Not *I, we.* We are going to find a way. It will take real chutzpah – a Jewish word for tough courage. But if I didn't think you could do it, I wouldn't even suggest it."

Tabitha sat on the edge of the chair. "Tell me. What is it? I'll try anything."

"It won't be easy. You must confront your father. You need to be very direct and describe to him what he did to you and how this is ruining your life. You need to tell him what you think of him for committing such a terrible sin. You might suggest that he seek treatment. Be prepared for rejection, though. A classic narcissist will never allow you to control his life or to even make suggestions. What I'm afraid of, my dear, is that your father might again commit a similar sin, perhaps with another wounded soul. You have the power to not let that happen."

Tabitha seemed shocked, but before she could speak, Rabbi Kadish went on. "I think it's the only way, Tabitha. If I thought for one minute you could not handle it or that you would be hurt by it, I would never suggest it. But in front of me I see a lovely, intelligent, sensitive young lady with, yes, chutzpah – and plenty of it."

A small smile worked its way around Tabitha's lips. "Will you help me?"

"I will be there for you at any hour of the day or night. But honestly, I don't think you'll need me. Think of who you are and who you'd like to be, and you'll do just fine."

"We have spring break coming up. I wasn't going to go home, but I will now. I will.

CHAPTER TWENTY-FOUR

"The evil that men do lives after them."

The trip to Emporia was long and tedious. A bus, a transfer, a train and finally, a cab gave Tabitha time to think and rehearse. After months of visits with Rabbi Kadish, Tabitha finally garnered the fortitude to confront her father. She had already made the decision to never come back to the place she once called "home" but what of Crystal? Through difficult years, Chrystal had been her rock – as real a mother as she could ever have hoped for. In a weak moment, she'd told Crystal about the money Jed took from her, but she never even hinted about his visits to her bedroom. If Crystal were to find out about that, she would want to leave immediately, but where could she go? Tabitha thought it best to wait until after graduation when she'd have a place of her own. Then, she could send for Crystal.

The taxi rounded the corner and began to slow down. "This it, young lady? Which house is yours?"

"It's the one next to the church."

The driver pulled to a stop and flicked the switch on the meter. "That'll be $3.30, but since you're probably a college kid I'll just make it $3.00 even. And don't worry about no tip, either. You just tell your pa that Willie says to have a nice visit."

Tabitha was relieved that it was late. Her father would no doubt be in bed and she was too exhausted to put up with him tonight. Crystal was waiting, though, and ran down the steps with outstretched arms.

"My girl is here! I can't believe my Tabby is finally home!"

Tabitha never felt so loved. "Yes, Mamma. I'm finally here with you. And I'll be here for a whole week! I have so much to tell you! Bertha better make plenty of pecan cookies, 'cause we'll be drinking lots of coffee." Tabitha looked around. "Where is Bertha? I know it's late, but I thought for sure she'd be waiting with you."

Crystal lowered her voice and looked away. "Well, honey, you see...I mean... Bertha's not with us anymore."

Tabitha couldn't take in what she was hearing. "Not with us? What are you saying? She's not...not dead?" She trembled as her hand found the porch railing.

"Oh, no Tabby! Bertha's not dead! It's just that after you left Jed said..." Crystal turned from her.

"Go on Mamma. What did my father say?"

Crystal took Tabitha's hand and led her inside. "Well, Jed said that since you weren't here anymore, there would be no reason to have a housekeeper. He said that I could do whatever chores needed doin' and that he would be able to set a good example by giving Bertha's wages to the Ladies Aid Society."

Tabitha was seething but said nothing further. "Where is she? I need to know. I have to see if she's alright."

"Bertha's at the mercantile. I see her stocking shelves when I go into the store, but she don't say much. Looks kind of scared all the time."

Crystal took Tabitha's luggage and started upstairs. Tabitha stopped her as she approached her old room. She just couldn't step into the room that was filled with nightmares. She faked a smile.

"Oh, just smell the wonderful air coming from the back room! May I stay in there?"

Crystal had spent weeks refurbishing Tabitha's bedroom, but if her girl wanted to stay in the guest room, she would have her heart's desire.

Tabitha threw herself down on the cozy bed. "Mamma, I just want to stay up all night and talk, but my body's telling me there will be no more talking tonight. Will you make hoecakes and may I have breakfast in bed like I used to?"

. "Done! I had that planned when I heard you were coming. You sleep in as long as you like. I will tell your daddy you can't be disturbed. You won't see him 'til supper, though. Important church stuff, you know. He'll be disappointed, but he'll understand the need for you to rest."

Tabitha was elated. She would have the whole day to think about her plan. And she desperately wanted to see Bertha. For now, though, she would sleep the kind of sleep that would give her the rest and peace she needed to face the following day.

"You sure did justice to those pancakes!" Crystal shouted, as she looked down at the empty tray. I feel so good. It's like the times I would deliver your breakfast and we'd just talk all morning." She picked up the tray, pointing to the bathroom door. "Your bath is ready, love."

Tabitha hugged Crystal, grabbed a robe and went in for a good soak. "I wonder what time Bertha's free today. Does she work all day?"

"Let's see. Today is Monday. I think she works only half a day. If she does, she leaves at one. You might be able to catch her then. I'll just stay here and start workin' on that big dinner for tonight."

It was good to walk the streets of her hometown. It was nothing at all like the city she was used to now, but it was strangely refreshing. The window at Baker's Hardware store sported the same tired barrel of nails and hand saws and Margo, owner of the only women's shop, didn't seem to know pink was out now. No matter. It was fun and kind of reassuring to know that some things remained the same.

Tabitha spotted Bertha as she was leaving the mercantile. She ran up to her, and nearly knocked her over with a huge, engaging hug. "Bertha, it's me! It's your Tabitha!"

Bertha shielded her eyes against the afternoon sun and wrinkled her nose. "Why, saints preserve us, it is! It's my baby!" She took Tabitha in her arms and rocked her gently; then stopped abruptly.

"I...I gots to go on now," was all she could manage to say. Tabitha couldn't believe what she was hearing.

"You're leaving? Right now? You don't want to stay and talk or come over to the house? Why? Where are you going in such a hurry?"

Bertha whispered. "I just gots to go is all. Please, Miss Tabitha. Please don't ask no more questions right now."

Tabitha was disappointed and hurt, but she realized it had to be something important to cause her dear friend to act so strangely. "OK, Bertha. I won't. But can't we get together when you're free? I don't want to go back to school without talking to you."

Bertha turned her head to see if anyone was within earshot and began shuffling her feet. She removed a handkerchief from her apron pocket and wiped huge beads of perspiration from her brow. "Truth is, baby, I wants to...I has to talk to you, too. I been waitin' and waitin' for the good Lord to send you to me. I gots something real big goin' on inside and I knows it won't never be fixed until I talks to you 'bout it. Can you come to my house in an hour? Jes don't let anybody see you comin'. You know where I live. It's the only house on the river road by our old fishing hole."

Tabitha nodded and waved as Bertha left hurriedly. She found a spot on the steps of Ebner's Sweet Shop and checked her watch repeatedly, anxious for the minutes to fly. Finally, it was time to leave for Bertha's. She half-walked, half-ran the distance to the fishing hole where Bertha had long ago taught her how to catch catfish.

Finally, she was at the door of the only house on the street. She might have known this would be Bertha's place. The spotlessly clean, white porch was the perfect backdrop for the many pots of red and yellow flowers. The windows housed white curtains that seemed to sparkle in the afternoon sun. A bible rested on a rocking chair and both looked well-worn and loved.

It was clear that Bertha had been waiting for her guest. "Come inside, honey," she whispered, looking all around. "I don't wants nobody to see us together."

Tabitha understood what she was saying. No white person would ever come to visit the home of a black person. It just wasn't done.

Bertha motioned for Tabitha to sit at the kitchen table. "I made some lemonade." She set the glass in front of Tabitha, sat down herself and almost immediately began to cry. Not a whimper or a cry of elation, but a cry that let Tabitha know that there was something very wrong.

"Tell me Bertha, what is it? What's causing you all this heartache?"

Bertha got up to retrieve the bible. "As God is my witness, Miss Tabitha, I done something terrible bad. I's carried it with me all these years and I's had the misery ever since. You gots to believe that!"

"Well, I can't believe it if I don't know what it is. Please. There isn't anything that you can tell me that would make me turn away from you. Nothing. Please understand that and tell me."

"Miss Tabitha, I knows what your father done to you. I seen it. I seen it with my own eyes." Bertha's voice was getting louder and more forceful. "I seen it and I didn't do nothin' about it. That's it. That's the powerful sin I done, and I just gots to tell you everything."

Tabitha sat back, shocked. She said nothing for a few minutes; then got up. She thought she was going to vomit. She ran outside and down the block where she found an old log to sit on.

"She knew! Bertha knew! She saw what was happening and she didn't say a word – not a word. How could she? I didn't understand what was happening to me, but she did! She could have made my father stop or she could have explained to me that it was very wrong. She probably could have gotten him arrested. But she didn't! She did nothing. My best friend in the world did nothing!"

It was more than Tabitha could bear. Bertha had made a conscious decision to turn the other way. How could she? How could she have betrayed the person she was supposed to protect and love. Tabitha told Bertha nothing would come between them, but she was wrong. She could not forgive this.

Tabitha wanted to say the damage was done and nothing or no one could fix it. But, if there was more to the whole thing, perhaps she should hear about it. She wanted to know every nuance of what happened, especially as she would soon be confronting her father.

Bertha was out of breath from running. "Come back, chil'! I don't blame you for how you feel right now but I swear you needs to hear the rest of what I gots to tell you."

Tabitha did as Bertha suggested. She returned to the kitchen table but did not look at Bertha. "Well," she said. "Go on. I don't even know if I want to hear the rest, but we're into it now so we might as well finish. What more can you tell me?"

Bertha spoke quickly, afraid that Tabitha might leave again. "Here's the way it happened, so help me Sweet Jesus! I was workin' late one night and Pastor Jed must have thought I was already gone, but I was puttin' away the laundry in the bedrooms. When I got close to your room, I heard some strange sounds comin' from inside. It was a man's sound. Somethin' like that awful sound men do when they's having their pleasure. I didn't know what to make of it. I was sure it wasn't you in there with no boy, but I heard what I heard."

Bertha began talking faster and louder. "I opened the door a crack and seed it. I seen your father with his hands all over you. I could hear him telling you he loved you and that's what people do, especially daddies and little girls, when they love each other."

Tabitha took a washcloth, wet it, and placed it on Bertha's forehead. "You don't look well," she said. "I'm sorry you have to do this. Why don't we stop right here? It's just not worth you getting sick."

"No, you gots to hear it all." Bertha took a deep breath and continued. "After that ugly man done have his pleasure, he gets up and says it was important for it to be your very own secret. He say it's in the bible that if you breaks a promise you will surely burn in hell."

Tabitha felt sick, as all of the dreadful memories were once again in full presence. "Why didn't you stop him, Bertha? Why didn't you stop him right then and there?"

"I tried. I was jes plenty worried 'bout you. Where would you go? Lord alone knows I couldn't take you. Nobody in this town gonna put up with me takin' in a white girl. You gots no other kin, 'ceptin that mean old granny. I needed time to pray on it." Bertha drank a huge glass of water and wiped her brow.

"Next morning, I axed to see Mr. Jed. He say he was busy right then and he maybe see me the next day. I say, 'Oh, no you won't. When I tell you what I knows, you is gonna want to talk to me right now.' God gave me courage, Miss Tabitha. I walks over to him and points a finger right in his face. I seen what you is doin' to Miss Tabitha. You is a ugly, filthy, disgusting man to do that to your own daughter. And you, a man of God! I is gonna tell everyone I knows, Mr. High and Mighty Preacher Man, and when I gets finished with you, you ain't gonna be worth cat poop! You is gonna take care of that poor, innocent child. You is gonna sell this house and send Miss Tabitha off to a good boarding school where she'll get the kind of care she needs. So help me Sweet Jesus!"

Bertha couldn't understand the look on Tabitha's face. Was it possible Tabitha didn't believe her? She began to shake. "Oh, honey, you gots to believe me! Every word I's telling you is the God's truth – every single word!"

Tabitha touched Bertha's hand. "I know you wouldn't lie to me. It's just a lot for me to understand right now. There must be more. Tell me."

Bertha pounded her fist on the table. "Miss Tabitha, Mr. Jed say I was a dirty rotten nigger liar. He say he noticed I was losing my senses and that he tried to be patient with me. He say nobody in this town gonna believe me over him. He say, 'Who gonna believe a stupid old nigger over the respected pastor of their church?' He say if word gets out, I can expect a visit from the white robes, with his blessing. Then, all of a sudden, he kinda changed his tune. He had a smile on his face, and he tol me to set down."

Tabitha could not digest everything she was hearing. "He said that to you – the woman who raised his daughter and took care of his wife?"

Bertha went on. "Now, Bertha," he say, "We can work this out. I know you wouldn't want people to think you were losing your senses. How could you ever expect to get a job here, or anywhere, if you lie?" He say he was thinking of letting me go anyway because Miss Crystal could do all the chores now. He tol' me if I forgets the whole thing, he gonna get me a job at the mercantile.

Bertha's eyes became wide. "Then, Mr. Jed, he come over to where I was standin' and he take my hand and he twist it hard and he say, "Bertha you better never talk about this little misunderstanding to anyone. It would be dangerous for you. Yes'm. That's what he done to me."

"You see, Miss Tabitha, what could I do? Mr. Jed was right. The white robes be at my door. I didn't have no proof 'bout what I saw, and Mr. Jed tell everybody 'bout me losin' my senses. Who gonna hire me then? And I jes gotta work, honey! I just about get by now. The job at the mercantile is saving my life, but sometimes I don't want to live no more anyway, Miss Tabitha. Not for what I done to you!"

Tabitha enveloped Bertha in her arms. "I suppose you're entitled to cry right now so do it. Get it all out. Who could blame you for doing what you had to do to save yourself? Now, I'm going to do what I have to do to save both of us. We have only an hour or so before I'm due home and when I get there, I will have my day with my father. I've waited a long time. Now, you've helped stoke the fire."

"What's you gonna do, honey?"

"I'm going to let my father know exactly who he is and what he is and how he has robbed me and Mamma and Crystal and you of a life. Rabbi Kaddish told me to expect him to deny everything, just as he did with you. I don't have proof, either, but I will at least be rid of the burden I've been carrying around. I want to move forward. I don't exactly know what I want my future to be, but I do know that I don't want him in it."

"Mercy me!" Bertha shouted. "You really gonna do dat?"

"Yes. Tonight. Crystal has a meeting at church. I don't want her to know just yet. I want to tell her in my own way and in my own time."

"Lord Jesus! This is it! This is the time I been waitin' for!" Bertha said. "I gots more stuff for you to hear."

Tabitha thought she'd heard everything, but Bertha continued. "Honey, Bertha ain't 'xactly been doin' nothing about this whole mess. Things was eatin' at me a lot so I starts snoopin' around, tryin' to find out as much as I could about Mr. Jed. I figured if he was doin' that to you, who knows what other kind of mess he be doin'? I kept prayin' that the Lord put me on the right path."

Bertha pulled her chair closer, glanced over her shoulder, and began speaking in a near-whisper. "Then, one day, the Lord done it. Listen to this! You know Miss Claire, the keeper of the money at your father's church? Well, one day she done tol' her maid, Mabel, to fetch me, fast. Now, I don't understand what Miss Claire want with me. She already gots a maid. But Mabel, she tell me I gotta go because it be my Christian duty. She done tol' me Miss Claire be on her deathbed and is gonna pass any day."

Bertha began fanning herself. "Miss Claire, she couldn't hardly talk but she pull me close. She say she have somethin' real big to tell me before she die."

"Miss Claire said that? It must have been pretty important for her to tell you about it."

"She tol' me she want forgiveness, but that Jesus won't listen to her, a big sinner. She say Jesus would listen to me because I is a holy person. I say, 'Oh no, not me, Miss Claire. I ain't fit to ask Jesus for no forgiveness. No Ma'am! Pastor Jed's the only one can do that.' I tell her I's gonna fetch him right away."

Bertha began fanning herself faster. "Miss Claire, well, she start to cry. She say she can't tell Pastor Jed because what she wants to ask forgiveness for is about him - and her. That they was doin' some bad stuff together when your dear Mamma was alive and even when he was married to Miss Crystal. She done tol' me that he talked her into takin' lots of money from the church funds and give it to him. She say she done it because she was afraid of losin' him."

There might have been a time when Tabitha would have been shocked hearing this. Now, there was no shock, just disgust.

Bertha continued. "I was cleaning ol' Harry's house one day when he gets good and drunk. He tol' me he was goin on retreat with the men of your church and Pastor Jed. He say the pastor let the men bring lots of booze to the cabin. He tol' me they would bring in women from that awful house over in Big Creek and Pastor Jed, he jus' look the other way."

"Is that the end of it, Bertha? I don't know if I can take any more," said Tabitha.

"You needs to hear everything. When we sees him tonight, he gots to know we got plenty on him."

"You said *we*. Are you coming, too?"

"Sure am, honey. Nothin' keeping Bertha back now. I been waitin' and waitin' for the right time and now it's here."

"What else? Tell me fast."

"There's plenty. Miss Flora, she my friend ever since I took such good care of her when she done birth little Mae Ann. I axed her did she ever think Pastor Jed was doin' something not right? She say, 'Oh, Bertha, I'm so glad to get it off my chest! I never told another living soul. I was afraid to say anything because I thought no one would believe me – not even my husband. You know how the men are with Pastor Jed. It's all about keeping secrets. He knows stuff about them, and they know stuff about him."

Tabitha noticed Bertha shaking and insisted she sit down, but Bertha was anxious to continue. "Miss Flora keep goin' on like she want to tell everything. She say, "Well, anyway, I was in the supply closet at Christmas getting the decorations out when Pastor Jed came in and shut the door. At first, I thought the door had accidentally closed, so I reached around to open it when, all of a sudden, he pressed himself up against me. He said he could tell that I really didn't want that door left open. He said we could have a little Christmas cheer."

"I axed her did she slap his face or anything. She say no, she didn't want to make no scene on account a everybody say she lie and her husband would be plenty angry."

"Bertha," said Tabitha sadly. "I wish I wouldn't have to hear all of this. Can you imagine how I feel, knowing these horrible things about my own father?"

"I knows, honey. But you can't change what's been done. Only thing you can do now is get the whole thing over with so you can try to forget, and forget you will. There's plenty of good, lovin' men who work hard to make a woman happy. You'll see. Someday, you'll find that man just like I did. My Calvin was the Lord's companion."

"I hope you're right, Bertha. But for now, let's get this done. I want to go back to school to get ready for graduation. You'd better be prepared, though. I'm sure my father will to tear you to pieces. Remember, we have each other now and we have lots of proof. He can't do anything to either of us."

Crystal greeted them at the door. "I was getting a little worried, Tabby, but now I see you've brought Bertha!" She wiped her hands on her apron, gave Bertha a warm hug and shouted, "Jed, look who's here! You're getting two of your favorite people at once. Here's your Tabby and Bertha's with her. Can you even believe it?"

Jed looked up from his newspaper and stared at Tabitha for a minute. "Well, daughter, you…you certainly have changed. And for the better, I might add. Come here and give your daddy a big kiss!"

Tabitha turned away. "I'm starting with a cold. You might not want to risk it."

Jed turned to Bertha. "What are you doing here?"

Crystal raised her voice. "Why, Jed Whittier, what an ungodly thing to say! Bertha's family! She's gonna sit right down and have dinner with us," Crystal announced.

The look on Jed's face gave away his distain. "Are you insane, woman? Bertha has never in her life sat at our dining table and she will not now. I won't have it!"

Tabitha intervened. "You're right. She never has. But she will today."

Crystal took Bertha's hand and whispered, "Don't pay him no mind. Men get grumpier every year. When that thing of theirs begins to get smaller, their mouth begins to get bigger, if you know what I mean!" The two women laughed heartily as Bertha helped Crystal with the meal.

The conversation over dinner was stilted and formal. Finally, Bertha changed the mood. "You sho is a good cook, Miss Crystal," she said numerous times.

Crystal responded, "Well, I had a good teacher!" She looked at the clock. "Just look at the time! I wish I didn't have to go to that meeting, but it wouldn't be right, me bein' the preacher's wife and all."

Tabitha got up and began clearing the table. "You go right on, Mamma. We're just going to sit here and chat over dessert."

Jed had no intention of chatting. He had enough of these women who didn't seem to know their place. "I have a meeting, too," he said, "and while I'm gone be sure to get rid of any evidence of Bertha's place at the table."

"I think you should stay, Father," Tabitha said, firmly. I promise that what Bertha and I have to say is far more important than anything you could possibly have to do."

"Listen, I…"

Tabitha looked at Jed squarely and pounded on the table. "No! I will not listen to you. You will listen to me! You will listen to every word I have to say. Now, sit down. This will take some time."

Jed began waving his dinner napkin in Tabitha's face. "Is that what that Catholic school is teaching you – to be impudent and disrespectful to your father?"

"For your information, that Catholic school taught me that there is another way of life, one that's about peace and love. By the way, my Jewish friends taught me that I am a talented, worthy person who is deserving of respect. And Bertha, my dear Baptist friend, brought me up to understand that I can turn to the bible to find direction and comfort."

"What in the name of God are you talking about, you smart-ass bitch? I gave you everything. I gave you a home when your mamma got sick. I could have sent you to live with your grandmother, but did I? Did I? No. Then you wanted to go to that Catholic school that cost a fortune. Did I say no? This is the thanks I get. A daughter who forgets everything I gave her. Get out of here!"

"Oh, make no mistake. I never forgot what you gave to me. You gave me something that I will never in my life forget. And, as for "that Catholic school," it was Crystal who paid out of her own money."

Jed's face was red with anger. "I refuse to listen to this garbage. I'm leaving."

Bertha stood up and pointed at Jed. "You ain't gonna leave when I tell you what I knows about you and Miss Claire!"

Jed flopped down into the chair. "Just what are you talking about?"

"I'm talkin' about you havin' your way with her. She done told me everything. I knows all about the boathouse where you first done it and all the places after that, even when Miss Anna still lived and even after you married Miss Crystal. I knows about how Miss Claire gave you money from the church funds – lots of money."

"You are a dirty rotten liar! How dare you say that about me? You are going to burn in hell for even suggesting that I could…"

"No, I think you gots it all wrong. You, sir, are going to hell."

Jed reeled. "Everybody knows you're losing your mind. You won't get a soul to believe you and they'll put you away. I'll personally see to it!"

Bertha opened her purse and removed some papers tied with a string. "Here's your proof! These here letters were written by you to Miss Claire. I gots the rest at home. Everybody knows your handwriting. Some people would say they're dirty. I say for you, callin' yourself a man of God, they are the work of the devil."

Jed was sweating profusely. "I don't care what you have from that old maid. I have plenty of friends in the church that…"

"No more, you don't. Those men done looked the other way with Miss Claire and the others, but they ain't gonna turn their backs on what you done with the church money. And, if you think you done heard it all, the worst part is coming. You tell him, Miss Tabitha."

Tabitha spoke, her voice shaking. "Why did you do it to me? Why did you lie to me for your own satisfaction? You knew I was just a vulnerable child who yearned for your love. Why did you use me? Why did you let me believe that I had to allow your hands to explore my body in exchange for your love? Why did you ruin my entire life?"

Jed's fury was growing. "Lies! More lies! Who's going to believe you?"

Bertha spoke up. "They will, Mr. Jed, they will. I done tol' you before I seen what you was doin' in Miss Tabitha's bedroom. That's when you threw me out, sayin' my mind was goin'. But it ain't, and I ain't afraid no more. God knows I is doin' the right thing and he's gonna take care of me. And Miss Tabitha, she gonna help me, too. I is gonna tell everything I seen, especially to the church leaders. And after they read these letters, they is not gonna say I ain't in my right mind. They is gonna thank me for tellin' them what they needs to know about their dear pastor."

Jed put his head in his hands. There would be no way to escape. Both women had the evidence they needed to have him sent to jail. The room was quiet now, save for the ticking of the old clock on the mantel, which seemed to be reminding him that time was running out.

Finally, Jed spoke in a voice that was barely audible. "What do you want from me. Obviously, you're looking for something. If it's money you're after…"

"Money?" Tabitha said. "Do you really think this is about money? I could have you sent to jail, but I'm not going to do that. I want justice! Justice for me and for my mother and for Crystal and for Bertha. That's all I want. You're going away. Tomorrow."

Jed got up to leave. "Sit down!" Tabitha commanded. "You need to hear this. The church attorney will be here shortly. You will sign the necessary documents to turn this house over to Crystal. She will see to it that the church is paid back in full – with interest. I've told Sheriff Harvey the whole thing. He wants me to press charges so he can take you to jail, but I've decided that spending some time in jail won't do. I want you to be free in a place where you'll have plenty of time to think about what you've done. I want you to understand what true suffering is and, when you finally do, I want you to beg Almighty God for his forgiveness. In the morning, the sheriff will deliver you to Dafuskie Island."

Jed screamed, "Dafuskie Island? That god-forsaken place isn't fit! I won't do it, I tell you! I'll take my chances here! The church people won't betray me."

Bertha pulled out one of the letters and handed it to Tabitha who read, "Claire, my love. I am sick with desire for you and can barely wait for our next time together at the boathouse. Meet me there after dark on Tuesday and greet me wearing nothing. I want to explore every part of you, darling, and I hope you want to do the same. Also, please bring the $5,000.00 we spoke about from the church account. We'll use some of it to have a grand weekend."

"So," said Tabitha. "It's your choice. Yes, Dafuskie is desolate and backward. No phones, no schools, no bridges, and about a hundred people who desperately want a preacher. You will be that preacher and you will keep clean. One false move and you will go directly to jail. And don't even think of escaping. Old Mac runs the ferry twice a day and he has his orders. Of course, you can stay right here in Emporia and face my testimony and all those letters in court."

Defeated, Jed muttered, "What about Crystal? She's coming with me, right? I mean, a man can't be expected…"

The swinging door to the dining room opened. Crystal stood, tears streaming down her face. "Expected to what, Jed? I came back to get my notebook and I heard everything. Expected to what? Expected to do without a woman – a crazy woman who does the cleaning and the cooking and the laundry and listening to her husband gripe about the bills or his aches and pains? A woman who shares a bed with this man for his own selfish pleasures and who never gives a hoot about her feelings or desires? Well, maybe some women, Jed, but not this one. This one would rather be alone forever than to be with you for even one more day!"

Jed stumbled over his words. "It's all a mistake, sweetheart. You didn't hear the whole story."

"I heard enough. And I'm sure there's plenty more."

Jed walked to where Crystal was standing. He put his arms out, a gesture to have her come to him. Crystal used all her strength and her rage to push him away. "Are you out of your mind? Don't you ever come anywhere near me again."

Jed's eyes widened as he held his hand up, ready to strike. Tabitha came between them. "Go ahead! Hit me!" shouted Crystal. You can't hurt me any more than you have already!"

Jed continued with his verbal tirade. "You stupid broad! Yes, broad! That's all you've ever been. You have no class, no looks, and no intellect. You should be on your knees, thanking me for even considering marrying you. God knows, I never loved you!"

"You're right, Jed. I was stupid. I actually believed all the rot you were handing me. My daddy gave me lots of good advice, but he never prepared me for the likes of you. It didn't take me long to find out that it was a huge mistake. By that time Tabitha was my very own child and I would never give her up."

Jed screamed, "I gave you a lot more than you deserved! I was a compassionate, dutiful man of the cloth who put the needs of others before his own. You pleaded with me to take you away from the city and I felt my offer to be the godly thing to do. Now, here I am, stuck with the likes of you!"

Tabitha cried, "Oh, Mamma, I am so sorry. I planned on telling you, but I wanted to tell you in my own way."

Bertha walked over and threw her arms around Crystal.

Through sobs, Crystal said, "I have my secrets, too. I've known all about the other women for a long time. There were times when I planned on leaving, but where would I go? A woman needs money put aside for her to have choices, but I…

Crystal didn't finish the sentence. She would not say anything about the tuition. "I just didn't have any money, and if I'd left, I was afraid I'd never see my daughter again."

Crystal threw her arms around Tabitha. "But what he did to you! Why didn't you tell me when I came into your life?"

"I think I was just too confused then. I was young and didn't even want you in my life. Besides, I didn't understand the things a young girl should know until you explained it all."

Tabitha clung to her mother, "Look, we can't go back. We have to stick together and spend whatever energy we have to make a real life for ourselves."

The doorbell interrupted. "That will be the attorney with the sheriff." Tabitha grabbed Crystal's hand. "Now, do what you need to do to get ready to leave. We're spending the night at Bertha's and the sheriff is staying. He can witness the signing and take my father to Dafuskie in the morning."

Tabitha felt more empowered than she had ever felt in her life – empowered and free. Totally and completely free. "Ladies," she announced, as they sat together over Bertha's homemade strawberry ice cream, "get ready." We will be leaving tomorrow morning. I called Iris and explained the whole thing. The Feldmans have room for both of you, and I'll be going back to school to get ready for my big day. No more sad memories or awful feelings that keep us from moving ahead. The word to remember now is "chutzpah!"

Part Six

1960 to 1962

Tabitha and Gerald

CHAPTER TWENTY-FIVE

"If music be the food of life, play on."

The party was in full swing. Tabitha's new family, Crystal, Bertha, and the Feldmans watched proudly as she received her degree. Now, they were ready to celebrate. Crystal saved for a long time to provide a party that would be second to none. Joe Pantos, owner of *The Dove,* would contribute to making it special. Joe had been a new entrepreneur when Crystal became instrumental in selecting just the right fabric he needed to have the dining chairs in his restaurant make a real statement. Now was the time for Joe to show his appreciation.

He began by sending his limo for the group, complete with champagne from his private collection. Tabitha clung to her bouquet of roses, the color and fragrance of which she had never experienced. The private room was decorated in blue and gold, Tabitha's school colors. Everyone agreed that dinner was a veritable feast. When the happy noise was dying down and the Baked Alaska lost its last flicker, Joe spoke up.

"So, Tabitha, how do you plan to pursue your career? Here in the city, the world is definitely your oyster. I have numerous connections, but I know Solly wants you to help run the business now, right Solly?"

"Yes, I would welcome that. But our girl will make her own decisions. She has talent that may be wasted in our shop."

Tabitha was quick to respond. "Thank you for your faith in me, Solly. You know how much I love working in the shop and being with all of you, but…" She reached into a small compartment of her purse, retrieved Henry's card and handed it to Joe, who examined it carefully.

"Young Henry Merriweather? Wow, I'm impressed! The Merriweathers frequent my restaurant and I do all of their big parties. I don't really know their son well, but if he's anything like his father, you can't go wrong. This is big stuff, sweetheart, you should give it serious consideration. If it gives you a foot in the door, why not?"

Tabitha thought about what Joe was suggesting. She didn't like the implication. She spoke up in a tone that was very much unlike her. "Not why not, but *why*? Why should I depend on someone else to get me a job that I am quite capable of getting myself?"

Joe smiled and took Tabitha's hand across the table. "You, my dear, are going to do it. You're going to knock them cold. You will be a successful woman in a man's world. If that's all you learned at college, it's enough."

Tabitha wanted to say that she'd learned nothing of the sort at college; that what she had learned was mainly about how to dress properly, how be a good and genteel wife and mother, how to set a proper table, and how to keep an intelligent conversation going during the cocktail hour. In short, she had been schooled to be an asset to her husband in the pursuit of *his* career. Her own career would be incidental at best. That's what she wanted to say. Instead, she just smiled and nodded in affirmation.

The evening was winding down. Joe walked the group out to the waiting limousine. He put his arm around Tabitha's shoulder. "Sorry if I offended you, Tabby. It's just that, well, you're so young and so kind of naïve about the ways of the world. Trust me, sweetheart, I'm a good deal older and a lot wiser. There was a time when I thought I could do it all, too. It wasn't long before I found out that it doesn't hurt to have a little help along the way."

Tabitha leaned in to kiss his cheek. "Thanks, Joe. I'm sorry I seemed ungrateful. I do understand that you're looking out for my best interest. Actually, I just may take what you've told me under serious consideration. And thanks for one of the best

evenings I've had in my lifetime. I hope I can consider you a
friend – no, a brother. I need a brother!"

Tabitha slept in the next morning and the morning after that and
the morning after that. She was sharing the bedroom that was
assigned to Crystal, but she soon realized that the
accommodations, though generous, would be insufficient and
cramped for three added women. She would have to find an
apartment of her own soon, but to do that she would need a job,
immediately.

That week was spent visiting professional employment agencies.
It was always the same. Fill out the forms and wait. "We'll be in
touch," was the standard response. It was a lot more difficult and
frustrating than Tabitha ever imagined.

"So much for a degree," she thought. "What now?"

Tabitha sat on a park bench near Central Park, combing the
paper, having her late morning coffee and bagel. Until now,
she'd never bothered to really look at the buildings nearby.
Today was different. Today, she stretched her neck high to
relieve a cramp, when she saw it – *Merriweather Bank of New
York* in large, brass lettering. "Holy Mary, Mother of God," she
said out loud. "It's Henry's bank! Right here in front of me is
Henry's bank!"

Tabitha chuckled as she spoke to the pigeons gathering around
the bench. "Do you think it's an omen? What do you say, do you
think I should give it a shot? Can't hurt, right?" One of the
pigeons moved closer and looked up at her. "So, you think so,
too! Good. Here's an extra piece of bagel. Save it for tomorrow
because I won't be here tomorrow. I'll be at the Merriweather
Bank!"

Though the conversation at the dinner table was loud and
exciting that evening, Tabitha could concentrate only on what
happened earlier. She'd called the bank, asking for Henry. She

was told he was not in and wouldn't be for some time. She was ready to hang up when she remembered the conversation she'd had with him.

"I have a card here from Mr. Henry Merriweather. He told me to call as soon as I graduate. I have my degree now and I just thought…"

The office secretary seemed bored and uninterested. "Well, I'm sorry, Miss. Mr. Henry Merriweather is not here so there's nothing…" Suddenly, her voice changed. She remembered something. "Miss, is there anything written on the card?"

Tabitha examined the card again. She'd never noticed it, but there were small, handwritten initials, *HGM*, on the back right corner. "Well, if you mean initials, then yes."

The woman's demeanor changed immediately. *This must be the person Henry told me to look for and to hire if she'd ever appear.* "You may come in tomorrow at any time that suits you, Miss. Please go to the personnel office on the fifth floor to fill out the necessary paperwork."

It was only a formality. The woman knew Tabitha would be hired without going through the necessary, rigorous interview.

Crystal stayed up late that night, making changes to Tabitha's only wool suit.

She would lower the hemline just a bit, remove the fabric flower, add a small amount of leather to the collar and try to find matching leather buttons. What no one realized was that none of the effort was necessary.

The Merriweather Bank was as impressive inside as out. The outside architecture was Art Nouveau, while the lobby spoke of Art Deco. She remembered it was Henry's favorite style. He had no doubt been responsible for acquiring the Gustav Klimt that was in full view at the entrance, and the Jean Durand chest placed discreetly in the corner. Tabitha lingered for a moment before she heard her name. "Miss Tabitha Whittier, I believe?"

Tabitha turned toward the voice. "Yes," she answered, squeezing her handbag. "I'm Miss Whittier."

"Follow me, please." The voice began walking toward the elevator. "Is there anything you desire? Water, juice, or morning coffee?"

Tabitha had no idea what to think or say. She'd never gotten this far on a career interview, but she was quite sure business was not conducted in this manner, especially with a novice.

"No thank you. You're very kind, though."

The voice just smiled. In a few minutes they were standing in front of a door marked *Justine Elton, Personnel*.

"Come in, Miss Whittier. This won't take long. Have a seat," the woman commanded, all the while thinking that, if Merriweather sent her, the die was cast.

Tabitha removed her gloves. "Shall I tell you what I do? I have some experience, but not much. I can type, though. Crystal said I had to learn before I went off to college because of term papers and everything. I worked hard at Solly's shop and I helped during Sabbath, and…"

"Whoa, slow down," said Justine. "Shall we say that I am not really interested in what you *have* done. Let's talk about what you *will* do."

Tabitha began wringing her gloves. "Oh, I see," she said. "I am so sorry. I just thought…"

Miss Elton interrupted her and replied, curtly, "My dear, please understand that you don't have to think. Not at all. You let me do the thinking. You are hired. Just fill out the required paperwork.

You may start whenever you like, and I will see to it that you are comfortable in whatever department suits you."

Tabitha did not understand. She thought Miss Elton's demeanor to be condescending and downright rude; the very characteristics she despised. At that moment the prospect of a good job was not the least appealing. No amount of special treatment was worth putting up with such insolence. She got up and started toward the door.

"I'm leaving, Miss Elton. I do not wish to be in your employ. I refuse to work for a company that does not allow me to think. I graduated Summa Cum Laude and have much to offer, but I see you are not impressed. Please give Mr. Merriweather my thanks and tell him he can find another errand girl!"

Furious, she turned to leave. Justine Elton was shocked. No one ever turned down an interview in this place, and she would be in big trouble with Mr. Henry if she let Tabitha go. Besides, she really liked the girl's spunk, not unlike her own.

"Wait," she called. Please don't leave. I…will you accept my apology? I really messed this up, didn't I? Can we begin again?"

Tabitha paused; then sat down. "Apology accepted. Please understand that I expect no indulgences. I want to begin on the ground floor like anyone else. I learn fast and will work diligently at whatever I am asked to do. I expect to be compensated accordingly, and if the work I do is not satisfactory, I expect to be told. Do we understand one another?"

Miss Elton swiveled her chair around to face the outside. "See the grand buildings around us? Take a good look. I have a feeling they're going to be part of your life for a long time."

She turned to face Tabitha and offered her hand. "Please call me Jussy. You may report for work on Monday at eight. You say you learn quickly. The computer department is just getting off the ground. I think it's a good fit for you."

Gerald Merriweather was getting off the elevator while Tabitha was getting on. She was so absorbed in what had just transpired that she took no notice of him. But Gerald noticed her. She was beautiful; lithe and willowy. He entered Justine's domain. "Hi, gorgeous," he said. "Who's the knockout that just left?"

Justin shook her head. She understood Gerald. They had shared a few drinks and a few brief encounters when they were both in need, but neither expected anything from it. She was one of the few women Gerald could trust.

"Tabitha Whittier. Henry set her up and I hired her." She shook a finger at him. "Look, don't go smelling around. She's a good kid. And smart. Leave her alone, will you?" Justine knew her request was futile. There would be no way Gerald would leave her alone.

Gerald blew her a kiss. "C'mon, Jussy! You know you'll always be my one and only. Just see that her paperwork finds its way to my desk, will you?"

"You're the boss. Somehow, though, I get the feeling that Mr. Henry isn't going to like this one bit. Just leave me out of it."

Gerald leaned across the desk and gave her a friendly pinch on the cheek. "My brother will be gone for another month or more. He need never know. Meanwhile, …"

Justine finished his sentence in thought. Meanwhile you'll have great fun at a new, short-lived game as you completely destroy another unsuspecting female.

As he was leaving, Gerald turned and winked. "Isn't it time for your annual review? I wonder if a handsome raise isn't in order?"

Justine smiled, knowingly. She suspected what was coming for Tabitha, and though she really liked her, she liked the thought of a "handsome raise" a lot more.

CHAPTER TWENTY-SIX

"Frailty, thy name is woman!"

Tabitha's new job meant a whole new beginning for her. She had been at the bank only two weeks but, in that time managed to find a suitable apartment. It would take some getting used to, to be sure. She wasn't used to doors slamming and people yelling in the middle of the night, but the activity made her feel alive, free and independent. There was no room for Crystal or Bertha yet, but she felt confident that it wouldn't be long before she might afford a larger place.

It had been an exhausting week at work. Today, Tabitha decided, would be the perfect day to try something special for dinner. She had little experience with cooking but her neighbor, Mrs. Morello, owned the little market downstairs and was happy for the opportunity to take her in as her own.

"What's your suggestion, Mrs. Morello?" Tabitha said, flipping through the woman's cookbooks.

"For beginners, I think you can try this casserole. I make it for my Salvatore, and he likes it. It's French, and I have all of the ingredients right here in the store. Make a good bread, too. I have an easy recipe for you."

"OK, my friend. Load me up with everything I'll need, and I'll start right away," Tabitha responded, happy to be doing something fun and different on this lovely Saturday. She returned to her apartment, opened the long window to the fire escape and began assembling, paring, and measuring. She discovered this to be a challenging task, especially the bread. But she finally got the casserole and the bread into the oven and poured herself a tall glass of wine, an indulgence she had just come to appreciate.

Tabitha sat before the open kitchen window, resting her feet on the sill and listening to Mr. Morello's opera music. She thought she heard the doorbell but didn't get up. *No one here knows me, except Mrs. Morello and she always yells. It's probably someone else's buzzer.* She took another sip of wine; then heard someone pounding on her door.

"Who is it?" she said, guardedly.

The voice from the other side responded. "Special delivery from the Merriweather Bank."

Tabitha recalled she was told she might sometime be required to work on the weekend. She supposed the delivery would be the pile of paperwork left behind.

"Just a minute," she replied, removing her apron and unlocking the door.

Her shock gave way to emotion. It was Henry, handing her a huge bouquet of the finest yellow roses.

"Oh, my gosh! Henry," she cried, "I thought you were gone! I mean, they told me at the bank you would be away for months! I am just so happy to see you." She threw her arms around him and realized, at that moment, how much she really missed him. She continued to hold him close; something that surprised them both.

"Come in." she said, leading him by the hand. "Come sit in the kitchen and tell me everything. I'm so glad you're here! I made a great meal and we can talk for hours and get back to being friends. I've missed you, Henry. Have you missed me?"

Gerald's thoughts were running wild. He had come here on the pretense that he misplaced some files and hoped Tabitha had taken them home, but this was actually better.

Oh, my God, she thinks I'm Henry! The two of them must have been cozy or something. Think fast, dummy! You want this lovely young thing and you don't know how to get to first base. She's giving you your chance. Don't screw it up. You can be Henry for a while. Who's to know?

"I see you're having wine. May I share some with you?" said Gerald.

"You want wine? Really? I've never known you to drink wine, Henry, but of course you may."

Gerald lifted the glass to his nose. "I really appreciate the gesture, but if we're going to spend time together you should let me bring the wine. When I see you next, I'll bring some Dom Perignon. It's a good wine for hanging out with a special friend."

Tabitha felt a bit embarrassed by the only choice she could afford. "I'm sorry," she said. "I hope you'll find dinner to be better."

Gerald inhaled deeply. "Ah, cassoulet! Let's see, mirepoix along with a couple of fresh tomatoes, Andouille sausage, three cloves of garlic, navy beans, and a bit of chicken stock. Is that freshly baked Tuscan bread?"

Tabitha was shocked. "Henry, how could you possibly know? You've never been the least bit interested in cooking! And how did you know about the bread?"

Gerald ran his finger over her nose a few times. "You have semolina flour on that beautiful nose of yours," he said, in a sensual way.

Tabitha remained in a state of disbelief. Whatever happened to the Henry she once knew – the Henry that knew nothing of fine clothes and good wine? This Henry's sweater was of the finest cashmere in a stunning blue that matched his eyes. He wore impeccable shoes of the finest leather, and she was sure his barber must have cut his hair one strand at a time. And the cologne! It must be from one of the finest perfumeries in France. It delivered a message that she was sure would drive any woman wild with desire. Tabitha didn't understand what had happened to Henry in Paris but, whatever it was, she liked it.

The two sat over dinner for hours. There was so much Tabitha wanted to talk about. The third glass of wine gave her the courage to ask. "Henry, why did you never get in touch with me while you were away? I know I probably gave you the impression I wasn't interested, but I really did think we could go on being friends. I have to confess that, when there were no letters or calls, I was a bit hurt."

Gerald had to think fast. "I really must apologize. You know how I am. My father sent me to Paris on a mission. It was a big deal. I worked day and night. I did think about you, a lot. But the days just seemed to bleed together, leaving no time for personal pleasure."

Gerald got up and turned on the radio to the most romantic music he could find. He pulled Tabitha to her feet and embraced her warmly.

"Dance?"

Tabitha recalled that Henry once told her he didn't dance. Tabitha was shocked. When did this happen? Certainly not in Paris if he was as busy as he purported to be.

"I'm not such a good dancer," she said, embarrassed at the thought.

Gerald took her in his arms gently and held her close. "There's nothing to it, really, just let your body go and feel the movement. Like this."

They swayed to the music, a natural, fundamental display, deep within the roots of sensation.

Gerald knew he had to slow down. He had time, and from the way this young woman was responding, it wouldn't be long before his plan would come to fruition. He decided it would be enough for now. He led her back to her chair.

"Oh, Henry. I just can't believe this! You're not the person I knew. I hope you don't mind my saying this, but Paris was good for you."

Tabitha poured espresso. "You know, I often think about how we met. I wonder how many couples can say they experienced such a chance encounter. Do you ever think about that?"

Gerald pretended to have a coughing seizure and ran to the sink for water. "I…of course! Wasn't that something? I know I'll never forget."

Tabitha recalled how she sewed Henry's button on during a downpour. "Did you pass inspection for your father that evening?"

Gerald looked at his watch. "Forgive me, will you? I don't mean to be abrupt, but I have to get back to the bank tonight to find those papers." He took Tabitha's hands in his. "When again? Is tomorrow too soon? What about brunch at Lindy's followed by a stroll and drinks at Tavern on the Green. Then, get into your best dress for dinner and dancing. Sound good?"

Tabitha responded, unconsciously squeezing his hand. "Sounds good. Sounds very good."

Tabitha couldn't wait to call Crystal. Crystal never heard that kind of excitement in her daughter's voice, not even when she received honors at graduation.

"Oh, Mamma, I feel wonderful! Remember the guy I told you about from the Merriweather Bank? You know, the one I said was nice but not my type. Guess what? He was here, Mamma. He just left. And he's not at all the way I remembered him. He's changed! He's so…well, worldly or something. He's handsome and charming and attentive and…"

"Tabby, slow down! Sounds like you got a major crush on him. I mean, take your time, honey. I want to know all about it, but I'd rather come over sometime so we can really talk. How about it? Let's do it soon. I really want to hear everything."

"Okay, Mamma, I promise we'll get together real soon. For now, though, tell Sister Veronica to pray for me. Tell her the guy I spoke to her about isn't what I thought he was. Tell her I'm as happy as I can be and that I'll talk to her soon."

Tabitha stayed up half the night preparing for the next day. She removed her daywear from the closet, examining each prospect and finally steam pressing the pleats in the lovely plaid skirt Crystal had labored over. With it she would wear the beautiful blue angora sweater Bertha gave her for graduation. It was the evening dress that would be the challenge. The only one she owned was from her college days, and the nuns saw to it that neither the neckline nor the hemline were revealing.

My first chance to take care of this monstrosity, she thought, as she picked up the dress and started ripping. *The hemline is going up and the neckline is going down.* She made a white silk cummerbund for around her waist and tucked in a few of the rejected rhinestones Solly had given her.

"There," she said, finally. "Straight out of Vogue. Henry's going to love it!"

CHAPTER TWENTY-SEVEN

"The prince of darkness is a gentleman."

It was all so new and exciting – the kind of world Tabitha had only dreamed of but felt she could never come to know. There was dancing at the Copacabana, strange foods from all cultures, exciting opening nights, shopping on 5th Avenue, complete with special gifts from Henry. There were Sunday dinners cooked together, and lazy, rainy Saturday afternoons spent just listening to music. Tabitha couldn't help but wonder, though, what happened to their museum time. It was what Henry once loved beyond all else.

One particularly dreary Saturday as they were stretched across the sofa, Tabitha brought up the subject. "Tell me, Henry, whatever happened to those great trips to our favorite museum? It seems as though you're avoiding it, and it's not like you."

Gerald was at a complete loss. He had no idea what museum or why it was so special. He faked a smile. "You know, sweetheart, it's just that I thought you should have all of the other fantastic experiences you've never had."

He thought hard; then remembered. He once heard Henry tell his mother he would be moving to a new residence. He recalled him saying he chose the location so he could be closer to the Metropolitan to take advantage of the lectures.

"We can go the Met sometime soon. Promise." He moved closer to Tabitha and took her in is arms. "Right now, though, we have something important to discuss – something I think is long overdue."

Gerald began slowly running his fingers up her arms, around her neck and over her ears. "Up until now, my love, we've held hands, had a few long hugs, and some rather perfunctory kisses. Don't you think it's time to move along?"

Tabitha guessed what Gerald was suggesting but this was new and uncomfortable. "I...I'm not sure I know what you mean,"

Gerald couldn't believe what he was hearing. "Well," he said, kissing her ear as he spoke. "You must know what comes next." He began kissing her, passionately, his tongue exploring her mouth. He opened her blouse, kissed her neck, her shoulders, and finally made his way to her breasts.

"Do you like when I do this?" he asked, waiting for Tabitha to respond in the way he was used to from other women.

Tabitha felt a sensation she never experienced. "Oh, Henry," she said, responding to his kisses. "I do like it. I love it, and...I...I love you."

Gerald wasn't ready for this. Most of his other conquests were like him – some crazy lovemaking, a roll in the hay, and a quick goodbye. No words were exchanged, and nothing was expected. This was different.

Tabitha continued. "Yes, Henry, I love you. I've never before known what love is, but I know now." She took Gerald's hand and put it over her breast. "This is what I mean. I do want you. Do you love me, Henry? Do you?"

Gerald stuttered. " Uh, s... sure, Tabby. Now, why don't we move to the bedroom."

From all that Crystal told her, Tabitha knew what Gerald had in mind. Crystal also instructed her to save her virginity for marriage. She rose from the couch suddenly, buttoned her blouse, and pulled back her hair, nervously.

"I'm sorry, Henry. I shouldn't have let things get this far. I just can't do what you're asking right now. It isn't right."

Gerald was trying to contain his rage. He lit a cigarette and poured a large glass of wine. "I gotta tell you, Tab. There are things you need to know about men. They operate on an entirely different plane. Their desire takes over and they just can't deal with waiting for marriage. They move along to someone who will give them what they want with no strings attached."

Tabitha picked up the pillow and held it close to her. "It's just not me, Henry. I'm trying because I love you so, but I'm really confused."

"What the hell can you possibly be confused about? I wanna get laid, is all. If you really cared for me, you'd be glad to take care of me. Hopefully, you'll have a good time too, and you might want more. That's all there is to it."

Tabitha bristled at Henry's language. It wasn't like him to be so crude. She thought back to the time Crystal was explaining intercourse to her. She remembered her saying that it was wrong to give yourself to a man before marriage. She hugged the pillow tighter as Gerald went on.

"It's time you understood that things are changing now. Your thinking about saving your virginity is archaic. Modern women laugh at the thought. Guys really don't give a hoot. To them, your virginity isn't worth a plug nickel. It's time you stopped being so sophomoric and began to...well...grow up!"

Tabitha was shocked and hurt at what she was hearing. "You mean that if I don't go to bed with you, you'll leave me?" She tried hard to keep what she thought were stupid female tears from arriving, but she could not. "Henry, you can't mean it! I know I don't understand some things, but I'm willing to learn. I don't think it's unfair of you to say I have to grow up."

Gerald poured himself another drink. He had made Tabitha very unhappy, something he really did not want to witness. He was shocked to discover that her feelings really mattered—something new to him. There were a couple of women in his past that may have had a fleeting moment of feeling, but it never lasted. Mostly, they wanted what he wanted. No expectations, no promises, no ridiculous small talk. Just sex.

Tabitha was different. She was involved. She hung on his every word, agreed to his every comfort. It seemed all she wanted from him was just to be in his presence. It was all so different to him. He needed time to understand his extreme discomfort.

Tabitha went into the kitchen. She needed to continue the conversation, but it would be best said over a sobering cup of coffee. Neither spoke for a few uncomfortable minutes. Finally, Tabitha found the courage.

"Henry, you heard me say I love you, didn't you?" Gerald didn't respond. Tabitha went on. "You know, that was a difficult thing for me to admit. There's a lot in my past you don't know, and I never thought I'd ever say those words to any man. But I did. It's huge for me, Henry, and I'm proud of myself."

Gerald forced a half-hearted smile. "That's special. Thank you."

"Thank you? Is that how you respond? Like I'm helping you on with your coat or making your favorite dessert?"

Gerald looked down at his coffee. "I'm sorry. It's just that..." He recalled being unlovable and perhaps even unlikeable from the time he'd been a child. Love was something completely foreign to him. He wanted no part of it.

The ringing telephone saved him. Tabitha answered. "Iris!" she cried, her mood changing instantly. "I haven't heard from you in a bit. Is everything alright? I miss you all so much!"

When the conversation ended Tabitha said, "Imagine that! I was just thinking of having you come to meet my family and Iris took care of that by inviting us for Passover next week."

She gave Gerald a tight hug. "You know, my love, I think that's what's missing. You've never met my family. I know they're going to love you as I do. After we spend an evening together, I feel quite sure Crystal will believe you're the right person for me. If I get those vibes from her, I'll know it's right – right enough to come back to this apartment and be mature enough to go to bed with you, totally and completely and with no regrets.

Gerald sat, ignoring the documents piled high on his desk. He tried to fight the uncomfortable thoughts going around in his head, but they would not be ignored. Justine entered and walked around to massage his neck. "Methinks you may be needing this right now. Lean over and enjoy."

Her hands on him were not in the least suggestive; just healing. The suggestive part was over a long time ago. But she knew him well. She understood that this was his other self. The one she didn't see very often except when his father died or when he had to put his dog to sleep.

"Do you want me to know, or would it be too much?" Justine removed his tie and opened his shirt. Gerald leaned into her hands.

The room was uncommonly quiet. Finally, Gerald spoke. "You know me too well. Kind of dangerous, don't you think?"

Justine continued with her healing hands. "Uh, well, I suppose you can say I know you, love, but that would be in the biblical sense. Understand you? Well now, that's something else. I wish I could say I do, but I really don't. I don't think there's a person alive who really understands you, Gerald."

"Touché. I don't even understand myself."

"I might guess it's female trouble, but I've never in my life seen you being

concerned about any woman, including moi! But then, I really never expected it, did I?"

Gerald took Justine's hand. "You were a good sport. We had a fun time, didn't we? Did I treat you shabbily?"

"No, my friend, you did not. You wined and dined me and pulled out all the stops. In exchange, I pulled out all the stops. Not such a bad arrangement. Women do it all the time. Men aren't the only users!"

Gerald became serious. "Do you think most women think the way you do?"

Justine chuckled and began kneading harder. "They tell me women are starting to come into their own now. Home and hearth aren't as appealing any more. If they have the home, they want it to be big and beautiful, and the hearth will have to be cleaned by someone else because they're not going to do it."

"But they're not all like that, are they? I mean, there are those that still want a man only to love them, don't they?"

"Sure. But if you find one like that, hang on because they're becoming more and more scarce."

She took both his hands and looked directly into the crystal blue eyes that once caused her to melt." Gerald, my love, could it be? Could you possibly be thinking…"?

Gerald read what she was suggesting and faked a laugh. "Are you kidding? Me? I want no part of it. It's just that I got myself into something I can't quite get out of."

Justine pounded her fists into Gerald's neck. "Sure you can. You're a master. Every time you get into a situation and it begins to make you feel like you're losing control, you just disappear for a bit. Is this different?"

Gerald pulled her closer, teasing. "You know you're the only one for me, sweetheart. Now, go get my drink. It's three o'clock."

CHAPTER TWENTY-EIGHT

"What a piece of work is man."

As the time for Passover drew near, Gerald became more and more anxious. He couldn't come up with a reasonable excuse to decline the dinner invitation. He decided to give Tabitha one more night; then part company with her. Justine had taken care of the niceties - expensive wine for Mr. Feldman, imported chocolate for Tabitha's mother and Mrs. Feldman. Appropriate, but not over the top. He wanted to be sure there was no misunderstanding; that these were nothing more than friendly gestures.

As they entered the building, Tabitha did not hear Gerald muttering, "Christ, this is a dump. I can't believe people live like this!" He had never been in such a place, where there was no doorman, no one to take your car, no elegant floral arrangements in the entryway. Oh, he had "slummed it" a bit when he wanted a fast piece, but most of the women in his life were well paid and lived in glamorous penthouses, complete with private elevators. This place made him feel uncomfortable and unclean. He was secretly wishing he'd never put himself in this position. He regretted not ending it with Tabitha a long time ago or better, not having begun at all.

Gerald reluctantly climbed the stairs and stood silently as Tabitha knocked. The door was opened immediately and the loud voice from inside announced, "Oy, so formal we are! Since when? Since when must you knock on the door of your home? Come in here!" Rachel pulled Tabitha inside and hugged her heartily.

"Happy Passover, Rachel!" Tabitha took Gerald's hand and held it tight. "This is Henry. He's the guy I've been telling all of you about."

Rachel examined the polished gentleman in front of her. "Oy, mien heart!" she exclaimed. "Such a fancy guy, Tabitha. And not so bad on the eyes, even for this old lady! Come in Mr. Henry. Come into our humble home. Our family is waiting to meet you and it's almost time to start the Seder."

Gerald handed her the flowers and the candy without smiling. "The flowers are for you, and the wine is for Mr. Feldman. The blue box of chocolates is also for you and the white one is for Crystal."

Rachel turned over the wine bottle and the candy to read the label. "Oy," she said. "Solly, come here. We have a problem." Solly came at once. Rachel whispered in his ear and Solly also turned the wine and candy over, looking for the necessary *Kosher for Passover* identification.

"I'm sorry, sir," he said, seriously. I know you would have no way of knowing and we appreciate your kindness, but we cannot accept."

Gerald's shock was apparent. "What? Are you saying that this is not good enough or…"? He tried to offer the wine again. "I assure you this is one of the finest…"

Solly pushed his hand away. "As I say, I am so sorry. It is wonderful of you to treat us so kindly, but you see, this is considered unclean. The *Kosher for Passover* marking is absent. We cannot accept."

Gerald's face turned red. "I don't really understand what you're talking about, but it's your holiday. The rules are your rules." He shifted the packages around; then said, "Don't concern yourself a bit. I'll just put them over here on this table and you can partake when your holiday is over."

Rachel lowered her head as Solly went on. "You don't understand. We cannot have these in our home. Please put them outside in the hall."

Gerald, disgusted and rejected, did as was requested but to refuse his gesture was to him, unthinkable. He was trying to prepare himself for what he was sure would be a long night. He thought about leaving immediately but could not come up with a suitable excuse. He was sure he'd think of something. He thought of the times he'd walked out on less than this.

Tabitha took Gerald by the arm and went first to Crystal. "Mamma, this is my special man. I just know you're going to love him as I do."

Crystal never had a problem meeting new people, but this was different. She moved closer to him; then stepped back. Gerald politely reached out his hand to take hers. "It's a pleasure, Mrs. …" He struggled to find a title.

"Just Crystal will be fine for now."

And so it went with the rest of the family. Solly hugged him, running his hand over the expensive cloth of his suit. Bertha slouched in her chair, trying to make herself invisible. Iris, seated next to Gerald, looked at him, through him and around him. Her pulse raced and her heart began pounding. *My God, Tabby has my deli guy! Go for it, Tabby! Go for it!*

The candles were lit, a sign for Seder to begin. Solly handed Gerald a piece of cloth. "Here is a yarmulke for you, Henry. It is what our men wear to show respect for God. Just lay it on the top of your head."

Gerald had no intention of wearing the hideous thing over his perfectly groomed hair. "I'm sorry," he said, "I…I can't. I apologize, but you see…" He had to think fast. "It's just that I'm undergoing tests for allergies and I might have a serious reaction to the fabric. You wouldn't want me scratching my head all night, would you?"

Tabitha bristled, surprised at the remark. Henry had never discussed allergies with her. She began twisting her napkin. *Why is he being so difficult? He must know how important the yarmulke is in a Jewish household.* She wanted to say that but forced a smile and said, "Of course," and tried to dismiss the issue.

Solly was the first to speak. "So, Henry, I know you are not a Jew so I will explain the prayers and the food. It will be strange to you, but it is what God has ordained. You have a book of prayers in front of you and we will all take turns with the readings. I will start and the rest of you will follow. Be prepared, my friend. We will be at the table for a long time."

Solly began. "Blessed are you, Lord God of the universe." The wine was poured all around and more prayers were offered. Gerald took a sip of the cheap, sweet red but could barely swallow it.

"I hope it's not too much to ask," he said, "but this wine is…I think I'll pass on the red. Gives me a headache. I'll just go out into the hall and retrieve the bottle I brought."

Solly and Rachel exchanged glances again. Iris spoke. "Henry, what my parents are trying to tell you is that the wine must remain outside. Bringing it into the house is not permitted." She rose and headed toward the kitchen. "I'll bring you grape juice."

Gerald shot her a look of disgust. "No need, water will do."

The prayers continued. Gerald was becoming bored and hungry. He noticed a plate of crackers before him. "*I suppose I'll just have to nibble on these until the food arrives.*" He took a large bite of matzo cracker, but it was like nothing he had ever tasted. He removed it from his mouth and placed in on the plate in front of him.

Solly, visibly upset, raised his voice. "Mien God! Oh, mien God," he recited over and over. "May God forgive him!" He motioned for his family to join in. "May God forgive him," they chanted, rocking back and forth.

Gerald had no idea they were talking about him. "Mr. Henry," Solly said, "will you kindly join in with the prayer? It is you who has offended God and God will want you should ask forgiveness."

"I?" said Gerald. "What now? What have I done?"

"You have started to eat before the prayer and you used the seder plate for your scraps!"

"What seder plate?" said Gerald, examining the plate before him. "You mean my scrap plate? I didn't like my cracker, so I put it on the plate. That's what it's for, isn't it? I saw the charred egg and the bone and the discarded scrap of green and figured it was a scrap plate. What's wrong with that?"

Gerald felt himself becoming more defensive. He wasn't used to explaining his every move. Solly didn't appreciate his tone. "My friend, this is not a scrap plate. It is a special dish that represents everything holy. This egg with the shell left on is charred deliberately. It is a symbol of a sacrificial offering, and it reminds us that the hotter you make it for the Jewish people, the tougher they get."

Solly continued around the plate. "This bone which appears to be shriveled and old is actually representative of the outstretched hands of God." He pointed to the horseradish. "Brings tears to your eyes, right?"

Gerald shrugged his shoulders. "If you say. I haven't tried it."

"It's a reminder to look at your own bitter enslavements, like alcohol or bad habits."

Gerald chuckled. "I'll just pass on that. I don't have any bad habits."

Rachel noticed Solly was clearly upset. She tried to lighten the mood. "You may like this, Mr. Henry. We call it charoset. It is sweet with nuts, pears, apples, and cinnamon. It represents the mortar used by Hebrew slaves to make brick."

Iris held up a small piece of parsley. "See this? It makes us feel like aristocracy or nobility." She waved the stem in front of him. "But then, you won't need that," she said, sarcastically.

Gerald caught the implication and returned Iris's glare. He looked at his watch again. *God, it's not even nine! I wonder when I can leave and head out for Callahans.*

Gerald's discomfort continued throughout the meal. Strange food, strange aromas, strange language, a strange assortment of people that he could not understand and had no intention of understanding. He couldn't wait to leave, but the evening was yet young.

Finally, Crystal pulled her chair close to him. "So, Henry, I have to tell you I've never seen my girl like this. I'm so happy for her." Gerald smiled and nodded, politely. Crystal slapped him on the shoulder.

"Hey, it's okay! You can talk to me. I'm all for it! Any guy that makes my Tabby this happy is good by me. You're one of us now, right?"

One of them? Really? Loud-mouthed Jews. A fat, black mammy who doesn't know her place, and a mother with no class. Really?

"Well, Miss Crystal," he said. "How nice of you. I certainly would be one happy and privileged man to join your company. Fact is, though, it might be a while. I have business that will be taking me away for quite some time."

Tabitha dropped her spoon. "Henry, what do you mean? You didn't tell me you'd be leaving."

Gerald put his arm on her shoulder and lifted her chin. "I'm sorry, dearest. I just now found out. Since Father's death, the

French division is in sore need of my attention and I've been called to leave right away."

Involuntary tears welled up in Tabitha's eyes. "I'm sorry, Henry. Of course, I'm disappointed. I just thought…" She forced a smile. "How foolish I am, acting like a love-sick teenager. Of course, you have to go. It'll be okay. Really." She wiped her eyes and abruptly rose to collect her coat, say her goodbyes and end the evening.

Gerald's driver was waiting. The two distanced themselves in the back seat and said nothing. It was as if each was deep in thought, ruminating over the events of the past hours.

Gerald was the first to speak. "I really owe you an apology, Tabitha. I didn't want to spoil your evening by telling you sooner. I knew how upset you'd be about how long I'll be gone."

He kissed her hand. "You have to understand, my love, that if you want to be part of my life, this is the kind of thing that goes with it. We're a powerful, successful family and these things are to be expected. Can you handle it? I mean, I wouldn't blame you at all if you couldn't. I would be away more than I would be home."

Gerald was sure she'd say no. He prayed she'd say no. It would be the perfect opportunity to leave without looking like a rat. How could he tell her what he was really feeling – that he could never be part of the family he'd just shared an evening with. He needed "class" on his arm, as his father would have expected. Tabitha was sweet and innocent and, yes, "classy" in a homey kind of way. He was certain she would shine at the country club and would be able carry on even the most challenging conversation with the stuffiest of them. What was missing was name and lineage. She could never fit into the Merriweather image. And she was Catholic. That would never do.

Tabitha leaned over, took his arm and put it around herself. "Oh, Henry. I've come so far! You'll never know how much it's taken for me to really love a man. I mean really – like I'd do anything for him. I can't possibly allow my archaic feelings about making love get between us. In fact, darling, I've been sitting here thinking of giving you the perfect sendoff."

She kissed him warmly. "I'm ready, Henry. I'm ready now. I've had time to think about what you said. You were right. I really do have to grow up. As soon as we get to the apartment, I'll…"

Oh, my God! All this and she's ready to go to bed with me. Gerald responded to her caresses. Well, why not. Why not get what I came for.

Tabitha had been designing the moment for a long time. She came out of the shower, let her beautiful chestnut hair fall to her waist, removed the large bath towel, and got into bed beside Gerald.

Darling," she said, getting on top of him. "I may need some help. Iris has filled me in a bit and there were those library books and everything, but…" She took his hand. "You just guide me. Tell me what to do; what you want, and I'll do it."

Gerald began breathing faster. This woman was a real beauty who would do anything he asked. He was ready. He would use all his skills; gently first, while her virginity was yet intact. The fierce, raw part would be saved for a bit later.

He got on top of her, preparing to enter. Suddenly, he stopped. Something wasn't right. Something was happening to him that he had never in his life experienced. He was unable to continue. He tried every expert tactic and every vulgar word that usually aroused him. He pretended she was someone else, but he could not perform.

Tabitha was bursting with desire, not understanding what was happening. "What's wrong? Why are you stopping. Please don't." She took his face in her hands. "Listen to me. If you're worried about taking my virginity, you needn't. I want to give it to you, and only to you."

"No, Tabitha, it's not that. I know you're ready and I know you love me. It's just that…" Gerald pushed her aside gently, got out of bed, and lit a cigarette. "I don't know what was in those library books or what Iris told you, but there are times men have a problem. They just can't do it."

Tabitha was shocked. She'd never read about that. "Why? What's the cause? Is it something I've done – or haven't done? Just tell me!"

The room was silent. From a distance, Gerald heard the opening song in a nearby club, announcing that Saturday night would begin in earnest. It was an enticement for him to leave and put an end to this untenable relationship that had begun only as one of his crazy whims.

Gerald continued to smoke, pacing and letting out a mawkish sigh. "It's not you. Honest. You're a lovely, sensuous woman. Any man would be thrilled…"

"I don't want any man, Henry. I want you!"

"I'm just screwed up. You say you have baggage, and so do I. My head is messed up. If we make love now and I go away, I'll never be able to concentrate on my work. I'll be continually guilty about leaving you here alone. I just think it best to wait until I return. I hope you understand."

But Tabitha did not understand. She didn't want to understand. It was all too much.

CHAPTER TWENTY-NINE

"This above all, to thine own self be true."

The clock was striking ten when Gerald found his way to
Callahan's. He needed a drink. No, he needed to be drunk; good
and drunk. "Get out my reserve, Patty," he said to the bartender.
"I'm going to be here for a while."

He sat drinking; not wishing to be disturbed. Even the music
bothered him. "Turn off that damn rot, will you?" he demanded.

"Right away, Mr. Gerald," said Patty, complying immediately.
"And by the way, Miss Justine was just here looking for you.
When you weren't here, she said she'd just go back to the office
and cry in her own beer."

The message brought a smile to Gerald's otherwise somber face.
"She was, was she?" He grabbed the unfinished bottle and left to
join his friend.

Justine didn't see or hear him as he crept up and kissed her neck
"Well now, what's this I hear about your own beer? Since
when?" He plopped the bottle of expensive scotch in front of her.
"C'mon. Tell Daddy all about it."

Justine slapped him on the rear. "You scared the shit out of me!"
She gave him a serious hug. "But I'm glad you're here. Pour me
a stiff one and I'll tell you my tale of woe."

"You look lousy," said Gerald. I don't think I've ever seen you
like this."

"Thanks. You sure do know how to make a girl feel better."

Gerald pinched her cheek "Now, admit it. You look lousy. What is it? That old creepy McKenna from personnel bothering you again?"

"That's just a petty annoyance. This…"

Gerald was not one to recognize emotional pain, but he thought this is what it might look like. "Wow! This must be serious. Not pregnant, are you?"

Justine took another large sip of her drink. "I wish it were that simple, actually. I kind of wish I were pregnant. You know, married, a kid, a husband that I didn't really love but that I had to fake it with. That's easier. I can live with not loving the guy, but I'm having a hard time loving myself right now. Not even liking myself."

The drink went down easily. Gerald poured another double as Justine went on. "Yeah, I actually despise myself right now." She started to cry, partly from true emotion and partly from the generous quantity of scotch.

Gerald picked her up, placed her on the chaise and began rubbing her feet. "Relax. Father Gerald will hear your confession."

Justine began. "You understand me, Gerald, because you're the male version. You know, it's all about a good time. No holds, no responsibilities, no drama, just fun. Black, white, married, single and in between. To be honest, I actually prefer the married ones. We're after the same thing. The guy treats me well, has no intention of leaving his happy home, and that's fine by me. Well, it was perfect until Martin."

"I never heard about that one. Why didn't you tell me?"

"There isn't much to tell, really. Married. A prominent attorney. He gave me plenty of what I craved. Grand vacations, complete with wardrobe and jewelry from every port. Best food and wine. Daily massages. And I gave him plenty of what he craved."

"He must really appreciate your, shall we say, 'finer' qualities."

"Hell, yeah," said Justine. "So, I didn't think there was a thing wrong with it. You know, I put out and he's all in. Seemed like a fair deal to me. After all, you and I both know how I got to be head of Personnel, don't we?" Justine tussled his hair and whispered in his ear, "Remember that trip to Miami when…"

Gerald began laughing and hitting his knee. "God, Juss, don't let anybody hear you talk about *that.* Can you imagine if it ever got out?"

"Well, you're the one that said if you got you should use it, right?"

"I sure did, my friend. Use every little thing the good lord gave you. He was just mighty generous to you and me, and it wouldn't be right to disappoint him."

The conversation turned serious. "So, you still haven't told me what's ailing you."

Justine closed her eyes. "When we were together last night, Martin announced that he started divorce proceedings because he just can't stand to be without me. He made it sound like it was no problem – that his wife and five kids would be taken care of."

"So? So what? People do it all the time. I mean, just because you marry someone doesn't mean you'll love them indefinitely. People change. Women let themselves go. I, for one, could not accept that. You know how frumpy housewives turn me off. Who could blame him for wanting you?"

"You got it all wrong. She's also a well-known attorney. And quite beautiful. Don't ask why he wants me."

"And you, Juss?"

"For Christ's sake, no! I don't love him. I've never loved anyone and wouldn't recognize the emotion if it came up and bit me.

Problem is, I lied. I used him. I told him all along I was in love with him to make things, shall we say, 'easier.' I didn't think it would get this far. I believe 'home wrecker' is the term used for women like me." Justine picked up a cigarette. Gerald lit it, took a long puff and returned it to her mouth.

"A trusting wife and five great kids. They'll get the shaft and I'll be stuck with someone I don't give a hoot about. Get it?"

Gerald tweaked her nose. "If I had to guess, I'd guess you're having a crying jag. I'm quite sure it's not a guilty conscience. That would be very not like you. What the hell is making you so upset? Could it be that you care for him? That also would be very not like you. Why don't you just tell him that you want no part of being the cause of his divorce. Tell him you could not possibly be party to that, and you refuse to continue to see him."

"I've already told him. A dozen times. He won't accept it. He says he can get his lawyer friends to expedite the divorce. I think the only way out of this is for me to come clean. I have to tell him that I don't love him; that I never have. Actually, I will have to confess that I used him. As I said, I don't love the guy, but he's too nice a guy for me to just keep using. All the screwing in the world can't come close to the money he's spent on me."

Justine reached over for a tissue and the last of the scotch in her glass. "I never thought I had a conscience but, when it comes to kids, I guess I do. My father did it to us. I remember one Christmas when I really, really wanted a new sweater and he said Santa was broke that year. Later, one of my friends told me she saw my father going into Leanne Burns' house when Mr. Burns was away. She said he was all duked out and carrying a beautiful, gift-wrapped package. See! The presents we kids were supposed to get went to that woman. I never forgave my father, and now I'm just as bad."

Justine got up. "I need a hug, Gerald. A great big, serious hug. From you. I know I don't deserve it, but I also know you'll do it."

Gerald opened his arms and Justine fell into them. They remained locked together a long time. It was Justine that broke the silence. "Gerald, what makes us tick? You and me, I mean. We're not like most people. We use people. We hurt them. We're all about ourselves. Do you think we've got a snowball's chance in hell to do something to make us proud?"

Gerald held Justine closer, stroking her hair. "I don't know, love. I honestly don't know." He pulled her into the chaise. They remained that way until morning, in an embrace that spoke only of deep need and an emotion that neither could understand.

Justine was the first to rise, and by the time Gerald awoke his coffee was in front of him, hot and fresh. "You're a doll, Juss. Thanks."

Justine mumbled and went on preparing his daily routine. "Shower's ready," she announced. "I called Jacqueline about your breakfast and massage. Pierre is on his way to take care of your wardrobe. Do you feel like navy today?" she asked, retrieving the classic navy suit and white shirt from his office closet.

"I think not," Gerald said. Get Pierre to throw just some sweaters and pants in a bag. I'll wear one outfit now, and he can pack the rest. No sense being formal where I'm going."

"The chateau?" Justine knew him well. "Yep," he said, and playfully tossed his towel to her. "Whatever you do, Juss, don't tell anyone—and I mean anyone—where I am."

"What about your brother? Isn't he going to ask where you are? After all, you do have business connections."

"We do business through department heads. I'm quite sure he could care less about where I am. Call my secretary and give her the same directive. Tell her my assistant will take care of things in my absence. Be sure to tell her what I told you. No one is to know where I am or when I can be expected to return. You, however, can reach me on my private line whenever you like."

Gerald looked at his watch. "Christ, I have to go. "He tossed a few wadded hundred-dollar bills to Justine. "Here, my sweet, go get yourself a mile-high banana split at Rumpie's. While you're at it, stop at Adelle's. Tell Monique I sent you." He tossed her a kiss a went off.

CHAPTER THIRTY

"My heart is ever at your service."

There was only one thing Tabitha could do. It had been months of worrying and wondering, of sleepless nights and lonely days, of plaguing memories and relentless pain. In all that time there wasn't a call, a letter, or even a small note to indicate that Henry was alright and that he was thinking of her. She was no longer the happy, exuberant, bright-eyed, person everyone knew and admired. Now, she was a shell of herself, thin and gaunt and sick with worry. She had to find out.

Henry made it clear to her numerous times that no one from the bank must ever know about their relationship; that his father had laid down strict rules about employees dating one another. Tabitha promised she'd never say a word, but here she stood in front of Henry's office, preparing to beg for the information she needed.

She was ready to knock when she saw Justine heading toward the same office. "Well, hello, Tabitha! This is a surprise. Haven't seen you in a bit. Everything okay?"

Tabitha mumbled, turning to hide her true feelings. Justine went on. "Wow," she said, examining Tabitha's entire body, "you've lost weight!"

Tabitha lowered her eyes. "I guess. A little. Too many donuts during break time so I decided to just give it up."

"Give it up? If you don't mind me sayin' so, you went a bit too far. You used to have a knockout figure with all the right curves in the right places. What gives? You're not sick, are you?"

Tabitha fought the tears. She wanted to say that she was, indeed, sick. Sick with worry, sick with longing, sick with frustration. Instead, she said, "Oh, Jussy! I'm a mess."

Justine was truly concerned. "Come with me," she said, as she took Tabitha's hand and led her to the ladies room.

"Wanna talk?" she asked.

Tabitha was ready. She did want to talk. She wanted to tell her everything. Maybe Justine could tell her what she needed to know. Then she was reminded of the promise she'd made to Henry. She must never say a word about their affair. They would both be in trouble.

"Crazy me," said Tabitha. "crying over those silly computer documents. I'm having a hard time understanding how to fix the problem, and it's not like me." She forced a smile and put her hand on Justine's arm. "Must be close to that time. I become teary when I…well, you know."

Justine didn't buy it but decided that whatever it was that was ailing Tabitha was probably nothing she could fix anyway. She wet a paper towel and handed it to her.

"Here. It's not like a good gimlet but it'll have to do for now. Forget about those documents. Treat yourself to a great lunch and a big bouquet of flowers."

Tabitha smiled and tried to rejuvenate herself. "Thanks, Jussy," she said, starting to leave; then stopping. She tried to sound casual. "You know, Jussy, I might feel better if I could talk to Mr. Merriweather about it. I haven't seen him around for a while, though. Do you know where he is?"

Justine froze. "Holy shit!" She said, audibly. Tabitha responded, "What is it, Jussy?"

"Sorry for the vulgarity, Tabitha, but I just noticed a run in my brand-new stockings." She had, indeed, noticed a run. She noticed Gerald running from yet another distressing affair; another broken heart.

Damn him! I told him not to fool around with this one. She's too good; too fragile to be messed up by the likes of that brute. I'm gonna tear him to shreds!

Justine tucked a stray hair in behind Tabitha's ear. "I have no idea where Mr. Merriweather is. Sometimes he's away for months – kind of incognito, you know. He's under enormous pressure right now, so I imagine he's doing what he always does – finds some remote island and hides for a bit. Don't worry. I'm sure you don't really need him. You'll find a way."

Tabitha looked in the mirror and found someone she hardly recognized. She did not like the person looking back at her. Her feelings took over. *You are so wrong. You have no idea how much I need him.*

Justine painted a smiley face on the mirror with her lipstick. "Here's the rest of your day, my friend. Paint it happy. You have my permission to take off the rest of the day. Call your mom and take her to lunch. You'll both love that."

Tabitha began to feel better. She decided Justine must be right. After all, she'd been around the bank a lot longer and she would know all about Henry's habits. She resurrected whatever solace she had left. *Of course, Henry must be stressed and needing some time off, and if he's in some remote island there might not be mail or phone service.* She called her mother at once and arranged for a lovely lunch in the park.

Crystal's arms went around Tabitha, not wanting to let her go. She had been worried about her daughter for months, but seeing her today was wonderfully reassuring. She and Tabitha had always been able to discuss anything, but today was different. Now, Crystal could only guess. What she guessed was that it must have something to do with Henry, who seemed to have suddenly disappeared from the scene.

The two sat for a long time catching up on small talk –Tabitha's apartment, the fall fashion line, Iris' baby, Sally's new shop – everything except Henry. Finally, Crystal brought up the subject.

"So, sweetheart, you haven't said a word about that man of yours. What's happening in the love department?"

Tabitha expected the remark. "Well, Mother," she responded, lowering her eyes, "everything is great. I have to confess I'm a bit lonely without Henry but he's just so busy and all. And Lord knows I'm busy enough at work that I hardly notice his absence."

She pointed to the outside. "Wow, look at that blue jay. He sure looks hungry!"

From the time she was a young girl, Crystal could tell when Tabitha was lying. She would never look at Crystal directly but would turn her head and try to change the subject. She was doing it now.

"It's no use, Tabby. It's me. There's no sense in trying to hide it. If you don't want to talk, it's okay. You're an adult and free to make choices. But you're my daughter and I hope you know that I love you enough to not judge."

Crystal motioned to the waitress. "Please bring more tea. We may be here for a while." She looked at Tabitha. "Or not."

Tabitha nodded. "Yes," she said, "more tea would be great."

"Whenever you're ready," said Crystal, leaning back in her chair.

Tabitha began. "Mamma, you know how much I love Henry." Crystal answered but did not smile. "Yes, Tabby, I think I do."

"And you probably understand that there's nothing much I wouldn't do for him." Crystal knew. She could already tell what this was about.

"Oh," she said. "That."

Tabitha turned away. "Yes, that," she said quietly. Then her voice became louder and she looked at Crystal directly. "Well, that is I would have, but it didn't happen. Henry was so nice. He said it wouldn't be right because he'd feel too guilty leaving me alone after we…well, after that. But I would have, Mamma, I would have. Right at that moment I didn't care about right or wrong; about what you've always preached to me or about the Catholic Church that says it's wrong. I just wanted Henry and would do whatever I needed to do to keep him."

Crystal didn't respond. This was far too important for her to make a clumsy mistake. She needed a few minutes to think.

"Honey, excuse me but nature calls. I'll be back in a bit. Just hold that thought."

It was out. There was no going back now. Tabitha would tell Crystal everything. After a few minutes, Crystal reappeared.

"So, honey," she said, taking her hand and looking at her directly. You've told me how much you love Henry and how much you were willing to give to him but, Tabitha, you've never told me how Henry feels about you."

"He loves me, Mamma. He does. He told me so."

Tabitha rubbed her forehead, trying to bring forth the scene she'd played over and over. *He did say those words. I remember. I asked him if he loved me and he said, 'of course.'* There was a sudden stab of consciousness. *Wait! He didn't say he loved me at all. He responded to me. He never once said he loved me.* She recalled that it disturbed her, but not enough to have it make a real difference.

Crystal's thoughts took her back to when she'd met Jed. She remembered that he'd never said those words, either. She could almost hear her father's voice. *Daughter, if you're smart, you'll marry somebody who loves you more than you love him. If the only thing he wants is to take care of you, if he's true to you, if he's happy to be in your bed every night, hang on to him. You may not be all gaga over him at first, but once you grow up to where you know what good is, you'll love him. Guaranteed! Remember, knee-knockers don't work. If he's making your knees knock, chances are he's making lots of other knees knock, too. Get it?*

Crystal remembered every word of that conversation. Over the years she'd chastised herself again and again for not "getting it."

Now, her daughter was waiting for solace or advice from the person she most trusted. She had to be very careful.

"I think you may be surprised by what I have to say, honey. I'm actually kind of relieved."

Tabitha's shock was evident. "Relieved? Mamma! I expected to hear you say a lot of things. Disappointed, maybe, or shocked. But relieved? Why in the world are you relieved?"

"I've worried so about you, Tabby. About what happened between you and Jed. I've always been afraid that you would never in your life be able to be close to a man; to love a man and to make love to a man. The fact that you are able to respond in that way to Henry tells me you're healed. That's why I'm relieved."

"Oh. Mamma!" Tabitha said, "You needn't have worried. I trust Henry. He would never hurt me. He's too good."

Crystal recalled the Passover dinner, when she'd first met Henry. She had no real reason to dislike him, but there was something missing. There was a lot missing. And her daddy had always instructed her to listen to her "guts."

Tabitha went on. "You haven't seen the other side of Henry, Mamma. He is really very caring. He taught me all I know about the impressionists. He's shy and polite and very respectful of women. He adores his mother."

Crystal was more than confused. It couldn't be. The Henry she knew was an out and out snob and respected only himself.

"I suppose I just don't know him well enough, honey. We'll have to work on that when he gets home, okay?"

Crystal didn't want to go on. For the moment, things were better left unsaid. She needed time to assimilate all she'd heard. She gathered her belongings, hooked onto Tabitha's arm and left.

CHAPTER THIRTY-ONE

"Out! Out, damned spot!"

Gerald sat over his brioche and coffee, skimming the American newspaper. Bored and disinterested, he pushed it aside. He'd been at the chateau for a few months now and the isolation was beginning to get to him. He threw on a pair of shorts and headed for the patio, taking his phone with him. It was a habit, nothing more. There were no plans to make; no one to call. His old flames bored him now, and he had no desire to go out in search of new ones. He could count on it being the same – great wine, decent dinner, crafty flattery, vacuous promises, and bed. It was predictable. No excitement; no challenge.

He'd thought about Tabitha nearly every day and had to confess that what he'd done to that sweet girl wasn't fair – no, it was downright deceitful and dishonorable. He hoped she would have by now moved on to someone else.

Of course, there was Henry to consider, too. Holy shit! Henry's gonna bust a gut if he ever finds out! It was bad enough when he took the rap that time with Celine Harding. If he ever gets wind of this…"

Gerald needed to talk to Justine. She'd always been good for a laugh. He put in the call. "Hey, Juss, Gerald here. How the heck are you? I was just sitting here thinking

about you and thought I'd give you a call. I miss you, babe!"

Justine was happy to hear from him. "Well, what do you know? What or who's new in your life? Not like you to be gone this long. You must be bored to death."

"Yeah, I am kinda. I might think about coming home in a while, but…"

"But you have some unfinished business that is keeping you there, right?"

"Like what? What do you mean?"

"I mean Tabitha Whittier. You know, the girl you destroyed. That girl. Didn't take much to figure it out."

"C'mon, Juss. I don't know what you're talking about. Okay, so I took her out a couple of times. So what? It didn't mean anything."

"Not to you, it didn't, but it sure did to her. She's destroyed. Gerald, when are you going to stop using people? She's a really special girl and you sure did mess her up. You gotta do something."

Gerald slammed his fist. "Like what, Juss? Like what? I didn't ask her to get all carried away, did I? I never…"

"It doesn't matter what you never did, Gerald. It's what you did that matters. Remember when we had that talk about Martin? Well, I told him how wrong and how sorry I was."

"How did he react? Was he really upset?"

"Well," said Justine, pausing a moment. Best way I can describe his reaction is to say I should have sold tickets for that show! He called me every name in the book, including that "c" word. When the fog was lifted, I had to admit they were all true. He said, next to me his wife was a saint and that he was going back to her and try to make things right. Thank God, Gerald. Thank God that, for once in my life, I was actually concerned about someone else. It could have turned out to be a disaster, but it's okay now. I don't feel good about what I did, but maybe now he'll show his wife how much he appreciates her."

"I hear you, Juss, but what the hell can I do? I don't know how to make things right." Gerald took a long drag on his third cigarette. "I need you, Juss. Get on the next flight and come here. You'll know what to do, I know you will."

Justine's voice turned somber. "Listen to me, Gerald. It's time you graduated to long pants. I can't help you. I can make you understand what you've done but I can't make it right. Only you can do that. It's a lonely place to be, my friend, but maybe the two of us need to learn just what a heartache loneliness is. Whatever happens, I'll be here for you, and maybe even for her when things crash. Now, go do it. Love you, even though you don't deserve to be loved."

Crystal sat soaking her feet after a long day. "God, Bertha, what a day," she declared, sipping on her second cup of bracing hot coffee. "I'm gonna hit the sack early tonight. I thought I'd watch that old Fred Astaire movie on TV, but seeing him and Ginger move like they do would put me right out. How about a game of rummy?"

"Sure, Miss Crystal. I'll get the cards." Bertha started for the kitchen but returned with a large envelope. "I'm sorry, Miss Crystal, I done forgot." She handed the envelope to Crystal. "This here come for you today."

Crystal examined the package, curiously turning it around a few times before opening it. "It's from France! What in the world? I don't know no one from France. You, Bertha?"

Bertha shook her head vigorously. "No'm. Sure don't."

Inside the package there were two letters. The first said, "For Crystal. Read first." Crystal examined the second envelope that read, "For Tabitha Only."

"What the bloody heck, Bertha, bring me a letter opener. This looks serious."

Crystal carefully removed the letter addressed to her, then stopped and broke into a huge smile. "Bertha," she said, "I just bet this is it! It must be Henry asking for Tabby's hand in marriage. Oh, Bertha, she's gonna be so thrilled!"

Bertha looked at her. "Yes'm. Tabby sho is gonna be happy but…" She stopped and didn't go on.

Crystal said, "Speak up, Bertha. What are you thinkin'?"

Bertha looked the other way." Not for me to say, Miss Crystal. Yo her Mamma."

"Yes, and you've been like a Mamma to her for many years. Now, what's on your mind?"

"Well, Miss Tabitha she sho gonna be happy, but I jes don't think yo so happy with Mr. Henry."

Bertha was right. Crystal felt relieved that Henry hadn't gotten in touch with Tabitha. She just wasn't convinced he was for her. She hated to admit it, but when she looked at him, she saw Jed. She'd never wanted to tell Tabitha how she truly felt, but now she could only wonder if her decision was right.

"We'll never find out if I don't open this letter," Crystal said, tearing the envelope.

My dear Mrs. Whittier,

I am writing this to you by way of explanation and to ask a favor. I think we can agree that we both care for Tabitha. You have done so much for her, and I am quite sure she would not have turned out to be the beautiful person she is, had it not been for you. She has needed your love and your care through all these years, and she will need you now.

The other letter I have enclosed is for Tabitha. I have a feeling she will be quite devastated upon reading the contents. I would rather she not be alone when she does. I fully understand this is a sensitive task, but I also understand that you are the only person Tabitha will be able to turn to.

Forgive me for all I have done or have not done. I am sincerely trying to make things right.

Forever in your debt,

Gerald H. Merriweather

Crystal read the letter again and again. From what Henry was hinting at, she had a feeling the contents of Tabitha's letter might cause her daughter to become distraught. It had taken her years to get past the traumatic event that robbed her of her youth. The contents of this letter may be something she might never be able to handle.

The signature identified this man as *Gerald* Merriweather. What was that all about? Crystal could not wait. She would invite Tabitha to come tomorrow.

Bertha didn't disclose anything that happened, but she asked the Feldmans if they might give over the apartment the next day so that Tabitha and Crystal might have some much-needed privacy.

Crystal called her daughter. "Hey there, honey, "she said, casually. "I'm glad you're coming over tomorrow. There's a piece of mail for you. Looks kind of important."

"You sure it's not just junk? I can't imagine what else it would be."

"Doesn't look like junk, Tabby. How 'bout coming over for breakfast? I'll make your favorite pancakes."

Tabitha arrived early next morning, pretending to have an appetite. "You said pancakes, Mamma, and I'm ready. Bring them on!" Crystal set the dish in front of her along with a cup of steaming hot coffee.

Tabitha looked around. "Am I eating alone?" she asked. "Where is everybody?"

Crystal struggled for words. "Everybody went to visit Iris today. You know, the new baby and all." Tabitha ate a few bites of pancakes.

"Where's the mail you told me about, Mamma?"

Crystal's hand shook as she poured coffee. She'd thought about it all night but could not come up with a decision that satisfied her. Should she prepare her daughter for what she thought was to come, or would it be best if she were to say nothing? She opted for the latter and just handed the envelope to Tabitha.

"Here it is. You'll notice it's been opened. That's because it was addressed to me."

"To you?" said Tabitha. "Then why did you say it's for me?"

"Please, Tabby, I think when you read the letter you'll understand." Crystal took a tissue from her apron pocket and wiped her brow.

Tabitha noticed Crystal's uncommon anxiety. She pointed to the chair next to her. "Sit down, Mamma. You don't look well."

Crystal was happy for the invitation. She pulled up a chair and examined Tabitha's face as she read:

> My dear Tabitha,
>
> To begin, please allow me to apologize for being so selfish as to not have attempted to reach you in all this time. My insensitivity is unforgivable.

The problem is I am a real coward. A few months ago, I felt the strong sense to run, for reasons I will try to explain in this letter.

I am not who you think I am, Tabitha. My name is Gerald Merriweather. I am Henry's identical twin brother.

Tabitha reeled. "What? What?" She said aloud. Crystal put her hand on Tabitha's arm as she continued reading.

From the time we were just boys, I took great pleasure in playing conniving games, pretending to be Henry. Some of what I did was nothing more than a bit of fun; most was just plain ugly. I allowed Henry to take the hit for my obnoxious behavior, and he forgave me, most of the time. That is, until now. Henry removed himself from my life s few years ago, for reasons that, obviously, have nothing to do with you. He has no idea about you and me and what has transpired over the last months.

My brother is a very special man, Tabitha. He may lack the sophistication and the charm of the worldly lothario, but when it comes to character, I must admit, I couldn't even shine his shoes.

In a crazy way, you made me understand that I truly love my brother and, yes, I truly love you – maybe not in the way you've wished for, but in a much better, more satisfying way.

We've both learned a valuable lesson. I've learned that there are good, honest women like you in this world that might be completely destroyed by men like me. I hope you come to understand that there are ego driven, disingenuous men who will do you in for just a bit of fun and a few rainy afternoon trysts.

I don't expect you to forgive me and I don't expect Henry to forgive me. Actually, I will never forgive myself. But you will need to forgive yourself, Tabitha. Forgive yourself for not seeing the signs; for allowing yourself to love a lout; for being willing to give over something to him that was so precious to you.

I'm not sure where life will take me, but I've decided to leave the company and concentrate on where I might take my share of the Merriweather fortune and try to put it to use in a meaningful way. Africa maybe.

My mother once taught me about "noblesse oblige." I scoffed at the advice then, but her words have remained, and I'm ready to act on what she suggested. To be honest, I don't know if I have it in me, but I'd like to try.

As I say, Tabitha, I won't ask for forgiveness. It's much too much to ask. I ask only that, when you're ready, you find a man who is worthy of you and that you give him all of the love you are capable of giving. I will never forget you.

 With sincere and deep affection,

Gerald Merriweather

Part Seven

1963

Tabitha and Henry

CHAPTER THIRTY-TWO

*The web of our life is a mingled yarn, good and
ill together.*

The note Sister Veronica was holding contained only a few brief
words: "I need the roof."

The puzzled nun called Crystal immediately. "What gives,
Crystal? I'm holding a note that sounds kind of ominous. Is
Tabitha okay?"

Crystal began crying. "I don't know. She won't talk to me. She
doesn't talk to anyone. Father Reilly told me he's happy to see
Tabitha in church every morning, but I'm not happy. It's not like
her, and I'm worried. It's all because of that damned letter."

Sister Veronica didn't ask about the letter. She thought perhaps
that's why Tabitha needed to speak to her.

"Don't worry, my friend. I'll be seeing her soon and I'm sure
we'll sort it out. I have a feeling that a mini retreat will be just
the thing for her. She needs to be with us for the weekend and
it's the right time. The girls are on break, so the rooms are
vacant. I'll call the girl who now occupies Tabby's old room and
ask if it's okay for Tabby to stay for a couple of days. I'm sure
she won't mind."

Crystal found a glimmer of hope. "Oh, Veronica! If you could
only…"

"Go make yourself a martini. You concentrate on making
yourself a good one and leave the rest to me. Meanwhile, I'm
going to pray to the Holy Spirit for guidance. Can't hurt!"

Tabitha arrived, wearing a dismal outfit and an artificial smile. She gave her mentor a hug, but the nun felt the distance between them. She decided to dismiss it for the moment. Instead, she handed Tabitha a small gift bag.

"Just something to welcome you. Not much. Just some cookies from Sister Joseph and a bag of candied walnuts from Mabel in the kitchen." Tabitha accepted the bag with polite thanks.

"Well," said Sister Veronica, "this isn't the best part. That will come when we raid the freezer and make our own root beer floats. For now, though, you might want to rest. I have to be in chapel soon, so it'll be a good time for you to do that. Your old room is yours for the next couple of days."

Tabitha found her way to her room, but it felt strange and lonely. She was used to seeing her friends in the dorm, singing around the piano or playing bridge. She was used to hearing them all pile in on a Sunday night, vying for first place to tell of their recent "pinnings" or new boyfriends. She remembered being happy for them, but not so happy to allow herself to be like them. She wanted no part of it then. That was before Gerald.

The room was unlocked, as usual. Tabitha let herself in, got into her pajamas, and collapsed on the bed. The extreme quiet, the welcoming breeze whispering through the pines, and the earthy fragrance of late afternoon was the elixir she needed. She slept. Finally, Sister Veronica arrived carrying a large tray. '

"Mabel's pot roast Tab, complete with her special mashed potatoes and chocolate pudding cake." She put the plate before her. "But there will be no milk tonight," she said, reaching down into her deep nun's pocket. "Tah tah! she announced, animatedly. "Tonight, it's Blue Nun."

Sister Veronica struggled to open the bottle. "Don't laugh. It's all I could afford. As it is, I had to lie. I told Superior I needed a couple of dollars for mending supplies. Well, it wasn't such a big lie. I mean, a long glass of wine can mend a lot, right?"

Tabitha laughed. "Oh, Sister Veronica, I've missed you."

"Please. Just for tonight will you call me Helen?"

Tabitha was startled, but happy to agree. "Of course, Helen. I can understand why you might be homesick for it."

Sister Veronica removed the tray that had barely been touched. "I've missed you, too, Tabitha. I miss all the girls, but some are just, well, special. Now, is it roof time?"

Tabitha got up, stepped outside and held her hand out to her friend. "Be careful. It's dark out here. Don't forget the wine, cheap or not."

The two sat for a bit, reminiscing. Finally, Sister Veronica spoke up. "You're not here to talk about old times. Not really. What's this all about? I can tell Crystal's worried sick."

Tabitha decided that if she were to open up to her friend, she would have to disclose the entire sordid mess. She was ready now. She left out nothing, even though she found the ordeal extremely painful and embarrassing. She discussed her mentally deranged father and what he'd done to her. She talked about Rabbi Kadish and how long and hard he'd worked at helping to rid her soul of its demons.

Finally, Tabitha got to the subject of Gerald. "I loved him. Ronnie. Truly I did. I loved him so much I would have done anything for him. Kind of like my father. All I wanted was for him to love me. They both recognized my weakness. They used me and left. Now...well never mind. It doesn't matter anyway."

Sister Veronica couldn't let Tabitha see her emotions. She turned from her and took a minute to compose herself. "What doesn't matter, Tabby? Sounds like you're taking a pretty fatalistic approach. I can certainly understand, but it seems like you're stuck in a maze and can't find your way out."

Tabitha responded, "No, I think I have found a way. I've spent a lot of time making the decision. I think God put these things in my path to show me that the way of the world is not for me. He put these trials before me because He wants me to come to Him. He wouldn't hurt me like the others. You know I've thought about entering for quite some time. Now, I've made up my mind."

The night was growing colder. The wine bottle was empty. Sister Victoria needed time to think and to pray. She knew she could not do what needed to be done without help. She took her shawl and wrapped it around her broken charge.

"I see we have a lot of work to do. I think we should each get a good night's sleep. We'll be able to think more clearly tomorrow. Meet me in my room after breakfast. We have important matters to discuss."

Tabitha held up her hand to knock on Sister Veronica's door next morning but changed her mind and began to leave. She didn't know if she could go through the ordeal she was about to face. If she hurried, she could get the 10:00 bus back to the city and would then call Sister Veronica to explain. Instead, she heard her name being called from a distance.

"Tabby, here I am, dear. I thought I'd bring us extra coffee. We'll probably be here for a bit. Know what, Tabby? Crystal and I used to have a pact. Whoever it was that was having a bad day got to lie down on the sofa or the bed while the other listened and provided chocolate or tissues. Worked better than any shrink. Wanna try?"

Tabitha knew she had to stay. She shrugged her shoulders. "I don't know, Helen, it doesn't seem right, me lying on a nun's bed."

"Why not? If you're going to be one of us, you may as well start now, right?"

"Somehow I detect a note of sarcasm," said Tabitha, waving her finger at her friend.

"Sorry, I apologize. Just thought I'd add a bit of levity, but I realize now this is not the time. The matter is a serious one and it isn't right for me to make light of it. Let's get to the heart of things."

"What more can I tell you?" said Tabitha. I've told you everything that happened to me. Now, I feel I have a calling. I feel that God has put evil and heartache in my path to have me understand that I can leave the pain and sorrow behind and go with him. It seems I can only be happy for a short time. When I begin to enjoy life, or when I feel love coming my way, things fall apart again. There's got to be a message there."

"And you think the message is coming from God?"

"Yes, that's how I see it."

"You need to understand some things. First, if you think pain and suffering are reserved for those on the outside, you are most definitely wrong. At this very moment, Sister Claudia, my very good friend, is in the last stages of her battle with ovarian cancer. She's only thirty-five. If you wonder where I disappear to every afternoon, I put that time aside to be with her and Sister Adrian who has dementia. Sister Catherine is going through a tough time with discernment right now. She may leave us. So, you see, nuns are not exempt from pain."

Sister Veronica felt inadequate to the task put before her. She walked to the window, blessing herself and taking time to collect her thoughts. As she did, her eye caught her nightstand drawer, slightly ajar. It was the inspiration she'd prayer for.

"Tabby, please open the drawer to my nightstand." Tabitha thought it a rather irregular request, but immediately obeyed.

"What do you see in there?"

Tabitha reached inside. "Uh, two books and a yellow highlighter."

"Yes," said Sister Veronica. The books are my go-to favorites. My father's bible and a book of Robert Frost poetry. I would never use the highlighter on my precious bible, but if you open the Frost book, you'll see it is full of marginal notes and highlights. The books have something in common for me. There are beautiful messages in both. Sometimes I want to hear them in God's words; sometimes God gives the gift of language to others so they may inspire in a more lyrical, poetic way."

Tabitha picked up the *Robert Frost Poetry Book.* Sister Veronica put up her hand. "No need to open it. I can recite my favorite poem in every language!"

Sister Veronica closed her eyes and recited as though she were delivering the words to angels:

"The woods are lovely, dark and deep, but I have promises to keep

and miles to go before I sleep. And miles to go before I sleep."

"You see, Tabitha, the dark woods Frost speaks of is like a hiding place we've made for ourselves. Kind of like that special place under the porch where you hid to escape. You wanted to stay there forever. You found comfort in the darkness when your soul was in terrible pain."

"I remember. Sometimes I want to go back there again."

"Mr. Frost continues. He encourages us to leave that place because we do have promises to keep – promises to ourselves, to those we love and, yes, to God. If we remain where it is 'dark and deep' we will never be able to fulfill those promises."

Tabitha moved to the chair and took a long swallow of coffee. "I think I understand, but you made the decision to enter. Why is it not right for me?"

Sister Veronica smiled. "I remember how destroyed Crystal was when I announced my decision. I had lots of boyfriends. Charlie and I were nearly engaged."

"Were you really in love with him?"

"I thought I was. More than that, he was truly in love with me. He was everything any woman would want."

"What happened to make you change your mind?"

"If you mean a sudden revelation, it wasn't that. I kept putting Charlie off until I came to realize that, as happy as I was when we were together, I was even happier when I was alone. I felt a peace like no other while walking through the woods or spending an afternoon reading Milton's sonnets or Thomas Merton's 'Thoughts in Solitude'. That's when I knew. As happy as Charlie was making me, I wasn't working toward my own happiness."

"And you don't think I'm doing that?"

"I'm sorry, Tabby, I don't. The difference is that I chose the religious life while I was happily involved. Your reason for entering is that you want to go back to being under that porch. We don't have porches here. The convent cannot erase your bitterness and discontent. It will surface. You will carry it with you and possibly even pass it along, like some nasty disease."

"Okay," said Tabitha, "you're telling me how my thinking is all wrong. You're not telling me how I can make it right."

"I wish it were in my power, Tabby, but I'm not the one to tell you how to get happy."

"You mean I should talk to Crystal or Rabbi Kaddish?"

"No, I mean you should talk to *you*. Spend the rest of the day alone. Go down by the lake and sit in the sun. Take Frost with you. Study the words. Invite them in. Nurture them and have them become part of who you are."

As Tabitha was leaving, Sister Veronica called after her. "Hey, whatever happened to that nice guy you told me about?"

"You mean…you mean Henry? The real Henry Merriweather?" Tabitha had a faraway look in her eyes. Her voice cracked. "I don't know, really. It's just another one of my blunders."

Sister Veronica replied, "Last I heard, you weren't interested in him. Romantically, I mean. You said there was something missing."

"Yes, I did say that. It was all stupid. I think I was looking for the 'knee-knocker' stuff, as Crystal would say. I just couldn't look past the old-fashioned bow ties and what I thought were stuffy mannerisms to realize what a fine man Henry truly is. Henry and Gerald are twins that were raised in the same environment and enjoyed the same privileges. I often wonder what it was that made them so different."

Sister Veronica asked, "Is Henry gone from your life now?"

Tabitha nodded, sadly. "Yes. I'm afraid that, when he left for Paris, I gave him the impression I wasn't interested. I wasn't, then."

"And now?"

It didn't take long for Tabitha to respond. She'd been thinking a lot about Henry lately, and about how much she'd missed his friendship. "I'd love to have him in my life again, to go to museums and hang out at coffee shops and to just know that he's there for me."

"Do you think things might ever go beyond friendship?"

"I doubt it. I haven't seen him in a while. He's probably with someone else by now."

Tabitha got up, sighing. "It's all so confusing. You gave me a lot to think about, but for now, can we just go and make that root beer float?"

Sister Veronica found a gift-wrapped package at her place at dinner. "Oh," she said to the nun sitting next to her, "there must be a mistake. It's not my birthday."

Tabitha was quick to answer. "Does there have to be a birthday to get a small gift? Open it!"

`Sister Veronica opened the package, careful to not tear the beautiful silver wrapping. What she found was a book she had never seen, an artist's interpretation of Frost's "Stopping by Woods." The lovely ethereal illustrations left her breathless.

"From you, Tabby? It's absolutely gorgeous! But how…"

Tabitha responded, smiling. "I did spend time at the lake. Then I remembered the bookstore was nearby. I wanted to get you something to show my appreciation. I was elated to find this new copy. I was completely taken in by the illustrations, as I thought you would be."

Sister Veronica couldn't contain the tears. "I don't even know what to say. Thank you."

"No thanks necessary. Now, turn to the last page. You'll see it's highlighted."

Sister Veronica did as she was asked and found the words: "…but I have promises to keep and miles to go before I sleep."

Tabitha got up to give her friend a warm hug. "I want you to know you've brought me to the understanding I need to leave the place inside of me that is 'dark and deep'. I know I have promises to keep. It's going to take me a long time to do all I plan to do. Better start now!"

"You're not alone, sweetheart. This will always be your safe place. It may not be behind our convent walls, but it will be in front of them, and that's a good place to be."

CHAPTER THIRTY-THREE

"He that is thy friend indeed he will help thee in thy need. If thou sorrow he will weep. If thou wake he cannot sleep. Thus of every grief in heart he with thee doth bear a part. These are certain things to know. Faithful friend from flattering foe."

The long summer ended, taking with it steamy days and long, lonely nights. Finally, the glory of autumn found its way to Tabitha's heart, providing the promise of renewal she desperately needed.

Crystal was elated to finally find her daughter smiling and happy. Tabitha thought about leaving the bank and all its unpleasant memories, but she resolved to not give in to the heartaches of the past. Instead, she would forge ahead and find fulfillment, wherever the path might take her. She'd learned that it was irresponsible to depend on others for her happiness; that she was the master of her own fate.

Thanksgiving Day drew near. The Feldman clan gathered in the kitchen, cooking and baking and laughing. Then the conversation took a more serious tone. Rachel spoke. "So, tell me Crystal, since we are celebrating Thanksgiving, how do you feel God has blessed you?"

Crystal went to Tabitha and gave her a big hug. "Why this, of course. You know, Jed was a real rat, but the one thing I thank him for is my Tabby. My girl and I were both suffering, so I think the Lord gave us each other to help us get through."

"Speaking of Jed, have you ever heard anything more about him?" Iris asked.

"Not really. I read in the paper that there was a bad bout of influenza on the island and many died. He may have been one of them, I don't know."

Tabitha wiped her eyes. She didn't know if it was grief from remembering what Jed had done to her or from the fact that she'd never had a father.

Iris noticed. "Hey, let's just talk about something lighter. Like, what's something that happened to you that seemed terrible at the moment but turned out to be great."

Bertha put her hand to her mouth and cried, "I gots a good one! Once, nosy old Margaret from church was walkin' by the hat shop when I was inside, shoppin' for a new hat to wear to Viola's wedding. Well, I done seed this beautiful purple taffeta with a big, bright red feather. I knowed it was the hat for me, but when I axed Clementine the price, I near fainted. I jes couldn't do it. Now, Margaret she go into the shop after I left and she done buy that hat, jes to get me upset. You bet I was plenty mad. But the good Lord, he come through. When we was all outside throwin' the rice, a big bird come by and did a huge poop on Margaret and her hat. Everybody laughed so hard they didn't pay no attention to the bride."

The women roared. "That sure was a good one, Bertha! I don't know if anybody can top that," said Rachel.

"Uh, I might," said Iris, raising her hand. "Once, I was trying to make a real impression on my date. I kept going to the ladies' room all night, combing my hair and freshening my makeup. I was nervous and I had to pee a lot. When I came out, everyone was looking at me and laughing, hysterically. I didn't know it, but the toilet paper got stuck in my dress and I was carrying a huge tail of it behind me. When I found out, I wanted to die, but Michael just got up and removed it, as though it was a natural occurrence."

Laughter filled the room. Crystal said, "You poor thing! Did you ever go out with him again?"

"No," said Iris, "I married him!"

Finally, Rachel said, "So, Tabby, you must have something you want to add. We all have stories, right?"

"I don't really. I've never been involved in anything humorous. Most of my life has been pretty serious, I'm afraid."

Iris gave her a slight poke with a wooden spoon. "Oh, c'mon. There's got to be something. If there's nothing funny, how about telling of a moment when something good happened that wasn't planned but that turned out to be a really good thing."

Tabitha thought for a moment. "Well, I didn't plan to be a part of your family, but here I am. That's good, right?"

Rachel responded, "Of course right! There's got to be something else. We all told, now it's your turn."

Tabitha's cheeks turned red. "Well, I suppose if you want to talk about good things, I can tell you about how I met Henry. That was kind of funny. And it turned out to be a pretty good thing."

Bertha chimed in. "Yo never did tell us about how you met the real Mr. Henry. Was it a secret or something?"

"No," said Tabitha. "At the time it didn't seem like anything but looking back it was kind of funny. I mean how many guys are you going to meet over a lost button?"

"A button?" Rachel chimed. "I met Solly at the synagogue over coffee, but a button?"

"Okay," said Tabitha, "I'll tell you the whole thing."

The women smiled, listening intently to every word. "That's so romantic," said Iris at the end.

"Romantic?" Tabitha chuckled. "How can a button be romantic?"

Iris responded, "Oh, I don't know, it's kind of like fate. The two of you were meant to meet. I mean, there are a dozen fabric stores on this block, but Henry just happened to step into where you were working. I call that fate. You were meant to be together. I feel it!"

Tabitha laughed. "So, it was like you and Michael and the toilet paper?"

Rachel said, "And a good man he is, our Michael. So, he's not handsome and maybe not even good looking. In fact, he's …well, a little plain. He'll never be rich, but he's a good father and he takes care of our Iris so what more do we want, I ask you?"

Tabitha and Crystal looked at each other, knowingly. Crystal broke the spell. "Hey, ladies. We ain't having no pumpkin or pecan pies for tomorrow if we don't get goin." The women agreed and happily returned to work.

Tabitha stayed the night but arose early the next morning. "I noticed Solly got in a huge shipment for the holidays. I feel like working in the shop a bit before dinner. The Christmas fabrics must be stunning, and I don't want to miss seeing them. I'll just go down and unwrap the bolts and maybe put together a knockout display to surprise Solly."

She set about to her tasks, happy to be in familiar surroundings. She unwrapped several bolts of fabric and began looking for trims and buttons to match the lovely new colors. It was raining quite heavily now, but Tabitha felt the gloom almost inviting. The Thanksgiving smells of turkey and pecan pie found their way into the shop, making her feel comfortable and warm against the nasty weather.

Tabitha began working on changing the window display, thinking how she could make it special. *No red and green for Solly's. The whole block is filled with red and green.* She stepped back. *If I were going dancing, my dress would be…* Tabitha examined all the new fabrics; then put one against her cheek. *This is the one! Ashes of roses. It's perfect.*

She chastised herself for daydreaming and began removing everything from the previous display. As she turned, she noticed someone outside, staring at her. She felt uncomfortable and thought she'd go to the back room with Solly for the moment. Then the man rapped on the door, gently at first; then harder. *He knows we're closed . I wonder if there's some kind of emergency and he just needs to use the phone.* "I suppose it's safe <u>enough</u>. Solly's here," she muttered.

Tabitha went to the door, but kept it locked. She couldn't see for the driving rain, but she said, "Is there a problem? Can I help you?"

The man didn't move. "We're closed but if it's a true emergency I can let you in for a minute or so. My father is right here so he'll take care of things."

Tabitha opened the door. Henry walked into the shop, removed his hat and shook it vigorously. He smiled broadly, yanked a button off his jacket and handed it to her.

"I wonder if you might do me a favor?" he said, smiling.

Made in the USA
Middletown, DE
11 October 2020